GRUMPY COWBOY

A COOPER BROTHERS NOVEL, SWEET WATER FALLS FARM ROMANCE BOOK 2

ELANA JOHNSON

ISBN-13: 978-1638760290

GRUMPY COWBOY

1

William Cooper scanned for a parking spot, the lack of one sending annoyance through him. He should've known better, in truth. Everyone and their dog, and their dog's uncle, came to the New Year's Beach Bash.

He normally didn't attend things like this at all. It took a lot to get him off his family farm, which sat about a half-hour outside of Sweet Water Falls. No, that wasn't entirely true. He worked a lot with the hundreds of acres and thousands of dairy cows the farm had, and *that* prevented him from getting out into society.

He almost scoffed at himself for thinking the word *society*. If there was one in Sweet Water Falls, he certainly didn't belong to it.

An empty space caught his eye, and he swung his

truck around the corner to get to it. The early evening sunlight glinted off his windshield, but he made it into the stall. There he sat, trying to decide if he should get out or not.

He'd come all this way...

Which in and of itself would be a dead giveaway to everyone who got within ten feet of him and Gretchen Bellows. For the life of him, he couldn't stop thinking about the woman. He'd tried, and just when he managed to go a few hours with his focus on milk, money, or muffins, the blonde woman would get reintroduced into his life.

She'd been at Shayla's big tent reveal, and Will had been too. His brother was now engaged to Shayla Nelson, and Will had wanted to be helpful to both of them. He currently lived with Travis in a cabin on their farm, but things would definitely change come springtime.

Trav hadn't said anything to Will about where he'd live with his new wife, and there was another cabin out by Clarissa and Spencer, who'd just gotten married a few weeks ago.

They'd have the hard conversations, because they didn't hold back on those in the Cooper family. They had enjoyed a very nice cruise over the holidays, and even Will could admit he'd enjoyed himself more than he thought he would.

In fact, he could use a waiter to bring him a plate of tacos and a tropical smoothie right about now.

The weather in the Coastal Bend of Texas never really got cold, though it did rain in the wintertime. Not this winter, however, and Will finally killed the engine and got out of his truck. Heat assaulted him, and he learned the weathermen Daddy liked to listen to in the mornings hadn't been kidding.

His truck would be a furnace by the time he returned to it, though the sun should be long down by then.

Will took a deep breath and faced the beach. He'd found a spot on the second row over, and he smiled at his good luck. Someone had probably come early and then had to leave for an emergency. A sick child or one who wasn't behaving.

Will thanked his lucky stars, his eyes moving automatically to the food truck arena—and straight to the brightly colored vehicle with the caramel apples on the side of it.

Gretchen's truck.

He told himself he wouldn't go there first. He could check out the other festivities first. There was a beach volleyball tournament happening, and he could stand there and watch that for a while. Travis and Shayla were already here, and he'd told them he'd meet them for dinner. Rissa and Spence too.

The caramel apple truck would be there all night, and Will wasn't going to draw any attention to himself. None at all. Everyone in his family loved the caramel apples at Sweet Water Taffy—Travis couldn't stop talking about them.

His suggestion they go get one wouldn't be obvious. He'd make sure it wasn't.

His first interaction with Gretchen hadn't gone extremely well, and Will reached up to smooth his hand down the front of his shirt. She'd plastered caramel all over him in the drugstore, and he may or may not have barked at her.

Then run away.

It's fine, he told himself. He'd been around her a few times since then, and while he didn't currently have her phone number in his device, he knew where to find her.

As he moved from sidewalk to sand, he couldn't believe he even *wanted* the woman's number. He couldn't remember the last woman he'd been half as interested in, and he hadn't asked for a woman's number in oh, at least five years. Maybe longer.

He had just turned forty this past spring, and as he'd watched Clarissa and then Travis start to date, fall in love, and get engaged, Will could admit that he had something missing in his life. A hole a certain blonde could probably fill right up.

Don't be stupid, he told himself. He hardly knew Gretchen. He'd helped her set up at Shay's tent reveal, and he'd run into her at the mall once. He'd been into her chocolatier shop a few times, but she hadn't been there every time.

So while it was true that he barely knew her, he did

want to *get* to know more about her. That thought made his stomach tighten and his vision narrow. So much so that he'd taken several steps toward the food trucks before realizing it.

He wasn't going to go over there first. He made a sharp right turn and headed out onto the beach a little further. Trav had texted several minutes ago to say he and Shay had found a spot to watch the volleyball, and Will would join them.

His brother wasn't all that hard to find, what with his tall, Texan cowboy hat. He stood with his hand in Shay's, and the bright, white volleyball flying above their heads as Will approached.

"Howdy," he said, easing in next to Trav.

"Will." His brother seemed happy to see him, and Will hadn't expected anything else. They'd always gotten along just fine, even if they did argue sometimes. Everyone in the Cooper family argued; it was bred inside them. Will thought it had something to do with the redheaded genes they'd all inherited from Daddy, who had one of the worst tempers Will had ever seen.

Age had calmed him, as had Mama's illness. Daddy was downright kitteny sometimes now, and he'd broken up a couple of arguments recently that he would've fueled previously.

"Who's winning?" Will asked, shading his eyes despite the sunglasses he wore. He'd also changed out of his normal farm attire of jeans, long-sleeved shirt, and boots and into a pair of khaki shorts, a polo the color of limes, and a baseball cap. He didn't quite feel like himself, but he fit into the Beach Bash better than Travis did.

"Lou's Plumbing," Trav said. "We're cheerin' for them."

Will nodded like he cared, but he didn't. Still, he did like watching the volleyball, and the plumbing shop won a few points later.

"Let's find Rissy and get something to eat," Trav said.

Will nodded and tagged along, the third wheel to his brother and his fiancée. He realized that when they found Rissa and Spence, he'd be the fifth wheel. His gaze automatically moved toward the food trucks, because they would be headed in that direction.

Irritation spiked through him, and Will tried to push it away. The crowd here on the beach drove him batty. The sun was far too hot for December thirty-first. He should've just stayed home, where the air conditioning never stopped blowing.

Travis and Shay got swallowed up in a group of teenagers, and Will paused as he got separated from them.

Couldn't anything go right tonight?

Why had he come?

He looked over to the food trucks again, and his feet took him that way. "Apple sample?" someone asked on his left, and he hadn't even seen the woman standing there. She wore the same bright colors in her uniform as had been painted on the Taffy truck.

"Sure," he said, though he didn't want to talk to her. He took the apple slice and ate it in one bite, the sweet caramel and warm chocolate easing some of the grumpiness inside him.

"Oh, this one gets a whole apple," a woman said, and *that* voice lit him up from inside.

He turned to find Gretchen walking his way. Gretchen Bellows. She was blonde and curvy, with long legs and a smile that could charm snakes and cowboys alike. He stumbled in the sand, though he'd barely moved his feet. A grunt came out of his mouth, and he latched onto her arm to steady himself.

Horror struck him like lightning, and he yanked his hand back. "Sorry." He stepped away from her too, to have more distance. *A proper distance*, he told himself.

"It's fine. I've fallen twice today. This sand is so lumpy." She handed him a white-chocolate-coated caramel apple with plenty of cinnamon stuck to the outside. "Apple pie flavor," she said.

He didn't believe for a single second that she'd fallen in this sand. "Oh, I can't," he said, though he already held the apple in his hand. His face flamed with heat, but Will didn't know how to quench it. The moment his eyes locked onto Gretchen's, she'd see his feelings for her.

So he kept his gaze flitting around. "I just lost Trav and Shay. We were going to go get something to eat."

"You can put it in your truck," she said. "Or I'll hold it for you at mine."

"Is that the apple pie one?" another man asked, and Will looked at him. He practically salivated over the apple, and Will wanted to clutch it to his chest and tell him to back off.

"We have a lot more over at the truck," Gretchen said, and she turned to lead him that way. She smiled at Will over her shoulder, and the gesture dove right into his heart.

Feeling foolish, he smiled at the girl giving out samples, though her attention had been stolen by other people at the party. Will knew the feeling. He felt like he had fifteen hundred things going on at any one time, and he was responsible for everything going smoothly at the farm.

He maintained all of their equipment in the milking operation, and he managed the schedules for all of the cowboys and cowgirls who worked the farm with them, on both sides. On the agriculture side and the milking operation. He never got time off. He never slept more than six hours.

The cruise had shown him how wonderful it was to have a break, and he'd told himself that was why he'd come to the New Year's Beach Bash too. To find a few hours of non-work. To get a break.

He returned quickly to his truck and put the caramel apple on the seat before pulling out his phone and texting his brother that they'd gotten separated.

We just found Rissa, Trav said. *We're going over to the Hawaiian rib truck.*

I'll meet you there, Will said. Then he shoved his phone in his pocket and faced the beach again.

The Hawaiian barbecue tasted like meat candy, and Will enjoyed himself despite being the extra man out. He kept himself from looking over to Gretchen's truck too often, and every time he did, he didn't see her.

No one asked him about her, and no one suggested they get apples.

The sun set, and the beach bonfires got lit. Will yawned long before midnight, and he'd never intended to stay for the twelve o'clock countdown and fireworks show. After all, they had milking to do in the morning, and because it was a holiday, they'd delayed the chore an hour. From five to six, which was still really early in the . morning.

They couldn't just make the cows wait to be milked, no matter what day of the week it was.

"I'm gonna head out," Will said about ten-thirty, his exhaustion all the way down in his soul.

"We are too," Trav said, smothering his own yawn. "See you at home."

"Yep." Will would arrive first, because he didn't have a fiancée to drop off and kiss goodnight before he made the drive back to the farm.

Will didn't mind being at the cabin alone. He sometimes thought he'd like to live alone all the time. *And you will*, he thought. *Soon enough.*

Trav and Shay had set a May wedding date, and that was only five months from now. Will probably wouldn't like living alone then.

He opened the door to his truck and slid inside, realizing far too late that he'd set his caramel apple on the seat. He felt it smear across his backside, and he leapt out of the truck, a roar gathering in his throat.

"No," he managed to say, and the sticky, gooey, now-baked apple fell to the ground. "Stupid...who hands out caramel and chocolate in a heat wave?"

And better question: Who puts an apple pie apple on their front seat and then forgets about it?

Will looked down at the lump of fruit and dessert on the ground, and then gingerly touched the back of his shorts. No matter how he sliced it, he was going to have to ride home in white chocolate, caramel, and cinnamon. A lot of cinnamon.

"This is so stupid," he growled to the night air. "Who tells someone to put a caramel apple in their truck?" He turned, wondering if anyone had seen him slide into his dessert, though it sure seemed like everyone else was all-in for staying at the beach bash until the clock struck midnight.

Will couldn't wait to get away.

Footsteps approached, and then Gretchen herself appeared. She extended a wad of paper towels toward him, saying, "These are wet wipes, Will. Maybe they'll help enough so you can get home."

Pure embarrassment and strong humiliation filled Will from top to bottom. He couldn't make himself step forward and take the wet wipes from the woman he'd just insulted and insinuated that his idiocy was her fault.

2

Gretchen Bellows wanted New Year's Eve to be over. She took a couple of steps toward Will and forced the disinfectant wipes into his hand. "Sorry." She wasn't sure what she was apologizing for, but the grumpy cowboy sure wasn't saying anything.

She retreated back between the two vehicles and then got herself moving across the aisle to the van. Her vehicle was refrigerated, and she picked up the tray she'd gotten out when she'd first heard Will's frustrated voice.

The man spoke in a timbre that she seemed attuned to, and she'd known it was him instantly. She'd gone to see if she could help, only to hear him curse her and find more caramel dripping from his clothes.

She pressed her eyes closed in a long blink and then drew in a breath. "Two more hours," she mumbled to herself. She could do anything for two hours. Not only that, but business was very good tonight. So good that Gretchen was considering bringing the truck down to the beach every single evening.

People loved treats at the beach, and caramel apples were portable, as well as easily cut and shared.

She returned to the truck, climbing up the few steps to the narrow, galley kitchen. "More apples," she said, sliding the tray onto the countertop. Jonathan, her assistant for events, turned a harried eye in her direction.

"Thank goodness," he drawled in his Kentucky accent. "A mob of teenagers just came up, and I wasn't sure if I'd get away with my life." He held up a fistful of papers. "So I just took their orders and prayed."

He grinned then, and Gretchen returned the smile. Her aching back could wait. She'd swallowed some pills at the van, and she'd be fine. This was all good for business.

So much of what Gretchen had been doing for the past six months had that mantra attached to it. She could handle handing out samples in the mall, because it was good for business. She could show up at the sweet shop before dawn, because it was good for business. She could design and run polls, stop by other shops and stores to see what their bestsellers were, and spend evenings in her test kitchen at home, because it was all good for business.

Gretchen wanted someone to take her by the shoulders and shake her. Tell her that she needed to start taking care of herself, whether that was good for business or not.

At the same time, she didn't want to let down Aunt

Patty. She wouldn't. Her aunt had owned Sweet Water Taffy before Gretchen had taken it over, and in a perfect storm of events, which included Aunt Patty falling and breaking her hip, and Gretchen's father's chronic lung disease worsening, she'd returned to Sweet Water Falls.

Rather, she'd come to town. She hadn't grown up here, but in an even smaller Southern Texas town called Short Tail. The town sat inland a bit, and Gretchen maintained a country cottage about halfway between Short Tail and Sweet Water Falls. Then she could get to the candy shop and her father's in about the same amount of time.

Aunt Patty had been making a good recovery, and she'd started talking about coming back to work. But she didn't want complete control of the shop. Gretchen was fine running it, though she'd changed several things in the six months since she'd been at the helm of Sweet Water Taffy.

She needed another truck like this one, and this one needed an upgraded generator and the steps on the front of it replaced. With the increase in business she'd been drumming up over the months, she could probably afford both.

She had hired more people as the business had grown too, and that included Jon, who she'd brought on after the very busy event at Sweetspot. William Cooper had helped her set up then, but Gretchen's face still warmed with embarrassment every time she thought about him doing so.

She was a professional. She shouldn't have relied on a bystander to help her with her business. Thus, Jon's position had been created in Gretchen's mind, and he ran all of their out-of-shop events now. When she showed up with the van loaded with the copper caramel pot and plenty of truffles, it was Jon who helped her set everything up.

Not only that, but the man could charm anything alive and probably all rocks, and having him as the public face at their events and in the truck had increased their sales yet again.

Gretchen set to work fulfilling the orders Jon had taken while she'd been gone to get the apples, leaving her mind free to roam. It moved along paths labeled *Sweet Water Falls Farm* and *Will Cooper*, though she didn't really appreciate being blamed for his placement of the caramel apple.

The orders actually started to slow, and Gretchen glanced at the digital clock she'd velcro'ed to the wall. "Holy cow," she said. "It's after eleven-thirty."

"Some of the other trucks are closing up," Jon said.

"Let's do that while we can," Gretchen said. Jon would drive the truck back to the shop, while Gretchen would take the van home. She'd deemed tomorrow a vacation day, and she was looking forward to sleeping in and then making a late brunch for her dad and Aunt Patty at her childhood home.

She'd spend the day there, and while she'd like to

promise herself she wouldn't work, she knew she would. Daddy had a bit of yard work to do, and Gretchen loved puttering around in a flowerbed. She'd also go over this week's and next week's schedule, send work text reminders, and go over her events calendar for the next couple of months. She tried not to do a lot on her days off, but she hadn't mastered truly stepping away from the business yet.

A flash of sadness hit her as Jon shut the big doors on the front of the truck that meant they were closed. She couldn't help thinking of Malcolm and all she'd lost when she'd left the praline shop behind in New Orleans.

She pushed her ex-boyfriend, her ex-candy-shop, and her ex-life out of her mind. Candy-making was a messy business, and she set an alarm on her phone so she wouldn't miss the ringing in of the New Year, and then she got busy cleaning up the stoves and countertops in the mobile candy truck.

———

THE NEXT DAY, GRETCHEN SANG ALONG WITH THE RADIO IN her car, Aunt Patty strapped into the passenger seat, and plenty of brunch items riding in the back. They'd arrive in Short Tail in a matter of minutes, and Gretchen had achieved one of her goals for the day.

She hadn't gotten out of bed until nine o'clock, and for

someone who usually keyed their way into the candy shop by dawn, that was a huge accomplishment.

She made a right turn, and then a left. Daddy's house came into view, and Gretchen found herself sighing.

"Here we are," Aunt Patty said. She was Daddy's sister, and neither of them had moved too far from their childhood home. Gretchen's grandmother had died last year, and she currently rested in a town due west of here named Sugar Hill.

"We can go see Grandma on the way home," Gretchen said, glancing at Aunt Patty.

"That would be lovely, dear." Aunt Patty smiled and patted Gretchen's hand. "Let's go see how your daddy is doing."

Gretchen knew how he was doing. She saw him nearly every day, and on days she didn't, she texted or called. He wore a tube in his nose that fed him oxygen all the time now, and Gretchen had gotten used to the mechanical whirrings of the machine, and the somewhat robotic way he seemed to breathe.

She got out of the car and went to the back to collect the things she'd brought. Aunt Patty used a cane as she walked up the front sidewalk, and Gretchen went past her on the steps to the front porch and all the way inside the house.

"Daddy," she called, and a dog barked from outside. They were in the back yard, and Gretchen couldn't blame her father—or his dog, Howl—for that. Daddy's backyard had a tiny stream flowing through it, and when Momma had been alive, she'd cultivated the Garden of Eden back there.

Gretchen had loved growing up in the two-story house with a steep roof, and she'd come to help her two brothers paint it last year after their grandmother's death.

The back screen door screeched, and Howl's old-man bark filled the air. Gretchen grinned as she slid the tray holding the eggs, croissants, and ultra-pasteurized milk onto the counter before turning to greet the little white dog.

He was a squatty little thing, part schnauzer and part Maltese. He only stood twelve inches off the ground, but what he lacked in height, he made up for in bulk. He was a healthy thirty pounds, and while he looked like he could be picked up, no one—including him—was happy when someone tried.

Gretchen bent down to pat him, finding his groomed schnauzer eyebrows so expressive. "Howdy, Howly," she cooed at him. "Were you and Daddy out in the gardens? You better not have been doing anything."

She spoke in a baby-voice, but she meant every word. Daddy hadn't fallen and broken his hip, but he couldn't really cart his oxygen tank around the back yard. Momma had put in octagonal pavers, and the wheels of the tank got caught on the edges, the tufts of grass between the pavers, and everything else.

Just now, as he came toward her, the tank jammed

against one of the table legs. He yanked it free without even looking behind him. "Hello, sweetheart," he twanged at her, and Gretchen enveloped her father into a hug. "You didn't have to bring food."

"I did if I wanted to eat something besides sprouted wheat bread and mushrooms," she joked. But she wasn't really joking. She'd never eat half the things her father put in his mouth. She started unloading the items from the tray so she could go get the rest, saying, "I'm going to make those egg sandwiches you like. Cut up some fruit. Can we eat on the back patio?"

"Should be able to, yes," Daddy said about the time Aunt Patty made it inside the house.

"Reginald," she yelled. "Your oak out front looks like it might have a disease."

"She might have a disease," Daddy grumbled, to which Gretchen could only smile. Aunt Patty and Daddy got along just fine, but she liked to tell him all the things wrong with his yard and house, and he liked to tell her to mind her own business.

As that conversation started, Gretchen retrieved the fresh vegetables and fruit from the back of her car and got to work in the kitchen. Just as the egg patties came off the heat and she yelled, "Brunch is ready," into the living room, her phone rang.

It was Jon's ringtone, and Gretchen hesitated at the same time she jerked into motion. She should answer it. She didn't need to answer it. Not today. No one was working today. There was no emergency that *must* be handled before another breath was taken.

She let the call go to voicemail as she went to help Aunt Patty to her feet. She managed that only to have to kick her father's Army green camouflaged oxygen tank free from underneath the side table. He'd almost refused to bring the tank home with him, and Cory, Gretchen's brother, had finally convinced him by saying they could wrap the tanks in Army green camo.

Daddy had served proudly in the Army for several years, and that had done the trick. Gretchen moved at the speed of a snail behind her aunt and her father as they padded through the kitchen and toward the back patio.

"I'll grab this plate and be right behind you," she said. Her phone rang again, and annoyance and acceptance rang through her simultaneously.

She plucked the phone from her apron pocket and answered Jon's call with, "This better be life-or-death."

"I'm with a gentleman that says it is," he said.

"Who?" Gretchen demanded, her eyebrows drawing down. In her opinion, there wasn't anything worse than cold eggs, and with the sloth-like movement of her family members, that had already happened.

"Well," he drawled. "I was just at the shop to try out those grasshoppers. Remember you said I could come in to do that?"

"Yes," Gretchen said, though she had forgotten. "We're closed today, though."

"William Cooper doesn't seem to understand what that means," Jon said, almost under his breath.

"Wait. What? Will Cooper?" Gretchen's face flushed again, and the man wasn't even here.

"Just let me talk to her," came through the line in Will's sexy bark. Gretchen couldn't believe what was happening, and she checked the phone to make sure this call wasn't a prank.

"Gretchen?" Will's voice came through the line. "I just dropped by to talk to you for a second, but you're not here."

"We're closed today," she said as practically as she could. "Jon told you that."

"Mm, yes, he did." Will sounded like he didn't buy it for a second. "Listen, Gretchen, I'd love to see you face-to-face for just a second. Would you mind if I stopped by? It won't take but a minute, I promise."

"Stopped by?" she repeated as if no one had ever stopped by her house before.

"Yes," he said. "If you just give me your address, I'll swing by. Sixty seconds. It's important."

Gretchen had no idea what would be so important that he'd need to stop by, but she found herself giving him her father's address.

"Short Tail, huh? You live out there?"

"My dad does," she said. "I'll be home later today, if you want to wait."

"I don't," he said. "I'll see you soon." The call ended

without him handing the phone back to Jon, and Gretchen once again stared at her device like she'd just been the victim of a practical joke.

Then she immediately started calculating how long it took to drive from Sweet Water Taffy to her father's place. She knew the exact number of minutes, as she'd made the drive plenty of times after work.

She now had twenty-two minutes to eat and enjoy brunch—and convince herself not to throw up—before Will "stopped by."

3

W ill followed the directions on the screen in his pickup truck, his heart beating louder than the radio played. He couldn't believe Gretchen hadn't been at the candy shop, nor that his nerves hadn't given out yet.

Short Tail sat about twenty-five minutes past her sweet shop, and he wondered how she lived this far from work.

"She doesn't," he told himself as he peered out his side window. "She said her father lived out here." She hadn't divulged where she lived. Rightly so, as Will had gone into grump-mode and demanded her employee get Gretchen on the line.

Even when Jon had said she was spending the morning with family after the first phone call hadn't been picked up, Will had insisted. He wanted to sleep tonight, goldarn it, and until he apologized to the gorgeous Gretchen Bellows, he couldn't.

The map on his screen got replaced with Daddy's name and picture as a phone call from his father came in. Will reached to tap the *connect* icon as he turned onto the street Gretchen had given him.

"Hey, Daddy," he said, one thousand percent distracted. She was here, on this street, at one of these houses.

"You left in the middle of milking?" Daddy barked into the truck.

Will blinked, focusing on the situation at hand. He shouldn't have answered this call. "Uh, yes, sir," he said. "Travis said he'd cover for me."

"Travis is currently covered from head to toe in manure," Daddy said sourly. "Where are you? This better be somethin' like you needin' an epi-pen or something."

Will didn't point out that Daddy had used the word "something" twice in one sentence. His mind screamed at him to say that of course he'd been stung by a wasp. The biggest, nastiest, most poisonous wasp in the whole world, so he'd jumped behind the wheel of his truck and driven to the pharmacy...alone.

His conscience wouldn't let him do it. "Not exactly," he said. "Daddy, listen, I'll be back in two shakes, okay? I just needed to do something."

"What?"

Apologize to a woman ran through his mind, and Will let it come on out of his mouth.

Daddy made a grunt or a scoff, or maybe he was just breathing out. No matter what, Will had stunned him. He'd also done something Will thought impossible. He'd calmed his father's bark for long enough for the man to think before he spoke.

"All right," he said with resignation in his tone. "But make it snappy, son. We have work going on out here."

"I'm aware," Will snapped back. He wanted snappy? Will could give Daddy snappy.

"Son."

"I'll be back in a half-hour," Will said, already reaching to disconnect the call. He wasn't sure if he did or Daddy did first, but there were no goodbyes. The GPS map roared back to life, and Will squinted at it.

"Shoulda told Daddy I needed glasses," he muttered to himself. "That wouldn't've been a lie." He got the truck moving again, finding the quaint and quiet farmhouse just two more down the lane.

He turned down the driveway, easily spotting a dark minivan that must be Gretchen's. At the same time, she totally didn't seem like a minivan type of woman. She didn't have kids—at least that he knew of.

The grass grew in between the tire tracks in the driveway, and a huge oak tree stood guard in the front yard. Off to the side and on the way around to the back to Will's left sat a willow, and he could take a moment and breathe here.

If he didn't get out of the truck soon, he wouldn't, and Will unbuckled his belt and slid from the truck. Only the whispers of wind and the sound of a tractor growling in the distance met his ears, and this place reminded him so much of his family farm.

He did love working the family operation. Of course he did. He'd never wanted for anything different, the way Clarissa had. She'd gone off to culinary school, and then she'd tried to get a job in the city at a fancy restaurant.

Cherry had done the same, graduating in educational counseling, and she worked at a college in San Antonio now. Will knew the most about that, and while no one in the family had asked in a long while, being on the cruise together had brought up some renewed questions about how Cherry could stay away when Mama was so sick.

Will kept his mouth shut. He'd learned that was the best way to survive in the Cooper family. At least when it came to personal things, he didn't say much. If there was a problem with a cowboy or cowgirl, he could yell with the best of them. But matters of the heart? He shut right down.

Which was probably why his pulse banged against his ribs, begging him to get back in the truck and get on home. No one came out onto the porch or down the front steps to greet him, and the house had no sidewalk leading up to it. It had to be about a hundred years old, but it seemed to be smiling at him as he made his way across the lawn. Someone obviously took care of the yard, as the lawn wasn't overgrown, and the trees had neat and clean beds around their trunks. The house had been painted recently, in Will's estimation, and he could appreciate someone taking care of their property.

He'd just put his foot on the first step to go knock on the door when he heard a voice. "...fine, Daddy," the woman said.

Will froze. Gretchen.

"I don't mind doing the yard work. I'll just check out the front and then come do those weeds in the back." She came bustling around the corner, her eyes sweeping the street and then the driveway. She froze, her hands halfway into a pair of gardening gloves.

Will swept his cowboy hat from his head, because he was a right fool. The motion caught Gretchen's attention, and her eyes locked onto his. He expected his nerves to riot, but for some unknown reason, they...calmed.

"Howdy," he said, taking a slow step toward her.

The heat of the day thawed her—or maybe his voice, though Will told himself not to be arrogant and not to assume that this woman felt anything for him. Just because he couldn't stop thinking about her didn't mean she felt anything for him. Anything but loathing.

She came toward him too, finishing the job of putting on her gloves. "Good morning," she said professionally. She stopped a good distance from him too, her eyebrows up in a silent question of *Well? Your sixty seconds starts...now!*

"Listen," he said, clearing his throat afterward. "I just wanted to apologize about last night." He wrung the brim of his hat like it was full of water and he needed every drop to come out. "Of course it's not your fault I put that stu—apple in my truck and then sat in it."

Gretchen's features softened. She held out a pair of gardening gloves. "Want to help me with the weeds in the back?"

"Oh, uh, sure." Will said nothing about his promise to be back at Sweet Water Falls Farm in a half-hour. He took the gloves and put them on, finding them too small and snug but saying nothing.

"Good, because my daddy is driving me crazy," Gretchen said. "Maybe if you're here, he'll behave." She started back toward the corner of the house she'd hurried around a moment ago. "You didn't have to drive all the way out here to apologize."

"I did," Will said. "I couldn't sleep last night. I was a real—I was mean. I was just frustrated at myself for not remembering I'd put the apple on the seat."

"I get it."

"And that I couldn't eat it later," he said.

Gretchen glanced at him as he finally caught up to her. They walked side-by-side for a moment. "Is that right?"

"Which part?"

"That you would've eaten it later?"

"Of course," he said, glad she hadn't asked him why he couldn't sleep. Since he was going with all honesty today, he might have told her she'd been plaguing his dreams—night and day—for weeks now. Months maybe, except there was no maybe about it.

"Why do you find that hard to believe?" he asked.

"You don't seem to like sweets," she said. "That's all."

"I do," he said, focusing forward as they reached the back yard. Pure paradise opened up before him, right along with a bubbling stream. "Wow."

"Yeah," she said. "My mother loved to garden."

Will glanced at her, the sadness pouring from her so obvious to him. "How long has she been gone?"

Gretchen yanked her attention away from the bushes and flowers and trees and blinked as she stared at Will. "How did you know she was gone?"

He shrugged, his heart shredding along the edges. "My own mama isn't well," he said. "I think I could just hear it in your voice." He surveyed the land again. "Is all of this yours? All the way back to that fence?" A white fence sat in the distance, with a great pasture beyond that. Will could see horses back there, and he'd dreamt of a place like this for himself.

He had the small house out in the country, but no room for horses of his own, and the landscaping around the farm was for function, not beauty. Her mother had created this to be enjoyed and Will took a few seconds to do just that.

"Beyond," Gretchen said. "My parents had horses in the past."

"But no more," he said, not asking.

"My dad is on oxygen all the time now," she said quietly. "Come on. You might as well meet him while you're here."

"If I'm going to be doing the man's yard work, I suppose I should." Will grinned at her, and to his great surprise, she smiled back.

"You owe me, Mister Cooper," she said, and Will hadn't been out with anyone in a while, but even he recognized when he was being flirted with. He stared after Gretchen as she started walking again, and he didn't get going fast enough before she noticed.

She turned back to him. "You comin'?"

"Yes, ma'am," he said, jogging to catch her. She ducked her head and smiled, waited for him to catch her, and they shared something when he did. Will wasn't entirely sure what it was, and he didn't have someone at the farm to ask.

He did have a long drive home, and maybe Cherry wouldn't be working today. Of course she wouldn't, because it was New Year's Day, and she had a normal job with normal vacation days.

It was only cowboys who worked every day of the year. *And nurses and doctors*, Will told himself. *Pilots, truck drivers, Mother Nature, and the Good Lord Himself.*

They walked along a fence with flowers spilling from

baskets along the top, and Will's stomach clenched as an idea formed in his mind. "Gretchen," he said as they reached the corner of the fence and even more of the yard opened up before them.

She looked at him expectantly.

He just had to say it. Ask her. The words foamed in his gut, rolling upward and out of his mouth. "Would you go out with me?"

Pure shock covered her expression, and her eyes widened. "Like, on a date?"

"That's usually what a man means when he asks a woman out," a woman said, and Will whipped around and backed up at the same time, as if he might need to protect Gretchen from the hag who'd appeared out of nowhere.

An older woman leaned against what wasn't a fence, but a railing, a smile made of pure glee on her face.

Gretchen moved out from behind his weak protective stance and to his side. "My aunt Patty," she said. "Aunt Patty, this is William Cooper."

"William Cooper?" a man practically yelled, and Will thought he'd fit in real nicely at the farm. A thumping, rolling sound came across the deck, and an older gentleman appeared at Aunt Patty's side. He was obviously Gretchen's father, though he wore a line of disapproval between his eyebrows right now.

"Ain't no daughter of mine goin' out with a man with a name like that."

4

"Daddy," Gretchen said, exasperation exploding through her. It seemed to multiply with every half-second that passed. "My daddy," she said, throwing a look in Will's direction. She couldn't look at him, so she looked past him. "Reginald Bellows."

"Pleasure to meet you both," Will said diplomatically.

"I knew a guy named Will once," Daddy shouted, and Gretchen pressed her eyes closed in a long blink. She could say the next part. *Served with him in Korea.*

"Served with him in Korea," Daddy said, mimicking her thoughts. "He had a fake leg, that one. He'd hide things in it. Up to no good." He slid his eyes down to Will's legs, and Gretchen wanted the ground to swallow them both right into a hole that went all the way to Korea. "Do you have a fake leg, son?"

"No, sir," Will said, a smile in his voice. Gretchen

dared to peek at him, and sure enough, he wore a smile on his face. That so wasn't fair, because he was already stunningly good-looking while growling about his sticky shirt or griping about sitting in chocolate and caramel. Why did he have to be blessed with perfectly straight, white teeth too?

Will held up his hands, the ridiculously flowered gloves plain to see. "I just came to see about some weeds back here."

"Sounds suspicious," Daddy said. "Beth didn't mind the weeds. She said it gave the garden character."

"These weeds are choking out her strawberries," Gretchen said, doing her best not to roll her eyes. "Come on, Will. Let's get it done."

"Wait," Aunt Patty said, and Gretchen might just leave her here. She glared at her aunt, but she really needed to work on heating her gaze, because Aunt Patty didn't care at all. She continued with, "I want to hear how Gretchen's going to answer your question."

All eyes landed on her then, including Will's and Howl's. Gretchen heated from head to toe. She had no good reason to be attracted to Will, other than his physical looks. The man was a god, and he had to know it. He was single, and he had asked her out, and Gretchen would need a very good reason to say no.

He'd been helpful at the tent event at Sweetspot, and at some point during all of their interactions, she'd caught glimpses of sweetness behind all of his rougher exterior.

"It's fine," he mumbled, dropping his eyes to the ground. "It's no big—"

"Yes," she said over him. He raised his eyes back to hers, and Gretchen saw the hope and desire swimming there. "I'll go out with you." Her own surprise mingled with his, and they smiled together.

"Great." He cleared his throat. He looked from her to Daddy and Aunt Patty, then back to her. "I'll go start on the weeds." He walked away, leaving Gretchen with her family.

All three of them watched him walk away, his hatted head held high. Gretchen sighed and said, "Not a word, either of you."

"I'm surprised you said yes," Aunt Patty said. "I wasn't expecting that."

"Yeah, well, me either," Gretchen said, tugging her gloves on a little tighter. She tore her eyes from Will's back and faced her daddy and his sister. "Please, try not to burn the house down while I weed your strawberry patch."

"Oh, go on now," Daddy said with a hint of gruffness in his voice. "We'll be fine here." He turned away, dragging his oxygen tank with him.

Aunt Patty shot stars out of her eyes, and Gretchen did let her eyes roll then. "It's nothing," she said. "I'm not talking about this on the way home. If you're going to do that, I'm not taking you."

"You wouldn't dare leave me here with Reginald."

Aunt Patty's glee dropped ten notches as her fingers tightened on the top of the railing.

Gretchen took a step. "I would, Aunt Patty," she said over her shoulder. "I totally would." After all, she'd just said yes to a date with a man she hardly knew. A cowboy she'd never really had a good interaction with. A handsome cowboy she also couldn't stop thinking about, despite the hiccups between them.

Maybe she had something to smile about too.

———

THE FOLLOWING EVENING, THE BELL ON THE DOOR RANG AT the sweet shop just as Gretchen slid another tray of double chocolate brownies into the case. She wasn't working the counter for the nightly sweet tooth rush, and she turned to head back into the kitchen. She could monitor the status of trays from there.

She happened to glance up, catching sight of the cowboy hats who'd just entered. Just about every man in Sweet Water Falls wore a cowboy hat, but somehow, Gretchen recognized one of them.

The man wearing it was Will Cooper. That cowboy seemed to have only North Pole magnets in his body, and they were all attracting her South Pole ones.

She stalled, and their eyes met. He reached up and touched the brim of his hat. Gretchen smiled at him, her feet carrying her further behind the candy counter, right to the very end. "Howdy, Will," she said, her gaze stuck on his. "Travis."

"Ma'am," Travis said, but she didn't even look at him. She jolted, realizing how very much she was giving away, and she dragged her eyes over to Will's brother. He grinned like he'd just found out he held the winning lottery ticket, and Gretchen's face heated.

He indicated himself and Will, who hadn't said hello yet. "We heard you had some new treats in the store today. Grasshoppers?" He scanned the trays of candy in the case between them.

"Yes," Gretchen said as professionally as she could. "Those are Jon's creation. He has them over there, on demo, today." She nodded toward the other half of the store, where Jon had a small group of people around him.

Mostly women, but Gretchen wasn't going to tease Jon about his charm. If it brought in customers—male or female—and his candy was delicious, Gretchen didn't care why the people came.

Travis turned and said, "Thanks" over his shoulder as he walked away.

Will leaned against the candy counter, his eyes on his brother's back. "He has a real sweet tooth."

"Mm. But you don't."

The cowboy looked at her, his teal eyes blazing and bright. "I did, once," he said. "Got right addicted to sugar, and I had to make some serious adjustments when the doctor told me I had pre-diabetes."

Gretchen's eyes widened. "I'm sorry. I didn't mean to tease you."

Will grinned at her. "Sure you did." He looked back over to his brother, who held up a small package of grasshoppers and then a big one. "He's going to kill me one day." Will chuckled and pushed away from the counter. "Real good to see you, Gretchen."

He took a step away and then another one, and Gretchen couldn't believe he was going to go. Just like that? They hadn't made plans for their date. He didn't even have her number, as far as she knew.

"Will," she blurted, and he turned back to her.

Travis came up behind him. "The big one or the small? What do you think for dessert tonight?"

"I'm not going to eat any," Will said, his expression darkening. "I don't care."

"You're the one who wanted to stop here," Travis said, his voice as black as Will's usually bright eyes. "Did you not get her number?" He looked over to Gretchen, and she wasn't standing behind a steel wall, but a chest-high case made of glass.

"Travis," Will hissed out of the corner of his mouth.

Gretchen reached up to tuck her hair behind her ear. "He didn't get my number," she said, deciding to lean into the humiliation. It came often enough that she might as well. "Because he didn't ask."

"You were supposed to ask," Travis said. "Hurry up. We have to get back before Lee figures out we're gone." He bustled off toward the register, and Will watched him for a breath of time.

"Better get the big one," he called. "To appease Lee." He turned back to Gretchen, his smile timid and a bit trembly on his lips. "I wanted to text you last night about our, uh, date." He cleared his throat. "But I don't have your number, so..."

"So...can I have your number, Gretchen?" she asked, flirting with him. He didn't seem to get that she was, and she could admit she'd never been great at letting a man know she was interested in him.

"Yes," he said with a chuckle. "I'd love to have your number, Gretchen."

Only if you say my name like that again, she thought, but thankfully she didn't have to go into full-blow mortification mode as she didn't say it out loud. Instead, she read off her number, and Will put it in his phone. Their eyes met again, and the world did that thing where it stopped.

At least until Travis said, "Stop staring at her like that. It's creepy. And we have to go." He nudged Will, and the trance broke.

Air rushed into Gretchen's lungs, and she dropped her chin, sure her face was a flaming red ball of fire.

"I swear, Trav," Will bit out. "You're the worst brother ever." He started for the door without saying goodbye. Yesterday, as he'd left her father's house, their goodbye had been stilted and strange, but it was better than not getting one at all.

"I'm the worst brother?" Travis called after him. "I drove *you* here to get your girlfriend's number, because *your* back hurts. How am I the worst bro—?" The door closed behind them as they exited the shop, and Gretchen could only blink into the silence left in their wake.

"Girlfriend?" Gretchen asked only herself, and the refrigeration unit that kept the candy from melting in the Texas heat kicked on as her answer.

———

THAT EVENING, GRETCHEN PACED IN HER HOUSE, ELVIS watching her from the top of the couch. "I'm just going to tell him when he texts that I can't go," she said, looking at the gray tabby cat for approval. "Whatever night he suggests, I'll be busy."

She'd been thinking about Will for hours—nothing new—but this time, her thoughts had taken her down a more dangerous path. She didn't know the man. He didn't say goodbye to her. She wasn't even sure they'd get along for longer than ten minutes.

Every interaction she had with him seemed to get interrupted or ruined somehow, from her father and aunt overhearing him as he asked her out, to a strange half-hug goodbye while she still wore muddy gloves, to him storming out of the shop while his brother continued to spill secrets.

"Meow," Elvis said, and Gretchen went into the

kitchen. She worked in a frenzy to get the cat fed, chopping up last night's leftover salmon and mixing it with some wet cat food and some dry kibble.

She added a couple of cherry tomatoes and put the bowl on the floor. "Here you go, sweetie." Elvis jumped down and joined her in the kitchen, his tail held high. She slumped down the cabinets next to the cat as he started noshing on his dinner, wishing she could calm her racing mind.

"You're right," she said to the feline. "He was probably just embarrassed at the pharmacy that one day. Then a little awkward at the mall, because Travis said he was particular about his shirt."

Her brain started to quiet. "He was frustrated at the Beach Bash, and maybe he blurts some things out sometimes. He didn't *know* Aunt Patty and Daddy were going to be right there, eavesdropping."

In all honesty, she should've warned him that her aunt had such a tendency. "And his back hurts, so he asked his brother to bring him to the shop to get my number." She sighed then, because it was romantic that Will wanted her number.

She closed her eyes. "Maybe he hasn't dated in a while. He's just out of practice when it comes to saying goodbye." Heaven knew Gretchen wasn't great at anything when it came to men, and she had plenty of stories to tell too. Elvis had heard them all already, and she was pretty sure the only reason the tabby stuck around was for the salmon bowl Gretchen had just made for him.

Her eyes flew open. "Oh, no." She moaned as she got to her feet. "What if his back hurts because of the weeding?"

Elvis didn't even look up from his bowl, the glutton. Gretchen reached for her phone next to the cutting board to call Will and demand to know why his back hurt. She couldn't be responsible for that.

As she stared at her device, she realized she didn't have his number. He only had hers, and he hadn't used it yet.

"He will," she said, refusing to remove her eyes from her phone. "He'll text or call any second now." Her stomach grumbled, and she should make herself some sort of salmon bowl out of the leftovers, but she didn't.

Darkness had started to fall, so surely Will couldn't still be at work. He'd text or call any minute now...

5

W ill stole out to the back deck the moment Travis said he was going to go shower. His phone lit up the night, and he cursed the fact that he'd been at the farmhouse for dinner for so long.

Everyone wanted to hear about these grasshoppers, and not a single one of them didn't get claimed. Lee had given Travis a cock-eyed look and said, "Is that where you two went earlier today?"

Travis had simply grinned at their oldest brother and shrugged one shoulder with a mouthful of crispy rice, caramel, and chocolate in his mouth. Lee's pretend ire had disappeared the moment he'd taken a bite of the treat too.

None of that had helped get Will away from the family dinner sooner, and he didn't want to call more attention to himself than had already been done. Travis knew of his insane crush on Gretchen Bellows, but no one but Cherry knew he'd asked her on a date.

"You're not going," he told himself as he lifted his eyes from his phone. He couldn't see anything now, as the bright rectangle imprinted on the backs of his eyelids every time he blinked. The war that had been raging inside him since he'd left the cute little house in Short Tail yesterday continued.

He'd never had a normal interaction with Gretchen. Just when he thought he might be able to pull that off, something happened to twist things sideways. Yesterday, he'd acted like an idiot when it was time to say goodbye. Instead of just saying the word and waving like a normal person, he'd done some weird lunge at her to hug her. She'd patted him on the back, which might have been fine had she not been wearing muddy gloves.

Another shirt ruined, though she hadn't offered to pay for it this time. He'd run away from her too fast for that.

He shook his head, which only made him dizzy in the darkness, what with his eyes closed and everything. He breathed in as he opened his eyes, saying, "Nothin' goes right when I'm around her," in a quiet voice. It still shouted in the country stillness. "I don't see how I can go out with her."

Will wasn't one for spotlights, and he felt certain that any café, restaurant, or bistro he took her to would end in disaster. So he wasn't going to go. He was going to cancel the date.

One arm of his strategy yelled about simply not texting Gretchen. She didn't have his number, and maybe if he simply never used hers, that would be that. His heart fought against this strategy, because it would hurt her. The last thing Will wanted was to hurt a woman.

"Arrogant," he cussed at himself. Who did he think he was to think his non-text would hurt Gretchen? At the same time, he'd seen the interest in her eyes yesterday, as well as in her shop today. She flirted with him. If he didn't text her to set up their date, she would get hurt.

He couldn't do that.

He frowned at his device again, cursing Travis this time. His brother's mouth had gotten Will into hot water for the last time. And not just hot water with Lee, but boiling, scalding water laced with humiliation with Gretchen Bellows.

Stop staring at her like that. It's creepy.

Did you get her number?

You were supposed to ask for her number. Hurry up.

Will had never wanted to cut out someone's tongue as badly as he had at Sweet Water Taffy today. Maybe he had been staring at Gretchen creepily, but she'd looked steadily back into his eyes. That was how he knew he couldn't just ghost her.

No, he'd have to text her and tell her with concise words that he'd had a change of heart and didn't want to go out with her. He couldn't make himself do it, because

Will wasn't one to lie, and he was dang tired of lying to himself.

Hey, Gretchen, he thumbed out, his fingers moving fast over the phone. He'd once won a contest for the fastest texter, and he told himself to hurry up and get these messages sent. She wouldn't be able to respond fast enough, and then he could silence his phone, take his turn in the shower, and go to bed.

It's Will. Listen, sorry about my stupid brother's mouth in the shop today. I swear he lives to embarrass me.

He sent that message and immediately started typing out his next message. *It's really busy around the farm right now, and I don't think—*

His fingers stalled when a return message came in. *It's fine. Can I call you?*

"Call me?" he asked, as if he didn't know what those words meant. Gretchen didn't wait for an answer, as his ringtone cut through the silence on the farm in the next moment, and her name and number came up on his screen, covering the texting app.

Somewhat dumbfounded, he swiped on the call and lifted the phone to his ear. "Hey," he said.

"How did you hurt your back?" she asked. *Demanded* would be a better descriptive word, and Will turned in a full circle, trying to make sense of the question.

"What?" he finally asked.

"Travis said he drove you to the shop because your back hurts," she said. She could probably win a contest for fastest speaker for how quickly her words flowed from her mouth. "Tell me it's not from the weeding."

Relief rushed through Will. "It's not from the weeding," he said with a chuckle. "I mean, that sure didn't help, but that's not the reason."

"William Cooper," she said, plenty of snap in her voice. "Why didn't you say something yesterday?"

"I just said it wasn't because of that."

"You said it didn't help."

Will stared out over the pond, the moon casting a silver line across the surface of the water. "Remember I told you about the pre-diabetes?"

"Yes," she said, really drawing the word out.

Gladness moved through him, because her Texas drawl gave him another few beats to think. "I started working out pretty hardcore when that came down the line," he said. "I cut out all sugars. I lifted weights religiously. I hurt my back doing that." He supposed there could be worse ways to injure himself, including weeding her father's strawberry patch.

"Oh." Gretchen took an audible breath through the line. "Does it bother you a lot?"

"Not a lot," he said, hesitant to say much more about what yesterday had cost him. Daddy hadn't been happy at all by the time Will returned to the farm. He'd worked until nearly ten p.m., and he'd gotten the early morning shifts for the next ten days straight. He wouldn't be mentioning any of that to Gretchen.

He was forty years old, and a punishment for leaving the farm without asking or telling anyone where he was going—for almost four hours—made him feel like a fifteen-year-old who'd snuck off to see the girl he liked.

Of course, that was exactly what Will had done, so he'd taken his tongue-lashing and awful schedule like a man.

"How long ago did you hurt it?" she asked.

"Couple of years," he said.

"So you haven't had dessert for a couple of years?" she asked, a hint of horror in her voice.

Will smiled into the night around him. "Not a lot, ma'am."

"I wish you wouldn't call me ma'am," she said. "It makes me feel old."

"Sorry," he said quickly. "My mama taught me to be respectful."

"Mm."

The conversation seemed over, but Will didn't want to let her go yet. "I've told you about a couple of things now," he said. "What about you? Health conditions I need to be aware of? Dietary restrictions for dinner? Food allergies?"

Gretchen giggled, and Will knew in that moment he wouldn't be canceling their date. "I don't like shellfish," she said. "Everything else is fair game."

"I'm assuming we need somewhere with amazing dessert," he said.

"That's a given," Gretchen said. "Before I moved here, I

worked in a fancy restaurant in a big hotel in Dallas. I made the most amazing chocolate pear tarts."

"Wow," Will said with a chuckle. "Maybe we should skip going out and just eat desserts at your house."

"Mm, that's not how to get a woman to go out with you twice, Will," she said, her voice carrying plenty of teasing. "Make them cook for you on the first date? That's a guaranteed way not to get a second date."

"Noted," he said, and they laughed together. The natural low that came after the high slid into place, and he asked, "What's your week like next week?" He honestly had no idea what his week held. Sometimes things could change minute to minute on the farm, but Travis had managed to see Shay on a steady basis. Properly motivated, Will could find a way.

"I have to go help my dad on Monday, Tuesday, and Thursday," she said, her voice getting a bit quieter. "He's got a few medical things I assist with. I usually go after work, sometimes in the afternoon. Tuesday is an easy thing, and I could be back in Sweet Water Falls for dinner."

"I could meet you up in Short Tail," he offered. "Or we could go out to Sugar Hill. They have a fantastic little barbecue place out there."

"Yes," she said, but she didn't sound excited about barbecue. Will could eat it for every meal, but he kept his mouth shut. "I live out in the country about halfway between my shop and Short Tail," she said. "Are you wanting to come pick me up or meet me somewhere?"

"Pick you up," he said instantly. "My mama would fillet me into bite-sized chunks and serve me raw if I let you meet me somewhere." He grinned as he said it, though a human sushi bar was actually a really disgusting thought.

Gretchen laughed again, and when she sobered, she said, "Will, you should do what you want. Despite what your mama thinks."

"I do," he said, feeling somewhat defensive. "I want to come pick you up."

"Then there's this great place near my house," she said. "A friend of mine owns it, and their menu changes every night."

"I'll try anything," he said, realizing how fully committed he sounded. The unsent text on his phone told a different story, and he was suddenly so glad she could dial faster than he could text.

"I'll see if we can go on Tuesday," she said. "She only takes a certain number of diners, because all of the food is sourced locally, and they make exactly enough for their reservations."

"This sounds like a weird way to run a restaurant," Will said.

Gretchen didn't say anything for a couple of beats, and Will knew in that moment just how related to Travis he was. "I'm sorry," he said at the same time

Gretchen said, "She doesn't want a big, fancy, chain restaurant."

"I'm sure she doesn't," Will said, turning back to the house, frustrated with himself. "I'm sorry, Gretchen. It sounds fantastic." That was code for, *I just want to see you again. I don't care where we eat.*

"She's a great chef," Gretchen said. "I'll see what she has. It might not work out for Tuesday."

"Let me know," he said. "Barring any emergencies around the farm, I should be able to get away any evening next week." And that was how he went from having a normal conversation with a pretty woman to making himself sound desperate to see her again.

He cleared his throat, which didn't help, and when Travis opened the back door and asked, "What are you doin' out here?" Will decided he needed to wrap up this call lickety-split.

He glared at Travis, and they'd exchanged enough heated words on the way home from the candy shop for his brother to hold up his hands in surrender and retreat back inside the cabin they shared.

Will turned around and exhaled. "It was real nice talkin' to you, Gretchen," he said.

"You too, Will."

"Have a good night now."

"You too," she said again, and Will's pride grew and expanded.

"We'll talk soon."

"Okay."

He ended the call, because he couldn't come up with another one-liner he could say that wouldn't embarrass him and make things weird. He breathed in and then out, a smile stretching across his face. "That wasn't too bad," he told himself. Didn't mean dinner was going to go well, but he might have had his first non-awkward, non-humiliation interaction with the beautiful Gretchen Bellows.

Trav opened the door again and called, "Will, I need you in here. The sink smells like a beaver climbed inside and died," and Will had never been so happy to have ended a call before anyone, most of all Gretchen, could hear a sentence like that.

6

Gretchen looked up from her phone, the distinct feeling that she hadn't been paying attention racing through her. "Daddy," she said.

"I'm gettin' it myself," he grumped at her. "You're obviously busy with something."

She hurried to pocket her phone and fly after her father as he went into the back of the house, where the kitchen sat. "I can do it. You need to rest. The doctor said no more up and down. You sit for an hour, you get up for ten minutes."

"I've been sittin' for an hour."

He hadn't been, but Gretchen didn't argue with him. She hadn't been listening, and guilt cut through her like a hot, serrated knife. She watched as her dad got out the leftovers from last night and started to fork some pasta into a bowl.

"It'll split if you use the microwave," she said. "Do you want me to mix in some milk or cream?"

"I'm not going to heat it up." Her dad gave her a slitted-eyed look at took his bowl of macaroni toward the door he'd just come through.

Gretchen sighed and waited for him to be out of earshot. For a while there, he hadn't been able to hear anything she said. She, Cory, and Max had begged him to get hearing aids, something she regretted in this moment.

"Gross," she said under her breath. Who wanted to eat white macaroni and cheese cold? All congealed into a glob? Just gross.

"Do you want more coffee?" she called. "Tea?"

"Chicken broth," he yelled at her, and Gretchen filled a couple of mugs from the cupboard with the hot water from the electric kettle. She dropped in cubes of chicken bouillon and took them back into the living room.

She still wore her church dress, but Daddy hadn't gone to services today. She handed him a cup and sank back into her mother's recliner. "Max called this morning," she said. "He thinks he's going to come with the kids on the long weekend."

Her father's face frowned momentarily. "That's fine."

Gretchen waited, because Daddy had more to say. He always did when he started a conversation with a frown like that. "No Joan?"

"Daddy, Joan and Max have been separated for six months now." She sipped her broth while she gave her father some time to compute. He knew this, but he didn't understand it. He and Mother hadn't always agreed on everything—Gretchen knew no couple did—but he didn't understand a man splitting from his family.

"He'll bring the kids?"

Gretchen looked down into her lap, wishing her brother had told their dad all of this already. "He won full custody of the kids," she said quietly. "So yes."

"Full custody?"

"I told you there was a reason he split with Joan," Gretchen said. "It's not all his fault, and you'd do well to work on keeping your mouth shut while he's here." She gave her father a stern look, one she'd seen Mother give him a few times over the years. "He's already hurting, and he's doing the very best he can."

"Three kids, all alone."

"Yeah," Gretchen said, trying not to let her own displeasure and sadness enter her voice. She didn't have any children, as focused as she'd been on her chocolate-creation career. "They're doing okay. All of them. But it's a lot to handle, and they just need our love and support."

"I know that," Daddy said, and he put one of those gross globs of pasta in his mouth.

"I don't think you do," Gretchen said, taking the opportunity to talk while he couldn't. "You've been very critical of Max. Why do you think he didn't come home for Christmas?"

Her dad's eyes bugged, and he chewed at the speed of light. After he swallowed, he said, "He said he wanted a quiet few days at home with the kids. To give them stability."

Gretchen sighed, reaching way down deep for every ounce of patience she possessed. "I know what he said." She gave her father a smile, and when her phone buzzed in her pocket, her heart hammered out an extra blip. Perhaps that was Will. She worked hard not to pull out her phone immediately to check. "But Daddy, sometimes you judge just with your eyes."

Her daddy blinked at her. "I do?"

"Yes," she said. "Now, I'm going to check my phone, because it might be Will. I was texting him earlier, because remember he asked me out?"

"How can I forget?" Daddy asked dryly. He rolled those eyes—totally judging her—and added, "You talk about him every dang day."

"He's good-looking," Gretchen said in her defense. "And I haven't been out with anyone in a long time. You should be happy I'm going to start seeing someone." He was so different than Mother. Her mom had hounded her through her twenties to find a "nice man" and settle down. She'd been proud of Gretchen's accomplishments in kitchens and bakeries too, but she wanted more grand-children.

Max and Cory had three kids each, and Gretchen did love being their aunt. Now that she'd returned to the Coastal Bend of Texas, she felt ready to be a mother. At thirty-seven years old, she didn't have much time to build her family.

She pictured fair babies, with blonde hair and skin that freckled like hers. Will was fairly fair too, and she giggled at the words *fairly fair* in her head. She plucked her phone from her pocket to check her messages, but the few she'd gotten weren't from Will.

Her friend who owned The Culinary Cabin had finally gotten back to her. Gretchen's heart raced as her eyes scanned the texts.

We're full this week, Gretchen. I'm sorry.

We have an opening next Wednesday evening for two. Or next Friday for four.

Then we're into the next week, and it's mostly open, except for Saturday, which is already full. I'm doing those Very Veggie tours on Saturdays, and they come with a reservation for lunch or dinner. That's why Saturday is always full.

Gretchen's heart settled somewhere in the soles of her feet. She didn't want to wait ten days to go out with Will, but she really wanted to take him to The Culinary Cabin on their first date.

Thank you, she typed out to Ingrid Olsen, her friend who owned and ran The Cabin. *Will you put me down for two next Wednesday?*

Will's schedule had seemed pretty open, barring any

emergencies around the farm. It was her schedule that felt stuffed to the brim, or sometimes overflowing, despite her Sunday afternoon broth party with her father.

A snore came from his direction, and Gretchen looked over to find him fast asleep in his recliner. He did that a lot lately, and her soul pinched and then warmed with love for her daddy. She took a quick snapshot of him and sent it in the sibling text she had with Cory and Max, saying, *he's asleep again. He does that a lot more often lately. Please come visit him when you can.*

Gretchen feared her daddy might not be with them for much longer, and the thought weighed heavily in her mind as she looked around the cluttered, dark living room. The very idea of cleaning out this house gave her hives, and she wondered if she'd be strong enough to do it.

After a deep breath, she knew she would be. She wasn't the oldest, but Daddy's estate would be split in thirds upon his death. She wouldn't have to worry about Cory taking something from her she wanted.

He lived out in the Hill Country, on his wife's family farm, which he worked alongside Vivi. Max lived in the Fort Worth area, now separated and taking care of all of his children alone. If Gretchen wanted the house and land, she could probably have it. She ran the candy shop, and she could see a future right there for herself.

In it, a certain reddish-blond cowboy emerged, and

she wondered if William Cooper would ever leave his family's generational dairy operation to live in this hundred-year-old house twenty minutes away.

She wouldn't know if she didn't ask. "Not on the first date," she murmured to herself, quickly navigating over to the text string they shared. Before she could start typing, Ingrid confirmed that she had Gretchen down for next Wednesday for two, and that made her smile.

The Culinary Cabin is full this whole week, she tapped out. *The soonest they have is next Wednesday, so I booked that. Is that okay?*

She sent that text, her mind firing at her to keep going. *We can go out before then. Anywhere is fine, honestly.*

Tuesday still? Will asked. *Or do you want to go on a day you're not busy with your daddy?*

Gretchen looked over to her snoozing father. She was busy because of him every day. He did have crucial medications she monitored on Mondays, and she changed his oxygen tank those days too. On Thursdays, she had to take him for his afternoon doctor's appointments, and then he always wanted to stop and get a double-decker chicken salad sandwich at Barney's in the mall. So that took up her whole evening by the time she drove, waited, got any new medications, asked her questions, and they got the sandwiches.

Tuesday, Wednesday, or the weekend, she told him. *Any of those work for me.*

I already talked to Trav about Tuesday, so let's stick to that.
Gretchen smiled at the speed with which his text came in. No typos either. *Okay,* she started to type, but she got another message from Will.

What are you doing right now?

Her pulse went crazy, and Gretchen looked up as alarm ran through her body. Right now, she was doing nothing. She sat with Daddy most Sunday afternoons, just to keep him company, talk about the candy she'd make that week, and spare herself from spending most of her time talking to her brother's cat.

She looked over at him, asleep. Cooing at Elvis might actually be a better use of her time...

Gretchen smiled as she tapped to call Will, a tactic that had worked to her advantage last night. His line rang a couple of times, and when he answered it with, "Howdy, Gretchen," it sounded like he might be a bit winded.

"Am I interrupting?" she asked.

"No," he said, but another voice came clearly through the line too, saying, "Get back in here! You can't get out of dish duty just because Gretchen called."

She started to giggle, but she pulled the phone away from her mouth to do so. She didn't want Will to think she was laughing at him—or worse, Travis.

"Leave me alone, Lee," Will growled. "I'm a grown man, and I'll get my chores done."

"Who's Gretchen?" a woman asked, her voice as old as Mother's had been when she'd died.

Gretchen sobered, because while weeding the strawberry patch, Will had said his mama wasn't well.

"No one," Will said. "Can't a man talk on the phone and not get questioned to death?"

"No one?" Gretchen asked, making her voice as lighthearted as possible. She stood and headed for the front door so she could talk and laugh and not disturb Daddy.

"We want to start the brownies," Lee said, his voice much closer. "Let me talk to her."

"You're not talking to her."

"She's someone," the woman said.

"Will," another woman called.

"I need five minutes," Will practically yelled into the phone. "I'll call you back." It sounded like a scuffle ensued, and then the line went dead.

Gretchen leaned against the porch railing and looked out over the deadly quiet street in front of her. A smile filled her whole face and moved into her soul. Will's family sure did seem...lively, and Gretchen could use a little more zest in her days.

Evening had started to fall before her phone rang, which was far longer than the five minutes Will had said he needed. Gretchen jabbed at the screen in her car to get the call to connect anyway, because his voice would be a welcome partner on her drive home.

"Hey," she chirped, wondering if she came through the speaker in his phone too loud.

"Let me lead with an apology," he said. "I'm sorry

about earlier. I should've known I can't answer a call in the middle of a family thing." He sighed, and she could imagine him shaking that head of his. "The problem is, everything I do is a family thing. So I guess that's the second thing you need to know."

"That you do things with your family?"

"We eat dinner together nearly every night," he said with a sigh that said it was akin to torture. "I cook on Fridays."

Gretchen's eyebrows shot right up, nearly flying off her face. "Every Friday?"

"I can switch the day around if I need to, but yeah."

Questions blitzed through her mind. She didn't know which one to start with, so she drove in silence.

"Anyway," Will said with another sigh. "I was thinkin' you might come out to the farm this afternoon, and we'd sneak into the Shoppe my sister runs and get some ice cream."

"I was at my daddy's," she said. "But I could've come." She reached a stop sign and looked right. Her mind slowed. "I just left his place. I could still come..."

"Could you?" he asked, the hope in his voice as high as the heavens above the earth. "I've got some things to do out in the barns, and the Shoppe is right across the lot from there."

"Okay," she said, flipping her blinker from left to right. "You were on dish duty this afternoon?"

"My oldest brother is an ogre," Will said, a dark tone to his voice. "You think I am, but you haven't met Lee yet."

"I met Lee at the tent thing," Gretchen said. "He did seem to be in a foul mood then."

"Oh, well, that was because—" Will cut off, his voice just going mute. "That was a hard day for Lee, that's all. But yeah, he cooked a lot today, and I said I'd do the dishes so he could take his son back to town."

"How's your mother? You didn't tell her about us?"

He cleared his throat, and his voice sounded gruff when he said, "No, ma'am. I didn't think there was much to tell yet."

Gretchen smiled into the nearly dark sky. For some reason, she liked this version of Will Cooper who felt put on the spot and out of his comfort zone. She had a feeling that didn't happen very often for him, and while he complained about his family, he loved them fiercely too.

"Anyway," he said. "Give me a holler when you get here. If you turn right off the dirt road instead of left, you'll be headin' out to the barns and the Shoppe."

"Yes, sir," Gretchen said, teasing him now. "I'll *give you a holler*." She giggled, glad when Will chuckled too. The call ended, and Gretchen basked in the fact that she and Will had made it through several conversations now without a horribly awkward exchange.

"Not in person, though," she said into the empty car, her hands suddenly kneading the steering wheel. Her headlights cut through the darkness, and Gretchen focused on the road ahead while she prayed.

"Please let us have a decent in-person interaction tonight. Is that too much to ask?" She didn't think so, and she pressed a little harder on the gas pedal so she could get to Will just a little faster.

7

W ill finished the schedule for the week, sent the texts, and silenced his phone. He always got at least a dozen text-backs about what day wouldn't work or if so-and-so could get off earlier than scheduled. He was honestly done with trying to herd cats around the farm, but he continued to do it, week after week.

He fed the horses in the barn and swept out the aisles. He'd just left the barn when a pair of headlights cut through the darkness and entered the parking lot just beyond the Shoppe his sister ran. That had to be Gretchen, and Will pulled his phone out to check.

Within five seconds, she called him, and he broke into a jog. He couldn't believe that forty-eight hours ago, he'd typed out part of a message to cancel their date. His nerves still weren't quite sure what he was doing, but he met her at her van as she opened the door and the light from inside illuminated a small space around her.

"Hey," she said, her voice warm and pliable. It sank right into his ears, and all Will could think about was holding her. So he took her into his arms and did exactly that. Gretchen stayed rigid for a moment, and then she melted into him. "Okay, so we're hugging hello." She giggled, and Will pressed his eyes closed for a couple of seconds.

He had no idea what he was doing. He didn't know what to say either. He was just so dang glad to see her. She calmed him, and made the black things in his life lighter. Everything that angered him simply didn't matter anymore, and that was something that only running had accomplished for him.

"Howdy," he said as he stepped back. A smile stretched his face. "I don't know why, but it's so great to see you."

Gretchen blinked, her own smile pasted to her face. "Okay, so we're going to work on how you deliver things."

Will frowned, not sure what she meant by that, and reached for her hand. "Is this okay?"

She slipped her fingers through his and squeezed. "This is fine."

He watched her, but she wouldn't look at him again. "I said something wrong?"

"It would've been better had you just said, 'it's so great to see you.' Not about why you don't know why."

Will's chest tightened and then released, the same way he flicked his fly fishing rod. Out and back. Out and back. He cleared his throat. "Okay. I can see that." He guided her toward the Shoppe and took the key from his pocket. "So my sister makes all the cheese and ice cream here. We sell it." He unlocked the door and took her inside.

"I had no idea this was out here." Gretchen looked around the Shoppe as Will fumbled to find the lights. He finally located the switches, and the Shoppe filled with light.

"This month's special is Berry Blast," he said. "It's pretty good." He dropped her hand to go around the counter and scoop the ice cream. The weight of Gretchen's gaze didn't leave his face, and he looked at her as he reached for a cone. "Cone or cup?"

"Cup, please," she said. She cocked her head. "Do you eat ice cream? I thought you were off the sugar."

"This is fruit ice cream," he said with a smile.

Gretchen burst out laughing, and for a reason he couldn't name—but he'd never say that again—he joined her. "It still has sugar, cowboy," Gretchen said between her giggles.

"Not as much though." At least that was what he was telling himself, and he was going to stick to it. He quickly scooped up some ice cream into a cone for him, and he reached for a bowl for her. "What flavor do you want?"

"The Berry Blast, of course." Gretchen's blue eyes dazzled him, and Will's heart dive-bombed through his body. He scooped up her dessert and handed it to her with a spoon, then washed up the scoop and picked up his cone.

Before he rounded the end of the ice cream counter, the bell on the door dinged. He froze, and Gretchen whirled toward the entrance. Clarissa stood there, both hands parked on her hips.

"William Iverson Cooper," she barked. "What are you doing?"

He lifted his cone, hoping his smile would work on his little sister. "Getting dessert?"

"You set off my alarm, you idiot." She glared at him, her expression changing to one of compassion and caring when she looked at Gretchen. "Hello. You must be Gretchen Bellows."

"Yes," Gretchen said, moving forward to shake Rissa's hand. "I didn't know we were out of bounds. He had a key."

"Traitor," Will said, his throat narrowing. Rissa was going to kill him.

"You have a key?" she asked, her voice this freaky-calm tone that sent chills through him. "That's interesting."

"It's right here," he said, hastening to get it from his pocket and hand it to her. "We're leaving." He stepped to Gretchen's side, who looked two seconds away from laughing. "Right, Gretchen?"

"Yes," she said, and Will silently begged Rissa not to say another word, at least right now. She was so much better than Travis, because she only nodded once as Will scampered out of the Shoppe, Gretchen in front of him.

Freedom tasted like fresh country air and a berry mixture of ice cream in his mouth. He darted around the side of the Shoppe with Gretchen, where they both dissolved into laughter once again.

"You didn't ask permission?" Gretchen asked. "William Iverson Cooper." She giggled again, took a bite of her ice cream, and looked at Will with stars in her eyes.

He told himself not to fall in love with her in a single evening. He'd made that mistake before, and he'd been paying for it for a long time. He could hardly help himself, however, and he just shook his head and took another bite of his treat.

It didn't take long to eat through a single scoop of ice cream, and he got to his feet. He extended his hand to Gretchen to help her up, and nothing had been right in the world without her fingers between his. Will gave her a shy smile and kept his gaze on the ground as he walked her the few paces back to her vehicle.

"Tuesday," he said into the stillness around him.

Before she could answer, the night lit up with blue and red lights, and a police siren went *whoop!-whoop!* seemingly an inch from his ear. Will turned around to find two cop cars screeching to a halt only feet from him, and an officer jumped from one of them.

"Hold it right there," he said.

"No!" Clarissa yelled from somewhere in the darkness. "I turned off the alert."

More headlights joined the party in the small Shoppe lot, and Will's countenance drooped to his toes as Daddy arrived in his big truck, then Lee in his.

"Alarms goin' off at the house," Daddy said, coming forward to see who the perpetrator was. "Will?"

"Sir, what's going on?" the officer asked.

"Nothing," Rissa said.

"It's a spreadable cheese shop," Will said into the chaos. "I had a key!" The only thing comforting him was Gretchen's hand holding tightly to his.

"I'm so sorry, Will," Rissa said, turning to face him with panic in her eyes. "I turned off the alert."

Lee met Will's eyes, and all he did was start to laugh. And laugh. And laugh.

"All right," Daddy said. "False alarm. Pack it up everyone. Time to go home." He gave Will a cocked left eyebrow that said he'd be in even more trouble if he kept going down his current path, then limped off to get back in his truck.

"Ma'am, are you okay?" an officer asked, and Will wanted to turn lion on him and roar that of course she was okay. He had a key, and they snuck two scoops of ice cream, for crying out loud!

"I'm fine," Gretchen said, and she stood partially behind Will while everyone left.

With his head hanging down, he finally faced her. "Sorry," he said.

"It's okay."

He looked up and into her eyes. She couldn't possibly think what had just happened was okay. "I feel cursed with you," he said, not quite sure why he let his mouth say things without consulting his brain first.

She flinched at his words. "Do you want to cancel for Tuesday night?"

"No," he said, reaching up slowly to run his fingers down the side of her face. Their eyes locked, and Will leaned toward her. He brushed his lips against her cheek and straightened before he made a bigger fool of himself. "If you're willing to put up with my mouth, and my insane family, and awkward exchanges every time we're together, and apparently a few cops every now and then, I'd love to see you on Tuesday night."

Gretchen smiled, nodded, and got in her minivan. Will stayed in the parking lot and watched her drive away. Then he looked up into the sky and blew out his breath. "Really, Lord? I had a key."

———

WILL GROWLED AS HE STRAINED AGAINST THE WRENCH, trying with every muscle in his body to get the nut to move. It finally did, releasing all at once and sending his elbow into the side of the machine.

He swore, but there was no one around to hear him. Travis had pulled over three cowboys from the winter wheat planting to deal with the milking today, due to this machine going down over three hours ago. Not only that, but the rain had turned every single thing at Sweet Water Falls Farm into muck and mud.

Will carried a lot of it on his jeans and boots, and he didn't think there was a shower on this earth that could get him clean enough to go out with Gretchen tonight. He sat up and rubbed his elbow, glancing at the analog clock on the wall in the milkshed.

Almost noon, and he didn't see the work he had to do letting up in the next six hours. "You should cancel with her," he said with a groan as he got to his feet. He reached for the package another of their cowboys had gone to town to get, and he got busy fixing the machine. Every cow they could get milked, rain or shine, needed to be done.

In this moment in time, Will hated every machine in the world. He installed the new pump and wrenched everything back together. After taking ten seconds to stretch his back, he walked toward the outer area of the shed, where the cows were chuted in to be milked.

"Try station seven now," he yelled to no one in particular. Several men worked to get cows—Travis called them Berthas—into position, and someone went toward station seven. A cowboy fed a cow down to the station, and the suction hoses got hooked to her udders.

A couple of moments later, milk sloshed into their canister.

Relief like Will hadn't experienced in a while cascaded through him, and he reached up and wiped his hand across his forehead. His stomach grumbled at him for something to eat, and he couldn't remember what he'd been doing when he'd gotten word about the downed compression machine in the milkshed.

Probably checking some other piece of equipment. The refrigeration unit in their storage facility had been on the fritz for the past month, and Will had finally gotten Daddy to approve the funds to fix that. They ran all of their milk through that fridge, and if it went down... Their losses would be catastrophic.

"The Smith's are here," someone yelled, and that was Will's cue to get moving again. Taylor and Bryant Smith owned one of the larger organic grocers in the state of Texas, and they'd been expanding their stores into Louisiana, Oklahoma, and Arkansas for the past year. They were the third largest client that Cooper & Co supplied milk for, and they came personally to pick up their weekly milk supply.

Will expected to find Lee out in front of the massive storage facility, and he did. All three men hovered under umbrellas, but Will simply walked through the rain. Maybe it would wash off some of the grime, the grease, and the gunk from the actual down-and-dirty milking operation.

"Here he is," Lee said. "I'll take Taylor to sign the paperwork. Bryant, you can go with Will and start filling your bottles."

Will put the friendliest business smile he could muster on his face, shook Bryant Smith's hand, and turned to lead him into the storage facility. It smelled like dairy and dirt inside, a scent Will was extremely familiar with.

Pure exhaustion flowed through him, and while Bryant went to load the first pallet of empty glass bottles they'd then fill with organic whole milk, he pulled his phone from his back pocket.

I'm so sorry, he typed out quickly. *But today has gone from one bad thing to another. The rain hasn't helped. Can we reschedule dinner tonight?*

He sent the message as Bryant backed the truck right into the facility, and Will started to close the doors. His phone rang, and irritation spiked within him despite Gretchen's name on the screen.

"Hey," he said quickly. "I'm with a client."

"Do you want me to come out there tonight? I can bring pizza or something."

Bryant dropped down from his truck, looking for Will. He raised one hand, his smile flying right back into place. He turned his back on the man before barking, "No."

"Will, it's not—"

"I'm not in the mood," he said, and he really didn't have time for this. He didn't know how to say goodbye. He didn't know how to soothe feelings. He shivered from the cold wetness that covered his whole body, and he really just wanted to get Bryant Smith's order fulfilled and the man on his way.

Then he needed to eat and shower, and he had zero mental bandwidth for Gretchen. Because of that, he said, "I have to go," and hung up. At least he thought he said that much. As he turned to go help Bryant, Will wondered if he'd really spoken that last sentence or not.

The probability that he'd just hung up on Gretchen Bellows like a great big cowboy beast intensified, and Will's shoulders sagged under the weight he carried.

"Everything okay?" Bryant asked, real concern in his voice.

No, Will wanted to rage into the sky. *Everything is not okay.*

Instead, he smiled and reached for the first bottle. "Yep. Let's get you gentlemen on your way. I don't think this rain is going to let up until next week."

With Bryant chuckling, Will's heart turned to stone because he *was* certain he'd just ruined everything with the only woman who'd sparked anything inside him in years.

8

ho's that who keeps texting you?" Karyn Harlow looked at Gretchen with surprise and curiosity in her eyes. She reached for another pod of edamame, but that didn't mean she didn't hear the buzzing of yet another text.

And then another one.

Gretchen swiped her phone off the table beside her and put it in her pocket. There, it could only rumble against her bones, making her weary from the inside out.

I'm not in the mood.

Will's words from two days ago still cut through Gretchen. She'd apologized via text for calling him when he was busy, and he hadn't responded—until now. Now, it seemed his fingers were on fire and his mind stuffed full of guilt, because he'd texted her at least fifteen times in the past sixty seconds.

"No one," Gretchen said, shooting Karyn a look she hoped told the older woman to drop it. She'd come to Karyn's for lunch today, because she'd taken a much-needed break from the candy shop. Jon was a wizard with guests, and they didn't need more truffles for their cases. They'd be out of brownies and pecan spiders by morning, but Gretchen didn't much care.

Not today, anyway.

"Sure," Karyn said as if she believed her. "I have *no one* text me five hundred times a minute too."

Gretchen let out all of her breath, the macaroni salad she'd been about to eat falling right off the fork as her arm sagged. It was too good to waste, but she couldn't bring herself to care right now.

"It's William Cooper," she said. "He asked me out last week, and by some strange occurrence I don't understand, I said yes." Gretchen looked across the table to Karyn. She'd stopped eating completely, and for once Gretchen was glad they were just at her house. Her two-year-old was down for a nap, and her older boy was at school.

"Then, there was this weird muddy hug, and a really hot cheek-kiss, but also cops, and the most delicious contraband ice cream." Gretchen tossed her fork onto the table. "We were supposed to go out on Tuesday, and he was grumpy about the rain and all the work going on at the farm. I called him, and he said he wasn't in the mood." Her chest heaved, and it hurt, and she just wanted someone to make it all go away.

Karyn blinked a couple of times, as if Gretchen had strung together a bunch of words in another language. "Let's circle back to the cops and the contraband ice cream," she said slowly. "But start with what happened after the call on Tuesday."

"I sent him an apology. He hasn't responded until now."

Karyn started waggling her perfectly manicured fingers. "Give me the phone."

"Karyn," Gretchen said, suddenly so protective of her device. "You can't text him."

"I'm not going to text him," she said fiercely. "I'm going to screen his texts to see if you want to read them or not."

Gretchen took out her phone and passed it to Karyn. "You like this man?" the older woman asked.

She didn't look up at Gretchen, which made it easier for her to say, "Yes," accompanied by a long, swoony sigh.

Karyn's eyes flitted back and forth as she read, only getting wider and wider as she did. She met Gretchen's gaze silently, and she handed the phone back. "You'll want to read those."

"All of them?"

"Quickly," Karyn said, her smile growing on her face.

Gretchen took a breath and held it as she looked down. Will had been sending a lot of texts, and Gretchen warmed with each one she read.

I'm so sorry stuck out to her.

I was just in such a foul mood hit her squarely between the eyes. *I get grumpy sometimes.*

I want to see you. No, I need to see you.

Please tell me I didn't fatally mess up.

And those were just some of the messages. She looked up and met Karyn's eyes. "Do you think he's sending all of these?"

She shrugged one shoulder as her toddler started to fuss through the speaker on the baby monitor. "I don't know, but he did win a contest once for fastest texter in Texas."

Gretchen sat very still, trying to absorb those words. "You're kidding."

Karyn stood and wiped her dark hair back off her face. "I'm not kidding. I have to go get Lucy up, and you need to go call your cowboy." She grinned at Gretchen, who stood too. She embraced Karyn, her heart pounding in a new way.

She still had to get out to Daddy's at some point today, but maybe she could make a little stop by Sweet Water Falls Farm first. Karyn detoured to go upstairs while Gretchen went out to the porch.

She waited until she was seated behind the steering wheel before she called Will, who was still sending her messages. The line connected, but he didn't say hello. More than one voice came through the line, and Gretchen heard, "Say hi, you dolt," in a woman's voice.

"Howdy," Will yelled into the phone. A big exhale

followed, and Gretchen wasn't sure what to say next. She blinked, seeing a Will-less future in front of her, and while a lot of their interactions hadn't gone terribly well, she didn't want to be Will-less.

"Will," she said diplomatically. "I took today off, and I was wondering if you might have a few minutes this afternoon before I drive out to my daddy's to visit."

Whispering came through the line, but Gretchen had a hard time distinguishing full words or phrases. "Yes," he finally said. "That should be fine."

Gretchen put her car in reverse and backed out of Karyn's driveway. "Are you with your sister?"

"Yes," he said again.

"Is she going to coach you through everything to say once I get there?"

"N-no," he said.

Gretchen smiled to the sky around her. The rain had moved on, but Sweet Water Falls was still wet. The farm would be, that was for sure. "Did you mean the things you texted, or were you just typing what Clarissa said?"

"Both," he said.

"Are you going to talk to me in more-than-one-word sentences?" she asked. "It's a long way for a yes or no answer." She came to a stop at the end of the street, once again presented with a left or a right that would take her to two very different destinations.

"Rissa's gone," Will said. "Listen, Gretchen." He cleared his throat. "I really am *so* sorry. I have these redheaded genes inside me, and sometimes they just come erupting out. My mama sat and listened to me whine all night last night, and you know what she said to me?"

"I have no idea," Gretchen said, making the right turn that would take her to the farm and not her father's.

"She said, 'William, it sounds like you like this woman a whole lot, and you better figure out how to apologize and then tame your inner grump.'"

"Texas Mommas," Gretchen said with a smile. "They're usually right. Mine used to tell me not to go kissin' boys on top of water towers. She said nothing good comes from a kiss on top of a water tower."

Will let a beat of silence come through the line, and then he burst out laughing. Gretchen joined him, glad all the tension between them had shattered. "I have missed talking to you," he said. "Did I hang up on you the other day?"

"Yes, sir," she said. "You sure did." She twanged out the words like they didn't sting at her, but his abrupt end to the call had needled her for over forty-eight hours.

"I sure am sorry, sweetheart," he said softly, and she caught a glimpse of the non-grumpy Will even though she couldn't see him. "How far out are you?"

"Fifteen minutes," she said. "I think the farm is about the same distance from my house as the candy store is, and as my daddy's place." She had no idea how she'd be ready to face Will in only fifteen minutes. Then she reminded herself that *he* was the one who should be shaking in his boots.

"I'm going to go grab the skillet cake Lee made last night, and I'll be at my cabin, okay?"

"Yes, sir," she said again.

This time, he said, "Okay, I'll see you soon, Gretchen," before the call ended, and then Gretchen only had to focus on not strangling the steering wheel for fourteen more minutes.

By the time she pulled up to the quaintest, most darling cabin in the world, her nerves had frayed all the way to the center. She didn't have to wonder if she'd found the right place, because Will sat on the front steps with a guitar across his lap.

He looked up as her tires crunched over the gravel in front of his cabin, and he practically threw the guitar to the side as he stood. He came jogging down the steps and the front sidewalk, and she'd barely had time to put the car in park and open the door before he arrived.

She put her hand in his offered one, the touch of his skin against hers sizzling hot. Their eyes met, and Will said, "I'm sorry. I'm so sorry," before he enveloped her in a hug. Gretchen wanted to be held by this man for a long time, despite his stressed-out, grumpy words from earlier in the week

"I shouldn't have called," she said against his shoulder.

He pulled back. "No," he said, his eyes blazing with energy. "None of this is your fault, Gretchen. I just...it's me.

Trav told me he asked Shayla to tell him when he's being this horrible person, and I guess I need that too."

Gretchen shook her head. "You know."

"Yeah." He slung his arm around her. "I do know. I'd had the worst day ever, and I really wanted to see you, and I was so upset I had to cancel. I didn't want to think about having to see you that night, and I didn't want our first date to be you bringing me pizza out here."

She drifted closer to his side as he took her up the sidewalk. The wind gusted, and he nearly lost his cowboy hat. He saved it by pressing down quickly on his head. "Tonight? Can I take you to dinner tonight?"

She shook her head. "I can't, Will. My daddy has a doctor's appointment in an hour, and we get sandwiches at this place in the mall every Thursday." She gave him a smile, but he didn't return it.

He stopped walking and cupped her face in his hands. "I'm sorry I made your life harder. I won't do that again, I promise you that." He dropped his hands, stealing his warmth and his affection from her. "But I understand if you just want to walk away now." His jaw jumped, and he looked over her shoulder and into the distance. "Might be best for you."

She let the wind tug at her hair and jacket without resisting them. "Will," she finally whispered, and that brought his attention back to her. "You're not like the other men I've dated, that's true. I worked for a bull of a chef in Dallas, and I had to close up my candy shop in

New Orleans when my business partner-slash-boyfriend stole from me."

She took a deep, deep breath. "When I look into the future, I don't see either of them. I see Sweet Water Falls, and I see Sweet Water Taffy." She gripped the front of his denim jacket, wondering how a man could make such a thing look so sexy. "I don't know about you and me yet, because we're just getting started, but I know I don't want to walk away right now."

He nodded, those blue-green eyes like hot fire in her soul. "How long can you stay?"

"Only a few more minutes," she said, thinking of the drive to get her dad and then get to the doctor.

Will looked up into the sky. "Okay," he said. "Let's go inside, because it looks like it might rain again."

Gretchen went with him, because she liked being at his side. She liked the sound of his voice in her ears, and she liked being able to share her day with someone with human DNA and who hadn't served in the Army fifty years ago. She could take a little bark from Will Cooper, and as he served her a piece of gooey chocolate cake, her world got a whole lot brighter.

"One of my goals this year," he said as he slid onto the barstool next to hers. "Is to take more time off. I need a break. I work too much." He took off his cowboy hat and tossed it on the counter. "Then I'm grumpy as can be, and I don't like being like that."

She took a bite of her cake, everything sugary and rich

exactly what she needed. "Me too, Will. I work too much at the candy shop. We can work on working less together." She grinned at him, and this time, he did smile back.

He leaned toward her and swept his lips across her cheek again. Gretchen leaned into his touch this time, his kiss a brand against her skin. "Tomorrow night," he whispered in her ear. "Can we go out together tomorrow night?"

He pulled back, and Gretchen caught the desire and hope swimming in his eyes. She wondered what he'd looked like when she'd called on Tuesday, and what color his eyes would be when he finally kissed her.

She nodded and forked up another bite of cake. "Yeah," she said. "We can go out tomorrow night."

9

Will threw the tie on his bed in complete irritation. "I don't have time for this."

"You don't need a tie," Trav said from the doorway. "Shay'll be here any second, and she could tie it for you though."

"No." Will glared at his brother in the mirror. "I should've left fifteen minutes ago." Someone had stopped by the office to talk to him right as he was getting up to leave. Of course. That was the story of William Cooper's life.

He turned toward Travis, feeling naked from head to toe. He hated it and reminded himself one more time that he *wanted* to go out with Gretchen. He *liked* her. He liked spending time with her and holding her hand, and he'd be lying if he said he hadn't thought about kissing her tonight after dinner. He had mints in his pocket and everything.

"Are you sure I don't need a tie?"

"You don't need a tie," Trav said, a smile touching his face. "I haven't seen you like this since—" Thankfully, he stopped talking, but the name hung in the air.

Tara.

"Yeah," Will said. "I just feel like a fool." He looked down at his shirt, which bore a collar and the color of lemon juice. "This shirt isn't right." He started undoing the buttons and flung it on the bed too. "It needs a tie."

"I'm coming in," Shayla Nelson called, and Will lost Trav's attention to his fiancée.

"In Will's bedroom," he yelled. "Come help him get dressed."

"Don't ask her to do that," Will grumbled, pulling a couple of polos out of his closet. These wouldn't require ties, and he wondered if he should change back into jeans too. He turned toward the door as Shay filled the doorway. Trav beamed at her and slid his arm around her waist.

She smiled up at him, kissed him, and then the pair of them focused on Will. "I like the blue one," she said. "With your hair color and that white hat."

"Great," Will said, already discarding the red and black one. "These pants? Or can I go back to jeans?"

"Those are great," Shay said. "They say I-thought-about-what-I'd-wear-tonight, and they look like you didn't just come in off the ranch."

"It's a farm, baby," Travis said, and somehow, that got Will to smile.

"Farm, ranch, whatever," Shay said, rolling her eyes. "Are we going to dinner or what? You made it sound like you might feed me at the farmhouse."

"Will's skipping out on his night," Travis said.

"I'm not skipping out," Will said. "We switched."

"So I'm cooking tonight," Travis said. "He's taking tomorrow." He left the room with Shay, the two of them still chatting, and Will took a moment he didn't have to look at himself in the mirror.

He'd shaved this morning, and only a little growth now covered his face. He'd showered, brushed his teeth, and used a couple of precious pumps of his grandfather's cologne. The polo was almost the same color as his eyes, with darker stripes of blue and navy running down it, and he could switch out his white cowboy hat for a ball cap of the same color and change his look entirely.

He didn't want to. He wanted to be a cowboy tonight, and he grabbed his wallet and shoved it in his back pocket as he turned to leave the bedroom. "I'm goin'," he said as he went into the living room. He shrugged into his leather jacket while Travis laughed about something with Shay.

Neither of them even seemed to notice that Will was there, and he paused again. The entire world froze, and he saw Travis and Shay living right here in this cabin together. As the heavens opened and told Will he'd be the one to move out and into the cabin next door to Spencer and Clarissa, he smiled.

That somehow drew their attention, and Shay scanned him from head to boot. "Gretchen is going to have to hold onto something when she sees you." She grinned at him, and Will reached up to tip his hat.

"Call me if you need me," Trav said. "I might have to call you to get out of the farmhouse tonight."

"If you do, I'll pour water in your bed." Will wasn't kidding either. He wasn't going to interrupt his first date with Gretchen to save his brother from an uncomfortable conversation with their dad. *Every* conversation they had was mildly uncomfortable, and Travis could deal with it.

Travis burst out laughing, and even Will smiled. He left the house and hurried to his truck. Twenty minutes later, he pulled up to the house at the address Gretchen had given him.

The little white brick house possessed charm, and Will felt life pulsing from it. The light green door bore a wreath, though Christmas had come and gone a few weeks ago. Bright bluebells and snowballs made up the circle, and the whole thing made Will smile. It screamed Gretchen, and he couldn't wait to see what the inside of her house looked like.

He got out of the truck and went up the walk, then the steps. She lived on a street with a few other people, but there was a lot of land here. Plenty of space for horses or cows, sheep and chickens. It didn't seem like she had any of those things, but a big, square patch of grass surrounded her place.

Her doorbell broke through the stillness out here in this more rural part of Sweet Water Falls, and Will wondered if she was in the town proper or not. "You drove to a Sweet Water Falls address," he muttered, quickly silencing as scratching happened on the other side of the door.

He squinted at the floor, and in the next moment, the door opened. Gretchen stood there, and it was Will who had to find something to hold onto to keep himself upright. He already found her gorgeous while wearing a T-shirt with an apron over it and a pair of shorts.

Tonight, she wore a black dress that swelled in the chest and hips and went all the way to the floor in layers of fabric. Wide straps went over her shoulders, and as he stood there staring and mute, she said, "Good evening, Will," and reached for her jacket.

He sprung into gear then, helping her into the denim coat with plenty of silver buttons down the front. "You smell nice," he said, unable to censor himself. Horrified, his tongue swelled and rendered him mute again. *Probably for the best*, he thought.

Gretchen grinned at him. "Thank you. It's a perfume I bought out in this tiny town in Louisiana. It's supposed to be—no, wait. You guess what it is."

Will took the opportunity to lean closer to her again, a gray tabby weaving between their four feet. He didn't

mind the feline, as he hadn't come here to see it. He took
Gretchen right into his arms, and she came real willingly
too. He lowered his head to get his nose closer to her neck,
and he took a long breath in.

"Smells like oranges and honey," he said. "Maybe
some lemon. Vanilla." He reminded himself the date
hadn't started yet, and he didn't need to be kissin' her yet.
He put proper distance between then and looked down at
the cat.

"You're right," she said. "It's an English tea party—the
perfume. Orange scones and butter and honey."

He met her eyes again. "I like it."

Her blue eyes danced with merriment. "I like your
shirt." Her gaze moved up to his hat. "And your hat."

"Thank you, ma'am," he drawled out, reaching up to
take off his hat and put it right back on. "What's the cat's
name?"

"Elvis," Gretchen said, toeing him back into the house.
"You stay here, buddy. I'll be back later."

"Yeowl," Elvis said, but Gretchen paid him no mind as
she stepped out onto the porch and closed the door
behind her.

"I like your wreath," Will said, reaching out to touch
one of the flowers. He saw little faces on some of the
snowballs too, and he realized they were snowmen.

"Thank you," Gretchen said. "I'm not great at decorat-
ing, but my sister-in-law and I did a wreath class one year
when I was visiting them in Fort Worth. I have one for

every month now, and that's about what I can handle as far as putting out holiday décor."

She slid her hand in his, and all of the jagged and upset pieces of Will smoothed and aligned. "I was thinking we'd try Italian tonight," he said, stepping to move down to the sidewalk. "You mentioned you like pasta, right?"

She had said it in a text last night. Will hadn't been on a date in a while, and he really wanted tonight to go well.

"I love pasta," Gretchen said. "Where were you thinking?"

"Wherever you want," he said. "Do you have an idea in mind?" He went with her to the passenger-side door and opened it for her.

She pressed in close to him. "I love the Cheese-It Bakery in Castleton. It's only twenty minutes from here, same as town."

Will swallowed, because she stood so near to him. She put one hand on his chest, and all Will had to do was lower his head and he could kiss her. "I've been to Castleton," he said instead, his voice made of gravel and dust.

Gretchen grinned and stepped up into his truck. He closed the door while she reached for the seatbelt, and Will took a couple of extra seconds to round the truck to get behind the wheel, needing the cooler night air to help lower his internal temperature.

Calm down, he told himself. *Be cool. Cool and calm.*

He started the truck and lowered the volume on the

radio. "Cheese-It Bakery," he said as he lifted his phone to type it into his maps. Once he had that set and running, he added, "Only seventeen minutes from here," with a smile in Gretchen's direction.

He backed out of her driveway, thinking maybe the hardest part of the night had ended. Then she said, "So, Will," and he realized he'd have to talk to her tonight. All night. And he never liked sentences that started with "So, Will."

"Mm," he said, tamping down his annoyance.

"I told you a little bit about who I've dated in the past," Gretchen said, her voice made of light and air. "What about you? Who've you been out with recently?"

Will's hand jerked on the wheel, and he dang near drove them off the road. He blinked and looked at Gretchen. "Did Travis set this up?" he asked.

Gretchen's smile faltered. It was false anyway, even if Will couldn't quite see all of it in the orange lamplight. "No," she said. She folded her arms across her chest. "It's fine. Never mind."

"No, it's okay," Will said, swallowing back his idiocy. "Sorry. It's fine. Let's see..." He pretended to think about who'd he'd been out with. It wasn't a long list, that was for sure, and he certainly knew the name of the last woman who'd carved his heart from his chest and sent him down this five-year-long road of celibacy.

He sighed, because he really couldn't lie very well. "The last woman I went out with was named Tara Wells," he said. "I fell in love with her pretty fast, and pretty deep, and it wasn't very pretty when she rejected my proposal."

Gretchen sucked in a breath, but Will didn't look over at her. The road was dark, and he needed to make sure he didn't kill them on the way to pasta bliss in Castleton. "Will," she said. "I'm so sorry. I didn't know."

"That's why you asked." He did look over at her then. Her arms had released, and she wore a genuinely compassionate look now. "Right?"

"I mean...yes."

"You didn't tell me anything about who you dated in the past. You said your boyfriend stole from you. That's it."

"That's a lot," Gretchen said.

"What was his name?"

Her arms cinched around herself again, and Will wished he hadn't asked. "Malcolm Adams," she said. "We opened a candy shop together in New Orleans. I thought we'd get married, work the shop, teach our children all of our ways with caramel and chocolate." She sighed, and Will really didn't like the sound of that.

"Things just don't work out sometimes," she said. "You know?"

"I've experienced that, yes," he said quietly. He reached over and took her hand in his. "I've seen people work through difficult things too, and they do stay together and work out. So it goes both ways."

Gretchen nodded and looked out her window. "Yeah."

"Do you miss him or the candy shop?" Will asked.

She swung her attention back to him, her hand tightening around his. "Neither."

"Then why are you sad?" He glanced at her but quickly put his attention back on the road.

"I don't know," she said thoughtfully. "There's this element of fantasy, right? The big house, the white picket fence, the children..."

Will wouldn't allow himself to clear his throat. "That fantasy comes true for people."

"I know," she said. "But not for me, it hasn't."

"Not yet," he said, looking at her again. "Right? It's not too late for any of that."

"Will," she said, her voice definitely brighter now. "How old do you think I am?"

"I have no idea," he said, and he did clear his throat then. "My mama taught me not to ask a lady's age."

Gretchen giggled, and that made Will smile. "You say anything else you want though."

He squeezed her hand. "I do?"

"Do you miss him or the candy shop?" Gretchen asked, dropping her voice and mimicking Will's. "Who asks someone that?"

"You seemed sad," he said, a fire lighting inside his chest. "I was tryin' to figure out why."

"You were tryin' to figure out if I was ready to date you or not."

"That too," he shot back. "Is there a problem with that?"

"Yes," Gretchen said, holding her own with him. "Not every woman is going to be Tara."

Will sucked in a breath and held it, wondering how this conversation had gone from her flirting with him about how old she was to the biting quality in her voice when she said *Tara*.

"I'm sorry," she said at the same time he said, "I don't think every woman is Tara."

Pinpricks of light appeared on the horizon, and Will kept driving. "I dated her for a long time, Gretchen. Three years. Before her, I hadn't dated in a while, and I thought she was going to be my fantasy, you know? That I'd have the cute house with the wreath on the door, and the kids in the yard, and there wasn't a candy shop, but they'd all come with me to the dairy farm, boys and girls alike."

He couldn't believe the words coming out of his mouth.

"Maybe there could be a candy shop," Gretchen whispered. "And a gray tabby cat named Elvis."

Will forgot about driving then. He looked at her and took his foot off the gas pedal so if they did crash, it wouldn't be fatal. "Maybe," he whispered back. "And the kids?"

"I want kids," Gretchen said, clearing her throat. She reached up quickly and swiped at her eyes, and Will wondered what he'd said to make her cry. "This is deep first date conversation," she said in a much lighter tone.

Will agreed, and he went back to driving. His mind

wouldn't let go of what she'd said, and when they pulled into the packed parking lot at Cheese-It Bakery, he knew he'd have to say what was in his brain.

He found a spot and pulled in, put the truck in park, and looked at Gretchen again. "Does your age have anything to do with having the kids you want?"

She smiled at him, and he liked the softness of it. She released his hand and reached over to cradle his face in that palm instead. "Do you always just say whatever's on your mind?"

"Not always," he said. "Just the stuff I know is gonna keep me up at night." He searched her face, almost desperate for an answer. "I'm forty years old. I haven't dated in five years, since Tara said no. I'm a redhead and hot-headed, and I swear, Gretchen, I'm doing everything I can to keep my temper in check when you're around."

He swallowed, because he'd said too much already. "Because I like having you around." He pressed his lips together, but he had one more thing to say. "I really like you, and I want to get to know you, and be with you, and I'm going to stop talking now."

Gretchen's eyes filled with tears, but she didn't brush them away this time. "I'm thirty-seven," she said, her voice a tad choked. "I spent a lot of my child-bearing years building my career, and I'm definitely second-guessing my life choices."

"It's not too late," he said.

"No," she said. "Not yet." She dropped her hand and

looked down into her lap. "I really like you too, Will." Her gaze flitted over to him and then around the truck. "Should we go in?"

"Yes," he said, his cells buzzing with a new kind of energy now. "Stay there, and I'll come get you." He slid from the truck first, and while he wanted to run around to her side and help her out, he took his sweet Texas time.

First to give her a chance to wipe her eyes and collect her emotions. Second to give himself a moment to enjoy the words *I really like you too, Will.*

He hadn't felt liked in a long, long time, and as he finally opened her door and found a smiling, shining Gretchen waiting for him, he wondered if she could ever possibly fall in love with a man like him.

10

Gretchen couldn't remember a better date than the one she was currently on. Sure, the conversation had been a little heavy on the drive to Castleton, but once they'd gone inside the restaurant, it had lightened up.

She'd gotten her "can't decide spaghetti," which came with marinara meat sauce and Alfredo sauce, and Will had professed his love for a good lobster mac and cheese. They'd talked about their siblings and their jobs, while staying away from the harder things like her mother's death and his mama's sickness.

She'd already confessed far too much to him that night as it was, and he seemed to feel the same way.

Now, he turned down her street, and a yawn pulled through her whole body. She couldn't contain it, and Will chuckled. "Tired?"

"Yes, sir," she said. "I'm not up this late ever. I go into the shop about dawn."

"I'm up at four-thirty to run every morning," he said.

Horror ran through her. "You're kidding."

"I'm not."

"You won't go tomorrow," she said, not asking. "That's in like four hours. Or will be, by the time you get home." He drove an incredibly nice truck, and the clock blinked like diamonds in white lights on the dashboard.

"I don't know," he said. "We'll see how I feel when the alarm goes off."

"Will," she said, helplessness in her voice.

"What?"

"You'll be tired."

"I'm a grown man," he said. "I know what kind of sleep I need."

"I feel bad."

"So our next date we won't stay out so late." He grinned at her. "The Culinary Cabin on Wednesday? Or did you want to maybe get together on Sunday? That's a slower day for me around the farm. I could go with you out to your daddy's."

Gretchen thought about it while he pulled into her driveway. The porch light shone in the midnight darkness, and her heart boomed in her chest. Surely this gentleman cowboy would get out and walk her to her door. Her lips tingled in anticipation of kissing him.

Would he even try to kiss her?

"Did I ask a really hard question?" Will teased. "It's okay to say no, Gretchen. I can wait to see you until Wednesday."

"Do you go to church in the morning on Sunday?" she asked.

Will sighed and reached to unbuckle his seatbelt. "Sometimes." He looked at her. "I'd go with you."

She smiled at him. "Great. I'll come pick you up, and we'll go. I usually go to my daddy's right after that, but you can follow me in your truck so you can get back to the farm if you need to."

"Oh, you're gonna cause so much trouble for me," he said, grinning at her. He got out of the truck before she could ask him what he meant, but she wasn't going to let this go.

He opened the door for her and crowded into the space as if she couldn't get down herself. She could, but she took his hand and let him slide his other one along her hip. "What does that mean?" she asked, staying close in his arms. "Why am I going to be trouble for you?"

"Remember my family?" he asked, his eyes a dark blue now. "We eat together every Sabbath Day. If I don't show up...they'll be all over me."

"Then we'll eat at your house—farm—wherever you guys eat, and then go to my daddy's." Gretchen grinned up at him, noting the shock as it marched across his face. "Oh, I see that's worse."

"Not worse," he said, backing up as she stepped

forward. "I'm just tryin' to imagine the hullaballoo if I show up with a woman to Sunday dinner."

"Because you haven't dated in five years."

"Right."

"But you told your mama about me."

"And Rissa."

"And Travis."

"Lee knows too."

"So no hullaballoo," she said, stumbling over the word. She laughed and added, "I don't know anyone who talks like that."

"Whatever," Will said, his arm tight around her. "Everyone in Texas talks like that."

They laughed together as they went up the steps, and Gretchen paused right in front of her perfect mint door with the very January wreath. She put both hands on Will's chest and leaned into him. "Thank you for tonight, Will. I had a lot of fun."

"Me too." He smiled at her, and his eyes dropped to her mouth. Oh, yes, he was going to kiss her. Excitement built in Gretchen's stomach, and her eyes drifted closed.

The wisp of his breath touched her cheek, and then a horn filled the air. A truck came roaring into her driveway, startling her and Will apart, the horn blaring as the lights illuminated them and the house.

"What in the world?" Will asked.

Gretchen started toward the steps, because she knew who owned this truck. "It's my neighbor," she said. "Something's wrong." She flew down the steps in her long skirt, already calling, "LaMar? Is Rachel all right?"

An older gentleman got out of the truck on the driver's side, and he said, "She's fine. We're fine."

Gretchen's heart wouldn't stop sprinting. Neither would her feet, and she ran past Will's truck to LaMar. "What's going on then?"

He reached back into the truck and pulled out a box. "Elvis got hurt at our place. We've been takin' real good care of him, and I've been watchin' for you to get home. I didn't want you to go in and be worried he wasn't there."

He handed her the box with Elvis cowering in it. He wore a wrap around his front right paw, and Gretchen couldn't believe this was what had interrupted her first kiss with Will. Her brother's bothersome cat.

She looked up at LaMar, feeling so out of sorts. "Thank you," she managed to say.

He beamed at her, tipped his hat, and got back in his truck. She took Elvis up to the porch, where Will had waited for her. "My neighbor," she said. "His wife has some health problems, so I thought it might be her." She held up the box. "It was Elvis instead. He gets out and into things he shouldn't."

She sighed as she opened the door and put Elvis inside. He yowled at her like that wasn't the treatment he expected, but Gretchen's exhaustion wove through her now too.

"I'm so sorry," she said, stepping into Will's arms again.

The moment was broken though, and she couldn't call it back now. "I'm keeping him for my brother as he goes through this hard thing in his life. His wife left, and he's got the three kids all alone. I guess Elvis was too much for him."

"Hmm, I can see why."

Gretchen smiled up at the cowboy. "I'll see you Sunday?"

"I can't wait," he said, his lips right at her ear. He touched them to her neck and stepped back. "I'll talk to you tomorrow."

"Mm." She walked to the edge of the porch and watched him descend the steps and then stride toward his truck. She couldn't believe she'd caught his attention, and while he had a gruff exterior, she knew more about the man underneath all of that now.

And she sure did like him.

"Meow," Elvis said pathetically, and Gretchen sighed as she turned back toward her house. She went inside and closed the door, then bent to pick up the tabby cat.

"You silly thing," she scolded him. "You interrupted my kiss with Will." How embarrassing was that? Her injured cat took precedence over kissing the handsome cowboy. Max was going to have some cat-tax to pay, that was for sure.

Humiliation dove through her when she remembered how she'd run from Will—and all for a cat who probably wasn't injured that badly?

So embarrassing.

She took Elvis down the hall to her bedroom, where he limped to the empty side of the bed.

"You're going to have to help me brainstorm a new plan to get him to kiss me on Sunday," she said pointedly, glaring at the feline. "So start thinking."

———

GRETCHEN REACHED TO UNTIE HER APRON, HER HANDS sticking to all the fabric on her shirt too. "Okay," she said with a huge sigh. Her heart raced, and her eyes darted around the candy kitchen. "I have to go."

At the same time, she couldn't go. Not with caramel-like-glue on every surface she could see. She and Jon had been making caramels for hours now for an event this weekend. She looked at the man, her eyes wide. She needed his permission to go before she could actually do it.

"Date with Will Cooper tonight," he said, giving her a smile that didn't seem very smiley.

"Yes," she said, still fumbling with the tie on the back of her apron. Her mother used to make her aprons that went on like smocks, and she could unsnap them from around her neck in two seconds flat. In moments like this, Gretchen missed her mother powerfully.

"He hasn't canceled?" Jon asked, and Gretchen stopped playing with the tie.

She reached for a roll of paper towels and a bottle of stainless steel cleaner. "Not yet."

"Because he did on Sunday, right?"

"Yes," she said. "His mama is real sick." She shot Jon a glance. "I understand that. I had to spend yesterday and Monday with my daddy, taking care of him."

Jon sighed and finished wrapping the last batch of caramels. He tossed them by the wax-paper-wrapped handful into the bin marked "vanilla" and sighed. "I know, Gretchen. I'm sorry."

"Why do you care?" she asked, glad the more difficult flavors of black licorice and cinnamon had been done for hours. "Besides me wanting to run out and leave you to clean the kitchen."

"Which I agreed to do," he said. "I booked this event, and you stayed to help me with the caramels." A hint of redness started to creep into his face. "I just think...this Will Cooper better be good to you." He turned away from her and flipped on the water at the industrial sink that ran along the back wall.

Gretchen stared at him for a moment, not quite sure how to digest his words. "He is," she said, her voice a bit high-pitched. "We're going to The Culinary Cabin. Remember that place I told you to take Diana?"

"Yeah," Jon said.

"You never did."

"I couldn't get her to go on a second date with me." Jon

turned around and gave Gretchen a glaring look. "So no, I never did."

Gretchen blinked at this man she'd hired a couple of months ago. He'd become her friend at Sweet Water Taffy, and she'd always gotten along with him.

"Never mind," he said. "You should go so you're not late for your date." He started scrubbing the counter in front of him as something strange shot through Gretchen.

Had she offended him by talking about her excitement to meet up with Will tonight? She'd told him about Will's difficult Sunday too, and maybe she shouldn't have. Perhaps she needed to simply treat him like an employee and not her friend.

She wasn't quite sure how to do that, but she did manage to untie her apron and hang it on the hook beside the sink. She washed up too, the water too hot but her mind circling too much for her to care that much.

After driving home without noticing anyone else on the road or if she came to a complete stop at any of the intersections, she dashed up the front steps and through the mint green door. "Elvis," she called, hoping the cat was here. She didn't want to leave out the fresh food if it didn't get eaten. If she did that, sometimes she got wild animals coming in through the cat door that led onto the back porch.

The cat appeared at the end of the hallway, and he'd probably been snoozing on her bed. "Come eat," she told him, and she flew through putting together his dinner. He got chicken, carrots, and peas tonight, which almost looked like a chicken pot pie without the gravy.

Gretchen very nearly tossed the bowl on the floor in her haste to get down the hall and out of her candy-making clothes. She hadn't checked her phone in hours, and Jon's question about Will canceling tonight rang through her head. She'd said he hadn't, but in truth, he could've but she hadn't seen it yet.

She stepped out of the black pants she wore to work, searching her pockets for her phone. It wasn't there, and panic ran through her. She felt torn in a hundred different directions, and she started to remove her shirt at the same time she ran back toward the hall, as if her device would be lying on the floor out there.

It wasn't, and Gretchen went into the kitchen just as her phone chimed. She'd left it next to the cutting board where she'd chopped the cooked carrots into uneven chunks for Elvis. The cat still chomped through his meal, and Gretchen swiped on her phone at the same time her doorbell rang.

Fear paralyzed her, and only her neck worked as she looked away from her phone and toward the door.

That couldn't be Will already. Could it?

In the living room, the grandfather clock she'd brought over from her parents' house after her mother's death started to sing.

It was six o'clock, and that meant the person on the other side of the front door definitely was Will.

Gretchen flew herself into gear, taking her phone with her as she dashed past the clock, which had started its march toward the six dongs it would eventually get through.

After all, she couldn't answer the door if she was undressed.

"I mean, you could," she said, flinging open her closet door. One day, she'd learn to lay out her date clothes before she left for work. "But I'm not sure that's the message you want to send."

11

W ill stood on Gretchen's front porch, the bouquet of flowers he'd driven to town to get starting to droop as his impatience grew. He'd already rung the doorbell twice, and he twisted around to look behind him for the fourth time.

His truck sat behind Gretchen's van in the driveway, so she had to be here. Right? He glanced to the left and then the right, but she owned enough land that he couldn't see her neighbor's houses.

"What will you do about it anyway?" he asked himself as he faced the January wreath on her door again. His hand twitched to ring the doorbell again, but he fisted his fingers into his palm to stop himself from doing it.

He took a step back and pulled his phone from his pocket, and he tapped a couple of times to get a call connected to Gretchen.

"I'm so sorry," she said, her voice made only of air. "I'm here, but I barely just got home, and I had to feed Elvis, and I'm not quite ready yet."

Will smiled, because he just liked the sound of her voice. "It's fine," he said, all of his annoyance gone now. "I can wait."

"The front door is open," she said. "You can come in, and I'll be right out."

Will wasn't sure he wanted to do that, but he didn't want to hang out on the porch holding this ridiculous bunch of roses either. He looked down at them, and said, "Okay, I'll do that."

"I only need three minutes."

"Take your time." He ended the call and turned back to the door. He did twist the knob and go inside just as Elvis jumped onto the back of the couch. He gave the cat a hat-tip and took a moment to look around Gretchen's house.

He hadn't been inside until now, and it felt like a place she would live. The furniture was a dark bluish-gray, with plenty of pink and yellow pillows in the corners. The windows had matching curtains, and the living room in the front of the house where he stood, flowed right into the back of the house where the kitchen sat.

Elvis gave him a cat-glare and proceeded to lick his jowls and then one of his paws.

An island ran right behind the couch, and it held the kitchen sink. The fridge stood against the back wall, along with her range. She had a decent amount of counter space, and he expected to find a stack of mail or a vase of flowers or something sitting there.

He found nothing. The counters were completely clean, except for a cutting board and knife right next to the kitchen sink in the island. A couple of pieces of abstract art hung on the walls in the living room, which had windows on two walls, and a grandfather clock ticked on his left right beside the hallway.

There were no family pictures, and no knick-knacks. The TV sat dark, with the remote control lined up beneath it in a near ninety-degree angle.

Will had no idea what he was dealing with here. He didn't consider himself a huge slob or anything, but Gretchen didn't even have a hook to hang her keys on anywhere.

"Sorry." Her voice preceded her down the hall, and Will lifted the flowers back to a position in front of him. She came into the kitchen, brushing her hand down the front of her blouse, which drew his attention there.

The fabric flowed like silk, and it reminded him of the pale orange he'd find in the perfect sunset. She wore a pair of navy blue shorts that went all the way to her knee, and a pair of bright white tennis shoes sat on her feet.

Will cleared his throat and stuck the flowers out a bit more. "Howdy, Gretchen."

She looked up at him, her bright eyes wide and filled with some emotion he couldn't name. She took a moment to breathe, and he watched her visibly relax. "Evening, Will."

He stepped toward her, and they met in front of the clock. She clasped her fingers around the stems of the flowers as he leaned in and kissed her cheek. "You look fantastic tonight," he said.

"I'm pretty sure I'm still sticky from head to toe." She stepped back, now beaming at him. "Thank you for these. They're beautiful." She inhaled the roses, her eyes drifting closed. She opened them and swatted Elvis away from the blooms. "Did you finish your dinner?"

She went into the kitchen and bent to pick up the cat's bowl. She put that in the sink with the cutting board and knife, doing it all one-handed while she held the roses. Then she got a vase down from the cupboard and looked at him.

"Sorry I'm so late," she said. "We won't be late to The Cabin, I swear."

"It's okay," he said again. "Why were you late? I thought you left the shop at three on Wednesdays."

"Jon booked this big party on Saturday," she said. "And he had to make five hundred caramels, so I stayed after to help him." She arranged the flowers in the vase and lowered it into the sink to fill with water. "And wow, you can not imagine the mess. It's a retirement party, and apparently this woman has a lot of friends who like black licorice caramel." Gretchen shuddered, which made Will smile and then laugh.

"You don't like black licorice?" he asked.

She looked at him as she turned off the sink and raised the vase out of it. "Does anyone?"

"I mean, my daddy does."

"Yeah," she said dryly, tugging a rose into a different position. "The generation older than us loves black licorice. They must've spoon-fed it to them in their baby cereal." She stepped back and admired the flowers. "These are so lovely."

Will wanted to say she was the lovely one in the room, but he couldn't. So he tucked his hands into his pockets and smiled at her as she came around the island and to his side. "Are you ready for this?" she asked.

"I've been waiting over a week for it," he said. "So I guess I better be, right?"

She grinned up at him, and Will had a vision of leaning down and kissing her right there, right now. His brain froze, and Gretchen's smile slipped. His eyes still worked, and he blinked.

"What other kinds of caramels did you make today?" He could smell the sugar on her, and that only drove his desire for her higher.

"Sea salt," she said. "That's my favorite."

"Mine too," he murmured, going with her as she moved toward the front door. "Do you need to put Elvis away?" He paused and looked at the tabby, who gazed right back at him as if he could see inside Will's head and knew he didn't want to be interrupted by the neighbor when he dropped Gretchen off later tonight.

"Oh, right," Gretchen said. "Come on, Mister." She unlooped her arm from Will's and scooped Elvis into her arms with a yeowl from the feline. She bustled down the hall and a door closed a couple of seconds later. "There. Now he won't be over bothering the Woodworths."

"Good news," Will said. They reached the door, and he opened it. She stepped past him, and Will honestly felt like the luckiest man in the world to be going out with her again. "How's your daddy?"

He saw her shoulders rise and fall, and he caught her hand in his as he stepped to her side at the top of the steps. "You don't have to say," he said as gently as he could. "I just noticed you didn't say anything about him in your texts over the past few days."

"He's...okay," Gretchen said. "I think he's getting more and more stubborn with every day." She gave him a brave smile. "What about your mama? Sunday was a bad day?"

Will's soul turned dark for a moment. He couldn't imagine a day on the Earth without Mama in it, but he knew he'd have to endure such a thing, probably sooner rather than later. "She's okay," he said. "She had a real bad night on Saturday, and Daddy was up with her a lot. They were both really tired, and even Travis couldn't get her out of bed."

He opened the door for Gretchen, but she didn't climb into the truck right away. "He's been goin' out with Shay a lot, and he was tired himself. So I went to help, and once we got Mama on the couch and Daddy frying eggs and potatoes, we went and got the chores done."

"There's some work that never ends, isn't there?" She looked at him with kindness shining in her eyes, and Will really needed someone to be kind to him right now.

"Yeah," he said. "I'm sorry about Sunday. I know I said I was going to try to take breaks and whatnot. Farm life is just so...unpredictable."

"So are sick parents," Gretchen said. "I understand, Will. Don't worry about it." She got in the truck then, and Will went to get behind the wheel. She directed him to the farm where they'd be having dinner, and Will knew the moment he turned down the dirt road that he'd feel right at home.

"This is incredible," he said, gazing at the dormant fields that had obviously been taken care of. "She's got stuff in some of these."

"She has a greenhouse," Gretchen said, a hint of pride in her tone. "She starts a ton of stuff inside in the winter and moves it into the fields later. Sometimes she harvests right from the greenhouse."

"Fascinating," he said. There was no fancy sign directing people where to turn or where to park. They weren't the first people to arrive, so it was pretty dang easy to turn into the next parking spot in the dirt field with a pink house in the background. It had a purple door and a lot of white trim around the windows and roof. It felt like the kind of house or cabin that Will would like to spend time in, and he grinned through the windshield at it.

"I told you you'd like this place," Gretchen said, and he switched his gaze to her.

"You sound so sure of yourself," he said. "I don't like frou-frou food."

"You and the rest of the cowboys in Texas," Gretchen said, rolling her eyes. "And yet, this place is booked out weeks in advance, and look, there's a cowboy going in right now." She unbuckled and added, "Come on, Will. We really don't want to be late. Ingrid serves appetizers, and I've never had one I didn't want to eat an entire tray of."

Will chuckled as he got out of the truck, and his smile remained in place as they followed the other couple toward The Culinary Cabin. A wrought-iron patio set sat out front, but they obviously wouldn't be eating there.

Gretchen led him up the steps to the porch, and Will's chest felt like someone had suddenly thumped on it with their fist. He couldn't quite catch his breath, because he wasn't quite sure what he'd find behind that door.

But he couldn't wait to find out, and he stepped with Gretchen, his hand in hers as tight as it had ever been.

12

Gretchen's excitement continued to rise as Will opened the door for her, and she stepped into The Culinary Cabin. The smell of rich, dark coffee hit her nose, and then someone said, "Welcome to The Culinary Cabin. We have two appetizers tonight. A fresh salmon kabob with a dill-lemon sauce or a short rib Gorgonzola bite."

"Wow," Will said, gazing up at the ceiling. Gretchen felt like that too, and she looked up at the vaulted ceiling —original to the house—and the ornate chandelier hanging there.

Giddiness pranced through her, because she'd wanted Will to like The Cabin as much as she did. "We'll have both, please," she said when it became obvious Will was going to gaze and not gab. She tugged on his hand to get him to move out of the doorway as another couple entered, and they stopped at a chest-high table without chairs.

"So they bring around appetizers in here," she said. "It's kind of like a museum. There's the history of Sweet Water Falls, some art by local artists. That chandelier was made by a Sweet Water Falls native named Vincent Gusteau, and I guess he died really young."

"This is incredible," Will said. "Not what I was expecting, but amazing."

"Coffee? Water?" a woman asked, and Will opted for water.

"For me too, please," Gretchen said. Once she'd left, she continued with, "Then we'll go out to the tables. You can see the farm better from out there. They'll serve the meal out there, and Ingrid herself comes out and goes through the menu. Then everyone gets served, and we can wander the farm for a little bit."

"It's almost dark," he said.

"They have some lights," she said. "But yeah, you won't be able to see as much as you do in the summer."

He beamed at her. "We'll have to come back in the summer."

Gretchen warmed from toes to throat, because if Will wanted to come back in the summer, that meant he saw them together in six months. "Sure," she said, the word barely making it out of her narrow throat. She wasn't even sure why she was so pleased, only that she was.

"Salmon and short rib," a man said, and she shifted so

he could put the plates on the table. Everything was bite-sized and easily popped into a mouth, and Gretchen reached for a salmon kabob. A piece of fish sat on the bottom and the top, with a blistered cherry tomato sandwiched between them.

"Do you like fish?" she asked Will.

"I do if it's like this." He picked up a kabob too, and said, "Three, two, one." He stuck his kabob in his mouth, and Gretchen did the same.

It was too much for her to have both bites of salmon, though she tried. She ended up giggling as Will grinned at her. "I win," he said. "I got all mine in one bite."

She shook her head and finished chewing in as lady-like of a fashion as she could. "It's not a contest, cowboy."

"It was real good," he said. "I liked that." He looked at the short rib. "Is this blue cheese?"

"Gorgonzola," Gretchen said, popping the last bite of salmon into her mouth. "I love this dill sauce."

Will grinned at her. "Yeah, it's on your blouse there."

Gretchen looked down, embarrassment streaming through her when she saw the glob of white sauce on her blouse. She quickly wiped it away and licked her finger. It sure seemed like she and Will were going to learn how to be comfortable with one another even when bad things happened, and she decided everyone spilled on themselves sometimes.

"Holy dairy cows," Will said with a moan. "I need five more of these."

"They'll bring more," Gretchen said, turning to find a waiter. She caught one's eye and raised her hand. He nodded, and she looked at Will again. "So, I saw you with a guitar last week. Do you play?"

"Hardly," he said, dusting his hands and reaching for a napkin. "A little. My granddad taught all of us, Cherry and Clarissa too. Lee's the real star with the guitar."

"Is that right?"

"Yes, ma'am," he said, smiling at her. "Trav and I just pluck around on chords."

"What about your sisters?"

"Cherry quit when she was ten or eleven," Will said. "She did piano for ages though. Rissa played longer, but I don't know that she's done anything with it since she went to culinary school."

Gretchen nodded and made room for another round of appetizers.

"What about you?" he asked. "Hobbies?"

"Hobbies?" she repeated. "Who has time for hobbies?"

He chuckled and bobbed his head. "Tell me about it."

"My shop and my daddy take all my time and energy," she said. "And then Elvis came to stay with me, and now I've got this cowboy I'm sweet on that I have to squeeze into my life." She was kidding, her tone clearly conveying that.

Will still looked at her with fire blazing in those teal eyes, serious as she'd ever seen him. "Is that a problem for you?"

"No, sir," she said, sobering too.

He fiddled with the toothpick holding his short rib bite. "You're sweet on me?"

"William," she said. "I told you I liked you."

"Liking someone is different," he said.

"Is it?"

"Ladies and gentlemen, we're ready to move outside to the tables," someone called. "Please come forward when I call your name and sit at the table you're assigned."

Will turned toward the man, and Gretchen's heart quivered strangely in her chest as she moved to stand beside him. Being sweet on him *was* the same as liking him. She hadn't revealed anything he didn't already know.

She cut a glance at him, trying to get a read on how he felt. The man was like a stone, and he'd drawn shutters over his expression. He seemed rapt on the man up front calling out names, and that only made Gretchen's legs shake a little more.

"Gretchen Bellows," the man called, and she and Will moved forward.

"Table six, please," he said, handing Will a single sheet of paper that looked like it was made from a specialty fiber. "This is our wine and spirits menu. Orders can be placed with your table host." He smiled and looked down at his clipboard.

Will led Gretchen to table six, his step sure and his voice silent. She wasn't sure how to break this ice she'd created between them. Or maybe he'd created it. Perhaps both of them. They sure had broken through a few awkward moments, and Gretchen took courage with that knowledge.

Will slowed and said, "That greenhouse is huge."

"Oh, there's Ingrid," Gretchen said, her soul lighting up. Ingrid saw her in the next moment, and her smile filled her face. Gretchen giggled as she left Will and danced over to her friend. "Look at you," she said, hugging the other woman. "You cut your hair and didn't send me a picture."

"Mm, I sure did." Ingrid gripped her tightly. "That is one mighty fine looking cowboy." She whispered the words, because Ingrid had tact and grace in droves.

"Yes, he is," Gretchen agreed as she pulled back. She looked into her friend's dark eyes. "Do you have a couple of seconds to meet him?"

Ingrid glanced toward the back porch, where another couple had just arrived. "I think so." She turned back to someone. "Martin, I'll be right back."

Gretchen turned to face the same direction as her, and the two of them walked toward Will. "William," she said. "This is my friend, Ingrid Olsen. She's the chef-owner of The Cabin." She smiled at Ingrid and then back at Will. She lifted an imaginary sledgehammer and got ready to swing it with all her might.

"Ingrid," she said. "This is William Cooper, my boyfriend."

His eyebrows went up, but the corners of his mouth

did too. He shook Ingrid's hand and said, "I can't wait to eat your food. Everything has been delicious so far."

"Thank you," she said. "What did y'all have?" She glanced between Gretchen and Will.

"We had the beef and the salmon," Gretchen said.

"Wonderful," Ingrid said. "Wait until you see the beets tonight. They make me so happy." She got called away in the next moment, and Gretchen watched her stride back toward the kitchen that sat off the back of the house.

Will indicated her chair, and Gretchen sat at table six. Above them, a canopy of mesh protected them from the insects, and only a few of the brightest stars had started to show in the near-darkness. Cement covered the ground and made the chairs and tables stable, and as Will sank into the chair opposite of her, Gretchen looked right into his eyes.

"You handled the boyfriend introduction well," she said, wishing she had a glass of water to hide behind.

"Did I?"

"Only raised eyebrows." She grinned at him and rested her chin in her hands. "No challenge to that?"

"Do you want me to challenge being called your boyfriend?"

"No." She reached for her rolled silverware and removed the utensils from the napkin. "Would you introduce me as your girlfriend?" She focused on spreading her napkin over her lap, her eyes cast down so she didn't have to see Will's reaction to her question.

"What if I did?" he asked. "Would you raise your eyebrows?"

"Maybe a little," she said, lifting her eyes back to his.

"And why's that?"

She didn't know how to articulate what she wanted to say. She couldn't just blurt out that he better kiss her that night or she might not think he was really interested in her. He seemed to be. He kissed her cheek. Brought her flowers. Held her hand. Asked her questions about her life, her temporary cat, her daddy, her hobbies.

"I think I know why," he said, glancing over to the nearest table, but the couple there seemed totally engrossed in their own conversation.

"Why?"

"Same reason I was a little surprised."

"Because this is our second date?"

"Because I haven't kissed you yet," he said, just saying the words right out loud. How he did that, Gretchen would never know.

She blinked and somehow got her head to nod. "Yeah...that would be nice."

Will's eyes shone with playfulness. Or maybe something else. "Would it now?"

Gretchen shook her head and rolled her eyes. "Come on, William."

He reached across the table, which held a cream-colored cloth, and covered her hands with both of his. "I like it when you call me William. Only my mama ever does that, and usually when I'm about to be in big trouble." He grinned, which was so unfair to every woman within the vicinity of his charisma. "But when you say it, I feel like I might win the lottery."

"I'm sure that'll happen," she said, teasing him. "Plus, I heard your sister call you William."

"Yeah, and I was in trouble."

Gretchen searched his face, catching movement just beyond him. Ingrid was about to go over the menu, and this conversation would die and another one reborn once they got their food. "The chances of winning the lottery are slim," she said. "But what are my chances of getting that kiss tonight?"

Will's eyes dropped to her mouth and rebounded back to her eyes. "I'd say high to very high. Maybe one hundred percent for-sure." He glanced toward the back porch as a bell rang. "Of course, I suppose it depends on what's on tonight's menu."

"Welcome, everyone, to The Culinary Cabin," Ingrid started, her own strong personality exuding out into the night. "We're thrilled to have you on the farm with us tonight. Our first course is French onion soup, made with a variety of sweet onions we grow plenty of here on the farm."

Will groaned under his breath, and his eyes shone with a teasing light as he said, "French onion soup? Can't kiss a woman after eating that..."

A COUPLE OF HOURS LATER, GRETCHEN LEANED AWAY FROM the plate of panna cotta. "I can't eat another bite."

"But there's only one left," Will said, still holding his dessert spoon in his hand.

Gretchen put hers down so she wouldn't eat the last bite. "You have it."

"I have all this pudding." He glanced down at his glass cup, which was almost empty. She couldn't wait to taste the chocolate on his mouth, and her chest heated with the very idea of kissing him that night. She'd been thinking about it all through the meal, and she wondered if he had too.

After the French onion soup, they'd been served bacon-wrapped sirloin steak, mashed purple sweet potatoes, and the cutest, smallest Brussels sprouts Gretchen had ever seen. Dessert was chocolate pudding and shortbread or a lemon-raspberry panna cotta. They'd opted to get different desserts and share, but she'd only taken one bite of the rich, dark pudding.

Will scooped up the last of the panna cotta and put it in his mouth. "I do like this," he said. "It's very tart."

"Refreshing," Gretchen said.

"My mama loves sour stuff," he said. "She'd love this."

"I'd like to meet your mama," Gretchen said. "Because we ladies who like sour in our desserts need to stick together."

Will put down his spoon and wiped his mouth. "I'd like you to meet my mama too." He'd been conversational during dinner, and they'd talked about the food and the farm and not much else. Gretchen knew there'd be plenty of time to get to know him, and it was nice to not have to be learning something new about him every second.

She had learned that he liked his bacon extra-crispy, and even men would eat vegetables if there was enough honey glaze to go over them.

"Your mama and your horse," she teased. "That's what's important to most cowboys." She put both hands on the table and leaned forward. "Do you have a horse, Will?"

"Yes," he said, his voice a bit guarded. "He's kind of like your cat. A little standoffish to people he doesn't know."

"What's his name?" Gretchen asked.

"Leonard," Will said.

Gretchen burst out laughing, sure Will was pulling her leg. He smiled, but he didn't join in the laughter, and she realized he wasn't kidding. "Leonard?" she repeated.

"He was a rescue," Will said. "I didn't get to name him."

"You can't rename a horse?"

"He likes his name."

Gretchen blinked at him, still trying to decide if Will was joking. He could flirt with her, and he could be playful, but he wasn't the kidding type. "All right," she said. "Leonard it is."

He tossed his napkin on the table, over the mostly gone glass of pudding. "Yep." He sighed and looked out into the darkness. "Should we go?"

"Sure," Gretchen said, standing up and putting her napkin on the table too. Will tossed a bill on the table, and Gretchen took one last drink from her water glass.

Somehow she walked back to the truck, and then before she knew it, Will had pulled into her driveway.

He held her hand on the way to the front door, and Gretchen wanted time to slow down now. Everything in the past half-hour had happened too fast, and she didn't want to miss her first kiss with this man.

Her pulse beat like a big bass drum as she faced him. She wanted to say something quippy like, *If my breath is too oniony, you can stop kissing me.*

She simply looked at him, the reverberations of her heartbeat filling her ears and throat.

He reached up and slid one hand along her jaw and neck to the back of her head. "I haven't kissed a woman in five years," he whispered.

"I'm sure you still know how," Gretchen said, taking a small step toward him. His hand brought warmth to her whole body, this single physical connection between them.

She put her hands on his chest, and they moved together—her inching up and him leaning down. His other hand landed on her hip, and her eyes drifted closed.

Will touched his lips to hers, and Gretchen felt like

she'd left her copper kettle over the flame for far too long. Heat soared through her, making her feel like steam was rising from the top of her head.

He moved slowly, almost experimenting to make sure he did remember how to kiss a woman. She slid her hands up and across his shoulders, then into his hair as he brought her closer and kissed her deeper.

All she could do was kiss him back and hope that she tasted as delicious as he did. She got chocolate and sugar and cream, and an earth-moving, life-changing kiss that shifted everything inside Gretchen's life.

13

Will could not remember a single woman he'd ever liked, much less kissed, before he touched his lips to Gretchen's. He lost himself inside that moment, and then pulled himself back, because he wanted to be present. He wanted to experience that smell of her, the taste of her, the way his back shivered as her fingernails slid along his ears and then into his hair.

He had no idea how much time passed, only that he kneaded her closer and kissed her again and again, needing to be as near to her as possible and explore every centimeter of his feelings for her.

They breathed together, and Will gently pulled away. His heart fluttered as if it had turned into a butterfly, and he felt the throbbing of his pulse in his neck. Though he didn't want to break the moment, but bask in it for a good long while, he opened his eyes.

Gretchen's eyelids trembled, and then her eyes came open too. He unknotted his fingers from her hair and ran them down the side of her face. "Okay?" he whispered.

"More than okay," she said back, those blue eyes burning in a way Will had never seen before. He wanted to light her up like this every single day, and he tried not to be too pleased with himself for a near-perfect evening. They hadn't argued; he hadn't gotten frustrated over anything; the food and conversation—and kissing—had been fantastic.

"I think you remember how to kiss a woman," she said, a smile appearing on her face.

"Mm, I suppose," he said, allowing himself to smile back. "Maybe I better do it again just to be sure."

Gretchen leaned into him, and he sure did like that. She made him feel strong and powerful, as if she needed him to hold her up. As if she needed him and only him in her life to support her.

She didn't, he knew that. She was a strong, smart, capable woman without him. But he still held her face in his hands and bent his head to kiss her again. His life lightened several more shades with this second kiss, and Will could only hope that he could continue to chase the darkness from his life with the help of his gorgeous girlfriend.

Gretchen pulled away first this time, and she tucked

herself into Will's arms. "Do you want to come in for a minute? I can make coffee or tea." She pulled back slightly and looked into his eyes. "Or I have some blueberry bars from this morning."

Will didn't have to think twice. He didn't consider what he had to do in the morning or how early four-thirty would come. "Sure," he said. "Coffee and blueberry bars sound great."

———

WILL'S BODY PROTESTED AGAINST ALL THE RUNNING. HIS muscles screamed at him to slow down, because they hadn't gotten enough rest in the past several days. He pushed himself onward, his focus on the ground and the music in his ears blasting away any of the country silence that existed as the sun crested the horizon.

He used to think about milking and machinery during his morning runs. Now he only thought of Gretchen. What he should text to Gretchen that morning, and if he could sneak away from the farm to see Gretchen that afternoon. Would she be driving to see her daddy, and could he go with her?

On and on.

The farmhouse came into view, and Will decided in that moment to stop there. He usually pressed past it, up over the hill in the road and on toward his and Trav's cabin. Then past it to Lee's, where he'd finally slow his pace to a walk and cool down by circling the pond while his heart rate returned to resting and his sweat cooled.

Soon enough, the morning weather wouldn't be cooling, and it would be hot in Texas twenty-four hours a day.

Trav's truck didn't sit in front of the farmhouse, which meant he wasn't there yet. Will had grown up in the very same house where he ate dinner most nights. He hadn't been able to see Gretchen again since they'd gone to The Culinary Cabin and then shared their first kiss.

Familiar darkness crept into his soul, despite his efforts to push it back out. "You'll see her soon," he told himself, though he hadn't dared set another date after he'd broken the last three for various reasons.

In truth, Gretchen had called to reschedule one of them, and Will had only been responsible for two cancellations. He couldn't help the weather, and he had no way of predicting how Daddy would feel on any given day, nor what problems would arise with their hired cowboys and cowgirls.

Three of them had requested less hours in the past week, which had left Will scrambling to post on the job boards to find someone new, as well as to cover the shifts they'd requested off. Thankfully, none of their machinery had gone on the fritz, and Travis and Lee had covered the milking side while Will had moved over to the agricultural epicenter of the farm.

Sometimes it was nice to work away from his brothers.

He found his temper not nearly as quick when they weren't around, though he did tend to make snap judgments and quick decisions about people when he shouldn't. Working with his men and women in the hay lofts, fields, and equipment shed had helped him get to know a couple of them better, and he'd had to reform some of his previous opinions.

Everyone in the family entered the farmhouse at will, and Will wasn't surprised to find the garage door unlocked, as well as the entrance to the house inside the garage.

Inside the house, silence prevailed, and Will glanced at the clock on the stove, realizing just how early it was. Not even six yet, though Daddy had been an early-riser for as long as Will could remember. He used to come into Will's bedroom, which he'd managed to have all to himself, and wake him about five.

"Milking time," Daddy would say, swiping Will's hair off his forehead. "Ten minutes."

If Will wasn't ready to leave the house in ten minutes, fire rained from heaven. At least it seemed that way to Will, as Daddy's ginger-haired genes didn't allow him to hold back his temper or his tongue.

Age had tempered him, and Will did enjoy seeing Daddy soften and take care of Mama the best he could. He'd been the strongest man Will had ever known, but he couldn't get Mama in and out of bed anymore. Travis had been coming in the mornings, and Will often came with him. Lee came in the evenings, and again, Will often came with him.

He'd always been stuck between the two of them—and in fact, was the very middle child of the family. He sometimes felt like a fulcrum, like everything in the Cooper family hinged on him, and he didn't know which side to hold up properly.

Will stepped over to the sink to wash his hands, the water coming out ice cold. It would take a few minutes to warm up, but Will got scrubbing anyway.

"Morning," Daddy croaked as he entered the kitchen.

Will looked up from the suds and running water, a smile instantly touching his face. "Morning, Daddy."

"Can you help Mama into the bathroom?" Daddy wouldn't look at Will as he spoke. He pulled open the fridge though he wouldn't take anything from it.

"Sure can." Will shut off the water and reached for a towel. Part of him wanted to wrap his father in a hug so tight that he'd know how much Will loved him. They talked in the Cooper household; it wasn't like Will hadn't told his daddy how much he loved him. It felt like it had maybe been a while, and Will had maybe caused a few too many problems lately.

"Daddy," he said, and his dad turned from the fridge. Will fiddled with the towel, wiping it between his already dry fingers. "Listen, I'm sorry if I've been a problem lately."

"Will," Daddy said. "You're not a problem."

"It's just—I didn't mean to make more work for anyone by leavin' to see Gretchen."

Daddy cocked his head. "I know that. You haven't been seein' her much lately."

"Yeah." Will reached to hang the towel back on the handle of the stove. "It's been busy."

"Trav manages."

"Trav's engaged," Will said. "I've been out with Gretchen twice."

"But you want to see her again, don't you?" Daddy leaned into the counter, and Will wondered how much of that was necessary and how much was just because.

"Yes," he admitted. "Our timing just hasn't worked out. Her daddy is sick, and he lives in Short Tail."

"You'll bring her to Sunday dinner this week," Daddy said, smiling at Will. "I know Mama wants to meet her, and I'll corral everyone and make them behave."

Will chuckled and shook his head. Despite his temper, Daddy couldn't really make anyone behave these days. He'd raised five headstrong children, with plenty of opinions and the loudest voices in Texas. They'd try, though, and Will loved them all for that.

"Text Trav that he doesn't need to come this morning," Will said. "I'll go help Mama."

"You call that woman too," Daddy called after him as Will started for the hall that led into the master suite. "Sunday dinner."

Will didn't answer, his mind buzzing with what this

weekend would be like for Gretchen. He was fairly sure she had an event, but he couldn't remember what it was. He hadn't been to town in over a week now, and he didn't keep up with the social events there anyway.

He rapped lightly on the bedroom door and said, "It's Will, Mama," before entering. His mother sat up in bed, several pillows propped haphazardly behind her. "You don't need to try to get up yourself," he said, hurrying now that he saw the evidence of her attempts to get enough support to stand.

Her left leg hung over the side of the mattress, and Will moved it further out, her right leg following it. He wrapped his arms around her torso as her legs moved, holding her up as carefully as he could. On the end of the bed, Queen Elizabeth the golden retriever watched.

"Morning, baby," Mama said, her voice raspy.

"You thirsty this morning?" he asked her, and she nodded against his shoulder.

"I'll get you in the bathroom, and then go grab you a drink," he said. "Ready?"

"Yes," she said, scooting to the edge of the bed, her arms up around his shoulders.

"All right. Three, two, one." He counted slow and lifted right after he said one. She pushed as much as she could, which was basically nothing, but he got her to her feet. He didn't release her instantly but gave her a few moments to steady herself.

"Thank you, Will," she said, pure gratitude in her

voice. "My pills are in the bathroom. I can just get a drink in there."

"You'll use the hand-bars, right?" he asked, though she did. Mama seemed to understand her limits. In the beginning of her illness, she hadn't, and she'd fallen four or five times before Cherry had come home and she and Lee had lectured Mama into submission.

Will had been present at the family meeting, and it still haunted him. He hated watching his mother cry, and he had no idea what it would be like to accept a devastating diagnosis. She'd been battling cancer for over five years now, and Will had seen her rapidly decline, then claw her way back inch by inch.

Her issues now had taken a long time to wear her down, and her decline had been slowly intruding on her daily activities for over a year now.

He helped her into the bathroom, where he'd helped Lee and Travis affix long silver bars to every available wall. They bordered the toilet and waited on the wall across from it. They'd put two in the standing shower, one on each wall. One sat just above the towel rack, and Mama reached for that one just inside the door.

"I'm okay," she said, though the walk around the bed and into the bathroom had winded her. "I need a few minutes, and then will you help me out to the couch?"

"Of course," Will said, his voice low and quiet. He reached to close the door behind Mama, and he leaned his forehead against the barrier between them. Helplessness washed over him in waves, and tears pricked his eyes.

He never let anyone see him cry. Ever. He rarely did anyway, but hearing his mama's labored breathing had punched him in the lungs this morning. He suddenly seemed to be leaking from every hole in his face, and he turned away from the bathroom and grabbed a tissue from his father's bureau.

He didn't want to grow old alone. He'd already spent four decades by himself, with varying periods where he'd had a girlfriend at his side. After he'd wiped his nose and eyes, he pulled his phone from his pocket and went to Gretchen's texts.

They'd been in contact; it wasn't like he never talked to her anymore. He just hadn't seen her in the flesh for eight days now.

"Too long," he murmured to himself as he tapped the phone icon to call her. A text simply would not do this morning.

"Will," she said, plenty of surprise in her voice. "What's up?"

"I miss you," he blurted out. "I hate that I haven't seen you in so long. I know it's Thursday, and you have your routine with your daddy." He turned around, his mind on the fritz. "But what about lunch? Can I bring you lunch? Even if I only stay for ten minutes, I'll get to see you."

As he spoke, he realized how vulnerable he'd just made himself. He heard the sound of his voice, and he knew it had been desperate. As he tried to decide if he cared that Gretchen knew he missed her and wanted to see her, she said, "Lunch would be wonderful, Will." She cleared her throat, and that made Will smile. "I miss you too."

14

"Will," Gretchen said, giggling as she tipped her head back. Will kissed her neck, and she enjoyed the feel of his hair through her fingers. He'd shown up with a couple of bags of food and wearing a cowboy hat, but she had no idea where either was at the moment. "My lunchtime is almost over."

"Is it?" he murmured, his lips coming back to hers. She could honestly kiss him forever, and she'd much rather do that than eat any day. She'd experienced several moments of doubt over the past eight days.

She'd gone through some hard things at work, with one of her best out-front employees putting in her two weeks' notice. Her family life felt like someone had put it in a salad spinner and just kept pumping that mechanism on top to make everything mix up more and more, faster and faster.

She'd wanted to tell Will about her brother deciding not to bring the kids to the area for the long weekend they'd just had, but Will had problems of his own.

You still should've, a voice inside her head whispered, and Will seemed to hear it, because he pulled away. He didn't back up, and she couldn't move away from the wall just around the corner from the sink, nor could she avoid his gaze.

"You okay?"

"Yeah," she said, finally able to look up and into those dazzling eyes. He wore compassion and desire there, one warring with the other. A vein of doubt seeped into her expression, and she gave him a smile. "Really."

"How's your daddy?" he asked, finally giving her an inch of breathing room. She quickly closed it between them again, not quite ready to let him go. He'd said he couldn't stay long, and they'd been kissing for a good twenty minutes.

"He's...fine," she said.

"Why didn't you call me?"

"And say what?" she challenged. "That he's telling the same stories over and over? That he keeps saying he's not going to go down without a fight? Which, by the way, I've heard five thousand times, and if I have to hear it again..." Gretchen shook her head, partly angry and mostly frustrated. Dejected. Hopeless.

She drew in a breath and sniffed back her tears. "I'm fine. How's your mama?"

Will gazed at her, his eyes still full of energy, full of life, full of disbelief. "Gretchen, it's okay to not be fine."

"Is it though?" she challenged him again. "Who's going to run the shop if I break down? You?"

"Yes," he spat back at her. "I could come help."

"When? Is that before or after you work sixteen hours on the farm?" Her chest heaved, and she couldn't breathe in here. This wasn't how lunch was supposed to go. She tried to move past him, but Will wouldn't let her.

"Hey, wait," he said, and his voice was so soft and so unchallenging that she waited. "Do you wanna know why I called you this morning close to six a.m.?"

She searched his face, but the man possessed incredible shutters. He never let anyone see what he didn't want them to, even her. "Yes," she whispered.

"I'd stopped by my parents' house on my run, because I'm just so tired. Daddy came into the kitchen and said Mama needed help to get to the bathroom. So I go do that, and it's horrible." He sighed and looked down at the ground, showing her the top of his head, where he had blond, brown, red, and even gray hair growing. She wanted to lift his face, lift his countenance, and lift his spirits.

He did that himself, a new type of blaze entering his expression. An angry, fiery blaze in those aqua eyes. "So I get her in the bathroom, and she's panting because it's so hard to walk the fifteen steps from the bed. I close the door, and I just stand there, and I want to cry." His voice broke on the last word, and that cracked everything inside Gretchen.

She took his face in one palm and slid her other along his waist. "Did you cry?"

"Maybe for a second," he admitted. "And all I could think about was you. I wanted to hear your voice, and I wanted to see you, and I absolutely couldn't let another day go by where we just texted or you called me on your drive home from Short Tail."

He leaned into her touch, and then turned his head and placed a kiss against her wrist. "I'm sorry life is hard for you right now. I will carry any burden for you that I can."

"It's not like you're just watching parades and enjoying the sunshine."

Will's anger dissolved into a smile. "True, but I did only run three miles this morning."

"Heaven forbid," Gretchen teased. "How will you look yourself in the eyes come this evening?" She giggled, and he chuckled, and when he kissed her this time, it was with new energy, new passion, and Gretchen wanted everything Will had to offer her. She could only hope she had something to offer him.

"...find her," someone said in the back recesses of her mind. By the time she registered Jon's voice saying, "There you are," she'd been caught kissing Will.

He backed up in a hurry then, stooping to grab his fallen cowboy hat and smash it on his head. He looked at

Jon and then Gretchen, a delicious blush creeping into his face.

Jon glared with the power of four suns. "There's a customer out here asking about a custom cake."

"We don't do cakes," Gretchen said with as much professionalism as she could muster. "Jon, have you met William Cooper?"

Jon nodded at him, no extended hand in sight. "Will."

"Jon."

Gretchen looked back and forth between the two of them, and she hadn't been around many dogfights, but this definitely felt like that. The tension rode on the air, and she had no idea why.

Jon exhaled first, his boxy shoulders relaxing. "I told Mrs. Lunt that we don't do cakes, but she's insisting you talked to her and said we could."

"Oh, Wilma Lunt. Right. I did talk to her a week or so ago. I'll be right out."

Jon flicked his gaze to Will again. "Okay, and then we need to get started on those mint wafer cookies, because they take forever to set." He turned and marched away, disappearing around the corner quickly.

Gretchen gaped after him, even when she couldn't see him. "Does he think I don't know how long it takes to make the mint wafer cookies? They're *my* recipe." She looked at Will, completely befuddled. "He's never acted like that, I swear. He's a nice guy. A *great* candy-maker."

"He likes you," Will said, the frown deep between his eyes.

Gretchen could not compute. "What?"

"He—likes—you," Will said just as darkly. "He's mad you're going out with me, and finding us kissing?" He shook his head. "He doesn't like me on principle, and he doesn't like you bein' with me."

Gretchen laughed, but Will did not join in. "That can't be it," she said, sudden worry gnawing through her. She couldn't lose Jon too. If he quit...Gretchen would seriously curl into a ball and sob in the corner.

"That's it," Will said. "Should we go eat?"

Gretchen looked around for the bags of food he'd brought, but she didn't see them. He walked around the corner and returned with them a moment later, all traces of ire gone from his face. "We can sit in my truck for a couple of minutes."

"All right," she said, thinking she better go talk to Mrs. Lunt first. "Can you give me a few minutes to talk to Wilma? I'll be right out, I swear."

"Sure thing, sweetheart." He brushed a kiss across her cheek, his gaze catching hers and holding. He didn't add anything else, at least not verbally. But Gretchen felt the searing heat of what he might've said flow all the way down her right leg to her toes, and then jolt up her left side in a powerful wave.

He went through the back door where he'd entered

the candy kitchen, and with flames licking through her, she went to talk to Wilma Lunt about baking her a cake.

GRETCHEN SURVIVED ANOTHER THURSDAY NIGHT WITH HER father. The doctor didn't have anything new to report, and the medicine her father took couldn't do more for him than it currently was. They got the same old sandwiches, and she listened to the Oldies station on her radio as she drove him home.

She tempered chocolate and made rose-flavored truffles for a bridal shower that weekend. She skipped church on Sunday and instead, took Aunt Patty to breakfast in a tiny café out in the middle of somewhere that didn't even have a name. Then they went to Daddy's for the afternoon, the same as usual.

More weekdays marched by, and the memories of kissing Will so passionately against the wall just inside the back door of the candy kitchen began to fade. She texted with him every day. He called her a time or two, and she returned the favor. They were dating, and she didn't doubt that they were together.

Life is busy she told herself more times than she could count.

He'd originally invited her to a Sabbath Day dinner at the farm, but he'd called in the morning and said tempers were high already, and perhaps she should come another time. She'd suggested a dinner date on Wednesday, but then the manager of a huge department store had stopped by five minutes before she was set to leave, and she wanted to hire Gretchen to make her "becoming famous" truffles for a massive sidewalk sale.

Thea's words, not Gretchen's, though she was glad someone had told Thea—the general manager at the largest department store in the mall—about her truffles. She suspected Karyn, but her friend wouldn't admit to it.

No matter who'd told her, Thea would bring in thousands of dollars and get Sweet Water Taffy out into the larger community surrounding Sweet Water Falls, and apparently everyone drove in for the Spring Sidewalk Sale at the beginning of March.

Gretchen felt like she spent a large part of her life behind the wheel of her car, but she wasn't driving where she wanted to go.

Another Thursday passed, and then February arrived. She'd started thinking about Valentine's Day weeks ago, because Sweet Water Falls did play home to about fifteen thousand people, many of them men who needed to impress someone on February fourteenth.

She'd been taking special orders for chocolates for weeks, and thankfully the cutoff date was January thirty-first. She couldn't exactly make the orders early, which made for a very busy February twelfth and thirteenth—and the fourteenth too, for those last day-of pick-up orders. But she did limit what else she stocked the shop with, a trick she'd learned in New Orleans from Malcolm.

She only put out what truffles she'd received orders for, so they could be perfect for Valentine's Day, and if she had any trouble fulfilling the orders, she could pull from her trays. Jon continued to make his grasshoppers and spiders, which were wildly popular, and she'd managed to hire several new employees to keep the front of the shop running smoothly during this very busy time.

"Gretchen," Jon said, none of the bite in his tone that he'd used with Will a couple of weeks ago.

She looked up from the milk chocolate she was tempering. "Hmm?" She'd thought a lot more about him "liking her" the way Will said he did, and she just didn't see it. He was professional, prompt, and proper. Nothing about his actions or attitude toward her suggested he didn't want her dating Will.

This Will Cooper better be good to you ran through her mind. He had said that to her, over a month ago, just before she and Will had gone to The Culinary Cabin.

"We're out of cream," he said, triggering something in her mind. "And Cason's just called and said they can't fulfill our order."

She looked down at the chocolate, working through the problem with the sweet stuff on her mind. Chocolate really could fix everything, and she saw the solution appear right before her eyes, in the shiny folds of the chocolate.

"I'll take care of it," she said.

"Do you want me to run to the grocery store and get what I can?"

"Is there some sort of cream shortage?" she asked. "We just need what? Fifteen gallons to get through the weekend?"

"That should do it," Jon said.

"Go get that at the grocery store," Gretchen said. "I'll call Cason and find out if they can deliver next week." She'd been ordering her cream and butter from the same supplier Aunt Patty had, a local pasteurization plant on the west side of town. Cason's EMC—Eggs, Milk, and Cheese—had been delivering eggs, cream, and butter weekly since Gretchen had arrived in town.

She didn't need cheese, though it was one of her favorite foods. But she did use quite a bit of butter in her creations, as well as cream in a lot of the fudge the shop offered. They'd gotten a big order of Fort Worth Fudge this week, and Jon was supposed to make that today.

"I'll go get it," he said. "We'll need it next week for Valentine's Day." He carried warning in his tone, which Gretchen did not appreciate.

"I'm on it," she said as sweetly as she could. "Let me finish with this round of truffles, because this chocolate is almost tempered, and I'll make sure we have all the cream we need for next week."

Jon nodded and started to return to the other half of the candy kitchen. "Wait," Gretchen called, reaching to flip off the flame beneath her double-boiler. "Is he sending butter still?"

"Yeah, he said the butter wasn't a problem. I guess he got some grocery store to pick up a huge order, and he says he can't keep our smaller unit and that he's real sorry." Jon shrugged, because this wasn't his problem.

It was Gretchen's, because she couldn't afford to pay retail prices for cream. She needed a restaurant supply price in order to make money on the candy. Her thoughts continued to bubble and boil as she finished her batch of truffles, and then she washed up and plucked her phone from her apron pocket.

A quick Internet search yielded her a number, and after she'd dialed it, a voice said, "This is Lee Cooper at Cooper and Co. What can I do for you today?"

Gretchen smiled up at the ceiling, the pleasantness in Lee's voice going against everything Will had ever said about his brother's sour demeanor.

15

Lee Cooper paced in the office inside the administration building. "This is a bad idea," he muttered to himself, not for the first time.

His son, Ford, looked up from the notebook on his lap, but Lee shook his head and Ford went back to his homework. Love swelled in Lee's heart, because his son was so precious to him, and he'd only had to ask once to get Ford to collect his homework and bring it with him this Saturday morning.

"How's the math?" Lee asked, forcing himself to walk over to the black leather couch where his son sat. He sank into the cushions where Will or Trav usually sat. Sometimes Rissa.

Lee himself usually sat behind the desk, something that had been happening more and more as Daddy had been pulling back. Lee needed to have an honest, open conversation with his father, but he hadn't been able to bring himself to do it yet.

Mama had just had a bad month. At least that was what Lee told himself. Daddy stayed in more when she wasn't well, and that meant Lee sat behind the desk nearly every day now.

He didn't mind the paperwork so much, especially in the summer months, when the heat could make a man want to stay in bed for another half-hour simply to gear himself up to go outside. He knew all the forms now, and he'd familiarized himself with all their corporate clients, which was the bulk of who Cooper & Co dealt with on a daily basis.

Trucks and tankers showed up at the farm every single day to fill their bottles, cans, cartons, or containers with the organic milk produced by the dairy cows on the farm. Lee tried to be present every time one of their top tier clients arrived, and he arranged delivery for a select few companies that weren't within driving distance.

In fact, Lee needed to call Fairchild Transport today and make sure the shipment to The Falls Grocer would go out by six tonight.

He'd do it after he checked on Ford's homework and met with Gretchen Bellows. His stomach swooped again, and he checked his watch as he looked at the math paper.

"Multiplication?" he asked, as Ford hadn't answered his question.

"I'm on sevens," Ford said. "They're not my favorite."

Lee didn't understand why anyone needed to learn to multiply anymore. He had a calculator on his phone and his watch, for crying out loud. "No?" he asked anyway. "What's your favorite?"

"Nines," Ford said. "I already checked them off." He looked up at Lee and smiled. "There's a trick to nines."

"Is that so?" Lee asked, grinning back at his son. He could see himself in his son's eyes, as well as the slope of his nose and the shape of his chin. Ford had his mother's darker hair, and his mouth sat somewhere between Lee's and Martha's. "Teach me the trick."

Maybe if he focused on his son, he wouldn't worry about going behind Will's back and signing a contract with Gretchen and Sweet Water Taffy to be their cream supplier.

He told himself—again—that Gretchen had called him. She'd asked him to keep it to himself for now, that she'd tell Will herself.

Lee had to trust her that she knew his brother and how to deal with him, but Lee had been around Will for forty years, and he knew with ninety-nine percent of his heart that his brother wouldn't like being in the dark about this new customer.

He focused as Ford taught him how to multiply nines, Lee found himself chuckling and getting all the answers right.

"Hello," a woman said, and Lee looked over to the doorway, though he knew it would be Gretchen Bellows.

His heartbeat flew up into his throat for all the wrong reasons. Lee wished it was because a beautiful woman had shown up on the farm to talk to him. Gretchen had, but for a completely different reason than Lee wanted.

"Howdy," he said. "C'mon in." He got to his feet and took the few steps to meet her at the door. He shook her hand and turned back to his son. "This is my son, Ford. He's just doing his math homework."

Gretchen grinned at him and said, "Nice to meet you, Ford."

"Is it okay he's here?" Lee asked. "I don't normally work in the office on Saturdays."

"It's fine," Gretchen said, switching her kind smile to him. "You told me he'd be here."

"Right," Lee said, trying to swallow his nerves. "Have you talked to Will?"

"It's on my to-do list," Gretchen said, nodding toward the chair. "Is this a sitting-down affair?"

"Yeah, sure," Lee said. He went behind the desk while she took a seat. "I've got your contract printed and ready to go over." He plucked it from the printer on the counter against the back wall and reached for a stapler.

One *cha-clunk* later, he laid it on the desk in front of her. "It lays out our policies for delivery of the product. We might have some issues fulfilling large orders, but you're doing such a small amount, I can't imagine we'll have a problem for you."

Gretchen picked up the three-page document and looked at it briefly. "I'm coming to get the cream," she said.

"Yes," he said. "I took out the part that outlines the delivery fee."

"Twenty gallons per week."

"Yes, ma'am."

Gretchen's eyes flew back to his. She set the papers back on the desk. "You sounded so much like Will just then."

"You really should tell him," Lee said, immediately wishing he hadn't.

Gretchen's blue eyes seared him as she reached for a nearby pen. She signed her name on the third page with a few flourishes and pushed the contract toward Lee, who needed to sign it. Then Sweet Water Taffy would be a client of Cooper & Co, and Gretchen would show up on the farm every Monday morning for her cream.

"Will's going to be put on my account, right?" she asked.

"I haven't spoken to him about it directly," Lee said. "You asked me not to."

"Thank you for honoring that," she said. "I'm on my way to speak to him right after this." She glanced at the papers, her meaning clear.

Sign it, Lee. Then I'm on my way.

Lee fumbled to find a pen, and then he scrawled his name on the appropriate line. He handed her the papers, and they both stood.

Gretchen's smile stretched across her face, and she shook his hand again. "Thanks, Lee."

"Good luck," he said, not quite sure why he thought she needed it.

"Dad," Ford said as Gretchen left the office. Some of the tension in Lee's shoulders relaxed now that this task was over, and he turned toward his son.

"Can we do the guitar lesson now?"

"Yes," Lee said, indicating Ford should get his things and come with him. "Let's go have our lesson and then play for Gramma. She'll like that."

"Can I do the one about the fox and the hound?"

"Yes, sir," Lee said. "After the lesson." He left the office with his son, and as they drove past the turn-off that went to the cabin where Trav and Will lived, Lee saw a minivan parked out front.

Lee hoped Will had had a good morning out in the fields, and that he'd be thrilled his girlfriend who he hadn't seen in a while had come to see him.

At the same time, Lee knew Will, and he knew the guilt that Gretchen had contracted with Cooper & Co to make sure she saw Will once a week would eat him alive. And while he'd hid it from her, Lee would most likely hear about it before night fell. Loudly.

He also hoped Will would figure out how to make Gretchen a priority, because she sure did seem to like him, and that was a feat for any Cooper male.

Lee certainly couldn't get anyone in the female half of

his species to stick around for more than a few conversations or a couple of dates.

He hadn't minded until Clarissa and Spencer had gotten engaged. Until then, everyone in the family had been single, and he didn't stick out so much.

But they were married now, and Trav and Shay would be in another few months. Will had a girlfriend, and Cherry didn't live here.

That only left Lee, and if he was the only single Cooper, the spotlight on him would be far too bright. He already had to handle the majority of the business on the farm, with everyone watching his every move. He certainly didn't need that pressure in his personal life too.

———

"You passed off your sevens," he said, slinging his arm around his son's shoulders.

"Just today," Ford said, beaming at the star chart on his classroom wall. Lee didn't come to a whole lot of school-related events, because Ford lived with his ex-wife, Martha, during the week.

Lee still talked to her constantly, as they were both determined to make sure Ford knew how very much he was loved by both of his parents, though they weren't together anymore. She told him about the conversations at parent-teacher conferences, and she took pictures of his report cards and sent them to Lee.

Tonight, she had a day-early Valentine's Day date with her new boyfriend—and the fact that she was dating someone seriously enough to tell Lee about the relationship was just another reason Lee needed to be out in the dating pool again.

Therefore, Lee had come to the math night at the elementary school. He'd already sat through the teacher's gushy welcome speech, and now Ford was supposed to take him around to different stations to show him all of the number knowledge he'd acquired this year.

A headache throbbed behind Lee's eyes, but he kept his smile hitched in place. He didn't have a significant someone to spend tomorrow night with for Valentine's Day, and he'd agreed to take Ford a day early for the weekend.

He hadn't heard a peep from Will about Gretchen's cream order, but his brother had texted to say he'd be leaving the farm tomorrow no later than five o'clock.

The fact that Will hadn't marched over to Lee's and then chewed him out for keeping Gretchen's secret demonstrated how much Will had changed in just a short time. Six weeks since the New Year's Beach Bash, when he'd sat in that caramel apple and started the ball rolling with Gretchen.

"Parents and students," someone said. "We're gathering in the orange kiva for a demonstration on some of our educational math games. It's out the door and to the right."

The teacher grinned and gestured people through the door like she was directing airplanes on a tarmac. Lee and Ford joined the flow of people leaving the classroom, and he turned right and went down the hall to the orange kiva.

With standing room only, he sent Ford up front to sit with a couple of his friends, and Lee pushed his cowboy hat further down over his eyes so he could observe the other parents there.

There had to be single moms with eight-year-olds too, right? Lee had no stipulations for a potential girlfriend. Heck, at this point, he'd take someone who would return a text.

"Ladies and gentlemen," a male teacher said from up front. "Children, give your attention to Rosalie Reynolds as she shows us one of the newer games she's developed to help students with their third grade math skills."

Lee turned his attention to the gorgeous brunette at the teacher's side, and everyone else in the school disappeared.

Rosalie Reynolds had dark ringlets that fell to her shoulders, and he'd bet with his whole inheritance that she hated her curls. Most women who had them did.

Lee sure did like them. He liked them a whole lot. His heartbeat picked up speed as she smiled, revealing straight, white teeth framed by pretty pink lips. She wore a blouse of butter yellow, coupled with a pair of dark brown slacks, the color of freshly turned earth out on the farm.

She started to speak, and while Lee didn't particularly

pay attention to her video game demonstration, he enjoyed the sound of her voice. Smooth and even, she'd clearly presented plenty of times in the past.

She could work a crowd, and she had the other parents laughing, then nodding, and at the end of her presentation, they all clapped and cheered.

Lee didn't even crack a smile. He was star-struck by the beauty at the front of the crowd. Her dark eyes scanned the crowd, and despite his pulled-down cowboy hat, their eyes met.

A jolt of electricity went through Lee, and he pushed away from the wall where he'd been leaning. Rosalie broke their connection, and humiliation filled Lee.

Surely she hadn't felt anything from him, other than the fact that he hadn't applauded her presentation.

The crowd swallowed her as children surged forward to play the game she'd demonstrated, and he lost sight of Ford. His son wouldn't go off with someone else, and he wouldn't leave the school without Lee, so he wasn't too worried.

The moment Rosalie stepped in front of him, he was. "You didn't like the game?" she asked, glancing over her shoulder. Those eyes came back to his, and Lee had no idea what to say.

In fact, he couldn't even speak. The seconds ticked by, each one louder and louder in his ears, and still he simply stared at the stunningly beautiful and smart Rosalie Reynolds.

16

Rosalie Reynolds gave the cowboy in front of her a few moments to think. He obviously needed them, and she was used to waiting. Autumn had taught her that. Working with game developers had too. Now that she had several products in her educational line-up, she'd learned even more patience when dealing with teachers, administrators, and superintendents.

What she didn't have a lot of recent experience with was handsome, dark, brooding cowboys who didn't clap after her fantastic demos. Rosalie normally didn't care how people reacted, though tonight's crowd had been exceptionally excited about the video game with a dragon hero that led children through their math facts.

It definitely felt more video game than addition or subtraction worksheets, and she'd spent a long time in development with parents, teachers, and children to get the game right.

The silence between her and Handsome thickened, and Rosalie glanced over her shoulder. "Do you have a child in third grade?"

"Yes, ma'am," the man said. "Ford's right over there." He nodded toward the mob of kids in front of the big TV screen mounted on the back wall of the kiva. "He's the redheaded one."

Rosalie spotted him easily, her smile also returning to her face without any effort. "Does he like math?"

"Depends," the man said.

She focused on him again. "What do you think I could improve about my demonstration or speech?" She wasn't asking to call him out, though her previous question may have been a bit confrontational. "I really want to know."

"Oh, uh." The man lifted his cowboy hat, showing all of his glorious, deep, dark auburn hair as he ran his fingers through it, pushing it back. He resettled his hat on his head. "It was fine."

"You didn't clap or anything." She tilted her head. "There has to be something I could do better."

"Everyone else was clappin'," he said. "You did fine." His eyes were the color of forests in the night, definitely green, but not emerald and not spring.

Autumn would call them "green like Daddy's Army gear." Rosalie's throat tightened at the thought of her four-year-old and her ex-husband.

James had the girl tonight so Rosalie could be here, and she was grateful for that. Autumn was so good to help her daddy around the house, and she adored his therapy dog. It was the guilt that got Rosalie every time she thought of the two of them together.

He made his choice, she reminded herself. She'd done the best she could with that choice, and she'd come a long way in the past eighteen months. Sure, maybe she still had some rocky road to tread, and she had the wild thought that it would be nice to go on the journey with the cowboy in front of her.

"I'm Rosalie Reynolds," she said, sticking out her hand and hoping to get Handsome's name. She'd noticed him in the back, leaning against the wall, before he'd shunned her near-perfect performance.

"Lee Cooper," he said, and Rosalie felt a certain level of victory for tonight. Even if none of the parents here and none of the teachers at Hanover Elementary purchased her software, tonight was a win because she now knew Lee Cooper's name.

"Is your wife around?" she asked. "Maybe she will have a better opinion of the software or the presentation."

"I'm not married," Lee said, pushing his hat further over his eyes. "Excuse me." He moved away as if he were water easing through cracks in the crowd.

Rosalie had never met anyone like him, and surprise moved through her as he went over to his son, bent down, spoke, and the boy turned to go with him. No argument.

No begging for the game—which plenty of other children were doing.

Someone appeared in front of her, blocking her view of Lee and Ford Cooper, and she had to blink to focus on the man's face. "We'd love to buy this for our son," he said, smiling at her.

Rosalie slipped into businesswoman mode, but the lonely woman inside her watched Lee walk away from the orange kiva, his arm slung protectively around his son's shoulders.

He didn't look back, not even once. Not even a flicker of his eyes toward her, and Rosalie told herself not to be silly. Her butter-yellow blouse was usually like a lucky penny, but perhaps it would be in the sales she could make tonight and not with a love match to a handsome, single father cowboy.

Her heart dropped to her stomach at the very thought of dating again, especially someone as no-nonsense as Lee Cooper. No wonder his son hadn't argued with him, and Rosalie told herself to forget about the man as he and his son rounded the corner and re-entered the classroom down the hall.

For the next hour, she did her best to focus on whoever was in front of her, answering their questions and taking their money.

She sold out of the games she'd brought, but Miss Bair and the other teachers said they'd send home her order form with their students next week.

As she pulled up to her house with all-dark windows, a sigh slipped from her lips. Autumn wouldn't be inside, and she'd forgotten to turn on the hall light so she wouldn't have to enter the house in the pitch blackness.

Thankfully, the outside lights triggered by movement, and they flashed to life as she got out of her car.

Tomorrow was Valentine's Day, and she'd scheduled herself to work from home. No school visits. No online meetings. No phone calls. No appointments, not even the fun ones like getting her hair or nails done.

She left all of her boxes and bags in the car, grabbed her purse and her keys, and went up to the front door.

A loud stomp sounded on the other side of the door as she fitted her key into the lock, and Rosalie sighed.

Autumn's pet rabbit had been left home alone for a while, and he obviously wasn't happy. He was a funny little thing with a great big attitude, and he wouldn't appreciate being left in the dark either.

"I'm coming," she said as another thump filled the neighborhood silence. Autumn had gotten him the day after James had moved out, and she'd named him The USS Thumper. For a while there, she'd insisted everyone use his whole name.

Thankfully, she'd calmed a little bit since the divorce, and Rosalie could just use Thumper now. She hated thinking about the way Autumn had named him the way the Navy names ships, because her daddy worked on a ship.

Well, he used to at least.

Rosalie finally got the door open and she stepped up and over the gate secured in the doorway directly next to the door. If that gate wasn't there, Thumper would be long gone in the night.

"I'm home," she said to him, her fingers sliding up the wall to the switch. The living room flooded with light, and Thumper stomped his foot as if to say *it's about time.*

"Let's get you fed," Rosalie said, dropping her purse on the couch as she walked behind it. She kicked off her shoes near the island and set about making up a bowl of veggies for Thumper.

Exhaustion filled her, and her mind wandered. She usually thought about the sales she'd made tonight, and she might even log them all in the financial software she'd purchased last year when she'd finally gotten her company off the ground.

But tonight, she could only think about one thing. Not a thing, a person.

Lee Cooper.

———

THE FOLLOWING DAY, ROSALIE WORKED A LITTLE BIT IN THE morning. She did get her receipts put into the computer. She brought in her demo boxes and sorted through them to make sure they were right and ready for next time.

She weeded through her emails and answered the ones she needed to.

Then she set about cleaning her house and straightening Autumn's bedroom. She wouldn't be back until Sunday evening, but Rosalie wanted to have a small Valentine's Day celebration with her then. So she decorated the girl's room with hearts and more hearts, all cut free-hand from pink, red, white, and purple paper.

Her daughter loved puzzles and word games, and Rosalie put letters on some of the hearts. Autumn would need to pull them all down and figure out the word, then she'd be able to find a basket from Cupid in that location in the house.

Rosalie put together the basket, which was complete with a stuffed teddy bear, chocolates, her favorite sour candy, and a card.

She hid it in the laundry room closet, right beside the cleaning pods and closed the door.

She tried to keep herself busy whenever Autumn wasn't home, but it was harder than she'd anticipated. She almost felt like a robot, completing tasks and moving through the motions without any feeling attached.

Her therapist would likely want to dissect that for the next several weeks, should Rosalie decided to divulge such a thing at her next appointment.

Thumper stomped from somewhere in the house, and Rosalie sighed. She's just started to boil some eggs to make into egg salad, which she fully intended to eat between two slices of white bread, when the front door opened.

"Mommy!" Autumn cried, and it took her a moment to struggle over the gate. Thumper came hippity-hopping from wherever he'd been angrily stomping in the house, and Rosalie smiled at her daughter.

Her insides quivered, because James wasn't supposed to bring her back until Sunday. It was Friday at noon.

"Hey, baby." She scooped her daughter into a hug and lifted her right up off the floor. "What are you doin' here?"

"Daddy has to go somewhere," she said, her child-like voice so innocent and so high-pitched.

Rosalie set Autumn on her feet. "Is he outside?" She didn't have a ramp for him to get his wheelchair up and into the house. He'd had his brothers come get his things and move him out, and then they'd carried him down the steps to his chair.

He'd never let her do that for him, and Rosalie hated this small, insignificant feeling inside her. She'd been willing to build the ramp. Move to a new house that didn't have so many steps. Help him any way she could.

He hadn't wanted her to. He didn't want *her* anymore.

Her heart cracked along one of the seams that had already healed, but it only went a little way.

"Yes," Autumn said, bending to pick up Thumper.

"I'll go talk to him," Rosalie said. "You stay here with your bunny. Oh, and there's a surprise for you in your room." She grinned at her daughter, glad she hadn't delayed in setting up the Valentine's Day hearts.

Autumn's face shone like the sun, and she skipped down the hall with the ten-pound rabbit holding on for dear life.

Rosalie faced the open front door, trying to calculate how much time had passed since Autumn had come through it. Only a minute or two. James couldn't expect her to come running straight out.

Her chest vibrated in a strange way as she stepped over the gate and crossed the porch. She told herself to be strong. No matter what he said, she wouldn't react. She could cry later, in private, long after Autumn went to sleep.

Her daughter loved her daddy with every cell in her body, and Rosalie would not do anything to combat that.

James sat behind the wheel in his enormous truck. It had been fitted with hand levers for the brake and gas pedal, so he could drive as usual.

His window was down, and he turned toward her as she reached the sidewalk and advanced in his direction. "Hey," he drawled out, his voice the one in her head that drove her to keep the house clean and her hair done up right.

"Hey," she said, keeping her voice light. "You're back early." She made it sound like he was supposed to drop Autumn off tonight instead of in the middle of the day, when really, he was two and a half days early.

"I know," he said. "I'm sorry."

Rosalie paused, because James rarely apologized for anything. He'd only said he was sorry a handful of times in their marriage, and one was when he said he couldn't stay in their marriage.

Despite everything, Rosalie still loved him, and she supposed she always would. He was the father of her child, after all, and she had to see him all the time.

"Listen, a really great opportunity came up at the naval base in California," he said. "I applied for the job. It was a long shot, but they called this morning, and they want me there as soon as I can get there."

Rosalie heard the words, but she took a few seconds to absorb them. "When will you be back?"

James sighed and that was when Rosalie knew what he'd really said.

"You're not coming back."

"It's an intelligence position," he said, staring out the windshield instead of facing her. "It's an amazing opportunity for someone like me."

Someone with no college education. Someone who couldn't walk. Someone who'd served his country for eight years, gotten injured, and then couldn't do the job he'd trained for on his ship.

Tears pressed behind Rosalie's eyes. "You're moving there today?"

"I'm going today," he clarified. "I'm not packed up to move yet."

"How long have you known about the job?"

"Four months," he said. "I've been doing phone and online interviews with them for two." He did look at her then. "This is how the Navy is, Rosa."

"I know," she snapped, folding her arms across her midsection. She took a deep breath and sighed it out. "Did you tell Autumn?"

"I told her I had to go for a while," he said. "I'll have to come back and get properly packed and everything." He looked at Rosalie with pure pleading in his eyes. She hated that with everything inside her, and she fought against the softness trying to surface.

"Okay," she said. "Please let me know when you come back, even if it's for an hour. Autumn will want to say goodbye." A real goodbye too, not whatever had happened this morning that Rosalie didn't know about.

"I will," James promised, but he'd promised her things in the past that hadn't come to fruition. He held her gaze, and so much more was said between them.

She wanted to tell him to take them with him. The three of them could relocate and start over. Maybe then they'd make it. Maybe then, the strong, confident man she'd married would re-emerge, and he wouldn't feel like he was shackling her with a lifetime of caring for him.

At the same time, Rosalie knew that man had died somewhere at sea, in an explosion on-board his ship that had killed three others and left him wounded.

She looked away, because no one could reclaim the

past. "Drive safely," she said. "Let me know when you get there. Send some pictures for Autumn."

"Rosa," he said, and she wished he wouldn't use her nickname. They weren't married anymore.

She nodded and backed up a step. She had to be strong. She could take care of Autumn all the time—she'd have to now. She couldn't send her four-year-old to California by herself, that was for sure.

She turned and walked away from James sitting in that truck, a brand-new level of hardness descending on her. She'd been a single mom before, but Autumn's dad was right here in town. Only five minutes away should she need help.

She was really on her own now, and as she stepped over the gate and into the house, her first tear fell.

17

Gretchen picked up Elvis's dinner bowl, where she'd served him a special Valentine's Day dinner with plenty of pink salmon, and put it in the sink right as the doorbell rang.

Her heart jumped up into her throat, and she swallowed it back into position. Will would be standing on the other side of the door, and Gretchen hadn't had a boyfriend on Valentine's Day for a long time.

Anticipation and adrenaline ran through her with the strength of river rapids, and she smoothed down the front of her dress as she walked toward the door.

She opened it, already smiling, and sure enough, Will stood there. He held so much in his hands that Gretchen could barely see his face peeking over the top of the stuffed koala bear, and she burst out laughing.

"Give me some of that," she said through her giggles.

She took the huge koala, as well as the twelve-pack of Coke Zero—her favorite soda.

"Evening," Will drawled, and she wanted him to drop everything in his arms and kiss her. He took the rest of it into the kitchen and started sliding it onto the counter.

She put the koala on the couch and the soda in the fridge.

"I got these amazing caramels at the best candy shop in these parts," he said, holding up a box of caramels that had come from Sweet Water Taffy.

She grinned and shook her head, wondering how she'd caught the eye of this man.

"The flowers are called tiger's eye," he said, handing her the bouquet of yellow-orange roses. "They stand for longevity, I think."

"They're beautiful," she said, bending down to smell them. The last bunch of roses he'd brought her still sat on the counter, and she looked at them. "You didn't have to bring all of this."

"I also got you the summer of coffee at Juice and Java," he said, ignoring her and holding up an envelope instead. "You can get unlimited coffee from Memorial Day to Labor Day with this pass."

Gretchen laid the flowers on the counter and plucked the envelope from his fingers. "I'll take that, thank you." She grinned at him, giggled again, and forgot about the unlimited coffee pass.

Neither of them had to speak, and they moved in

tandem. Will stepped closer to her, taking her in his arms and kissing her in one fluid movement. The man was made of grace and strength, kindness and muscles, and one of the best hearts she'd ever encountered.

He could kiss like he meant it too, and Gretchen sure did enjoy the stroke of his lips against hers and the way he seemed to know exactly where to put his hands to make her feel safe, cherished, and loved.

He pulled away far too soon in her opinion, and she tucked herself against his chest. "It's good to see you," he said, his voice stuck somewhere in his throat. "How was your week?"

"It was a week," she said. "You?"

"I scheduled myself for a day off, believe it or not."

Gretchen pulled away and searched his face. "You did? When? What day?" Why hadn't he told her so she could do the same?

He grinned at her, something in it a little naughty. Mischievous. "Monday," he said. "I was hoping I could convince this woman who comes and picks up cream at the farm on Monday morning to steal away with me for the day."

Gretchen had been extremely nervous to talk to Will about what she'd arranged with Lee. He'd taken it well, and she'd picked up her twenty gallons of cream on Monday morning, kissed her boyfriend for a few minutes, and said she couldn't wait for tonight's date.

"You don't give a woman much time to make plans," she said.

"You don't need to plan anything," he said.

"I run the candy shop," she said. "If I'm not going to be there, I have to make plans." Nervous energy ran through her, because she wanted to call Jon right now and find out if he could cover the day's sweets.

But it was Friday night on Valentine's Day. She couldn't call and ask him. He'd asked out a woman from his church, and she knew they had a date tonight.

"I'm sorry," Will said. "I wanted it to be a surprise. I could just come hang out at the shop?"

"No," Gretchen said. She'd never be able to work with him there, and Jon sure wouldn't like it... She kept that last part to herself and met Will's eyes again.

"I see the wheels turnin' in there." He smiled at her.

"I'll figure it out," she said. "The shop is pretty bare right now because of Valentine's Day. But I'll figure it out." She could go in on Sunday night and do a few things to restock. Jon could keep up with the rest.

"Let's go," she said. "We don't want to miss our under-the-stars reservation time."

"That we do not," Will said, tucking her hand in his. "You're all set? Elvis is secure?"

"Yes, sir." She grinned at him. "I can put those flowers in a vase later."

Will leaned forward and kissed her again, a short, quick kiss that left her unbalanced for a moment when he pulled away. "Nope, I can't kiss you again. Then we'll really be late." A flush worked its way into his cheeks, which Gretchen secretly liked. She loved the way he took care of her by opening the doors and walking her to her side of the truck. He'd been nothing but a cowboy gentleman with her, despite their awkward moments.

His blush had disappeared by the time he got behind the wheel, and Gretchen decided to dig a little deeper. "So," she said.

"No," he said, interrupting her next breath. "I don't like it when you start sentences like that." He tossed her a healthy glare and backed out of her driveway.

Gretchen blinked, trying to figure out how else to start a sentence. "Um," she said.

Will began to chuckle, and Gretchen's face started to heat. She was sure she carried the flush in her cheeks now.

"You can't start sentences without using the word so?"

"Why don't you like it?"

"Because," he said. "You make it sound like it's going to be a casual question, and then it's not. It's like this punch in the lungs."

Gretchen blinked, trying to absorb what he'd said. "A punch in the lungs?"

"What were you going to ask?" He looked over to her, not paying attention to the road at all.

Gretchen looked out the windshield and shook her

hair back over her shoulders. "I don't know. I've forgotten now."

"Oh, come on."

"No, really."

Will made a sound of disbelief combined with annoyance—Gretchen knew, because he'd made that sound while on the phone with his brother before. "You can say it."

"So I left a review for Cooper and Co," she said. "Oh my word. I just started the sentence with 'so'." She looked at him, her eyes wide. His shoulders shook as he laughed silently. "I didn't realize I did it so much."

Laughter burst from his mouth, and despite his earlier glare and her growing embarrassment, Gretchen giggled too. She might as well embrace her relationship with Will. He was going to say what was on his mind. They were going to get interrupted when they tried to kiss. Things could go from glares to giggles in less than ten seconds.

Gretchen found it all very exciting, and she turned toward him and crossed her legs, glad she'd chosen a skirt that would allow her to do so.

"So," she said, really enunciating the word. Will's laughter dried up and Mr. Growly Bear came back. Gretchen just grinned at him, because she liked him when he was soft and sweet, and she liked him when he was grumpy and glaring.

"Mister Cooper. If your girlfriend could get out of work on Monday, what do you have planned?"

He did the male equivalent of shaking his hair over his head, which was lifting his chin and looking out his side window. "I have a few things up my sleeve."

Gretchen laughed this time, because that was cowboy-code for *I don't know yet, but I have the weekend to figure it out.*

Now, she just needed to make sure she could cover things at the shop so she could spend the day with Will. Him taking a day off was a *huge* deal, and Gretchen determined she'd close Sweet Water Taffy for the day if she had to.

———

MONDAY MORNING ARRIVED, AND WITH IT, GRETCHEN showed up at Cooper & Co to get her cream. Despite her texting and asking every hour yesterday, Will would not tell her where they were going today.

She'd managed to go into the candy kitchen yesterday morning and make what she needed for today, and she'd asked Jon to act as the boss. He'd agreed, and while he hadn't asked, it was implied Gretchen would be out with Will.

She'd been to Daddy's yesterday, and she'd told him she wouldn't be by this afternoon. He could manage without her, and she'd put his medication in a clearly marked baggie and magneted it to the fridge. She'd call him later to make sure he'd taken it.

Excitement built in her chest when Will appeared, pushing the dolly carrying her crates of cream in front of him. She quickly put her van in park and jumped from it.

"Morning," she said, practically running toward him. She swept her hand down toward her feet. "How did I do?"

He stopped walking and let the dolly settle flat on the ground. Will scanned his eyes from the top of her head to her running shoes—which were a bright fuchsia and clearly not used much—a smile widening with every inch of her he saw.

"You killed it." He tipped the dolly again and continued toward the van. She met him before he got there, and he leaned sideways as she slid one hand up his bicep.

She kissed his cheek, wishing he'd turn his head and really say good morning. He didn't, but he chuckled, and that sent an additional dose of desire through Gretchen.

"Let me get this loaded," he said. "Then we'll get it dropped off, and we'll go."

"It's six-thirty."

"Did you want to go back to bed?" He grinned at her and left her standing on the path as he continued down it. She let him do all the work, admiring those pretty muscles as he lifted crates of cream into the back of the van.

One, two, three, four five, and the job was done.

"I'll follow you to the shop," he said, wheeling the dolly past her.

"Okay," she said.

Jon was at the shop already when Gretchen arrived, and the two of them hauled in the cream before Will pulled up. Jon eyed the big truck like it was made of snakes, said, "Have fun, Gretchen," and went back inside without acknowledging or waving to Will.

Gretchen didn't know what to do about that. She liked and needed Jon at Sweet Water Taffy, and she was falling in love with Will. Surely Jon would get over whatever bothered him about the cowboy, and Gretchen wouldn't ever have to address the issue with him.

She climbed into the truck and reached for her belt.

"All right, cowboy," she said. "I'm yours for the day."

nxiety seemed to accompany Will everywhere he went lately. He hadn't gotten up to run this morning, and he told himself that was why.

It wasn't because Gretchen sat in his passenger seat before seven a.m., telling him she was his.

For the day, he told himself.

She wasn't his forever.

Yet, streamed through his mind, but he really wished it wouldn't. He didn't want to move too fast with her, and while they'd technically been dating for a little over six weeks, she'd had to hire the farm as her cream supplier to make sure she saw him.

Humiliation and guilt made a dangerous cocktail inside Will, and he shouldn't have skipped running.

"Are we going?" Gretchen asked, and Will reached to put the truck in reverse.

"Yeah," he said. "We're going." He cleared his throat. "Okay, so listen."

"Nope," she barked at him. "I don't like it when you start sentences like that." She grinned at him as she spoke, but Will didn't think she was kidding that much. "You used 'listen' and 'so.' Both of those are off-limits."

"Fine," Will said. He would not clear his throat again. He would *not*. "I just think maybe you have some high expectations for today, and maybe you should lower them."

"Come on," she said. "You're not taking me to Disneyland?"

Will smiled, suddenly realizing that it didn't matter what he'd planned for today. She was just glad to be with him. The concept felt foreign for another breath, and then it seeped into Will's bones as fact.

He was glad to be with her, no matter what they did.

"Trav said The Bluebell Café has good breakfast," he said. "I can't imagine you've eaten yet." He looked over to her, and she shook her head.

"So—I mean, I thought we'd start there," he said, amending that pesky beginning word. "Then, I thought we could wander the Holy Cow boutique, because that seemed like something you'd like that you don't get much time to do. Plus, there's going to be a popcorn demonstration there this afternoon."

He looked over to her, trying to drive and gauge her reaction to his plan at the same time. He didn't care if they walked around town, as long as he got to hold her hand, talk to her, and kiss her.

That was all Will wanted. Time. He wanted more *time* with Gretchen, and he'd do whatever he had to do to get it. He'd spent a long time talking to Travis last weekend after Gretchen had stopped by the cabin on Saturday during his lunch hour and told him he'd have a new job every Monday morning—loading her cream for her.

He'd wanted to rage into the sky, but he'd held back. He hadn't told her at all how inadequate and how guilty he felt that she'd felt like she'd had to *hire his blasted farm* just to see him.

Travis had found a way to keep up with his work and make Shay a priority in his life. Will was struggling, but he was trying to do the same thing with Gretchen.

"That sounds fun," Gretchen said. "You like popcorn."

"I do," he said. "They're going to do the demo for different kinds. Caramel, putting on seasonings, taco-corn, that kind of thing."

"Fascinating," she said, and he found her grinning.

"Then," he said, and he failed in his quest not to clear his throat again. "There's this water circus I thought would be fun. It's later in the day. Then dinner. Then I'll take you home."

In his mind, there was plenty of time for talking before the circus, and plenty of time for kissing after. Gretchen agreed, and Will relaxed in his seat.

"Okay," he said. "The Bluebell Café, here we come."

"Have you been there before?" she asked.

"No," he said. "But Travis has, and he said it was good."

"I like their food." She reached over and took his hand in hers. "This is a good plan, Will."

"It's not that exciting," he admitted.

"A water circus? Are you kidding?" The power of her grin landed on the side of his face. "I can't wait," she said. "I've never been to a water circus."

"Me either," he said. "Which honestly, isn't hard. I haven't done much in my life but work on the farm." He glanced at her, hoping she knew that. "Listen, I wanted to talk to you about the farm."

"Listen, you did?" she teased.

He grinned too, realizing he did begin a lot of sentences that way. "Yeah, I...don't take this the wrong way or anything. It's not, you know, super urgent or anything."

"Okay," she said slowly, because he hadn't really said anything.

"I work on the farm," he said. "A lot. You've got Taffy." He'd heard her abbreviate the name of her shop to that several times. "I know you live outside of town so you can get to your daddy's place easier, and I'm just wondering... I mean, if we were to, you know, make it and get married." He cleared his throat so hard, it sounded like a tiger growl.

"Would you want to stay in your house or see if we could find a cabin on the farm?" He didn't dare look at her, because he'd invited tension into the cab with them.

"I don't know," she said slowly. "If I took a different

road, I could get to Daddy's in about the same time from the farm."

"Just something I was thinking about," Will said, his whole upper body burning now. "It's fine. Like I said, not urgent."

"Where are Travis and Shay going to live?"

"We haven't talked much about it," Will said. "But I'm going to tell him they should live in the cabin where we live now." He shifted in his seat, knowing Travis wouldn't want to feel like he was evicting Will.

"There's another cabin out by my sister I can live in."

"With your wife?"

"Uh, it's not a huge cabin," he said. "Maybe just the two of us. I mean, not us, but a man and his wife."

Her fingers around his squeezed. "I get what you're saying. You don't have to keep saying it's not us."

"I don't want to freak you out."

"I'm not freaking out," she said, but she'd turned toward her window and kept gazing out of it.

"Great," he said a little too brightly. "So maybe a couple. I wouldn't want to have a family there." And he wanted a family. He knew Gretchen did too.

She just nodded, and Will needed to move this conversation to something else. "Okay," he said. "You never did tell me where you found Elvis when you got home from your daddy's last night."

———

Hours later, Will was sure he'd experienced the best day of his life. The absolute best. After his initial awkwardness, he'd calmed down, and they'd been able to have normal conversations around their jobs, the things they liked, and the things they wanted in their lives. He hadn't found enough bravery to tell her he wanted her in his life, but she hadn't said anything like that either.

He'd found a loaf of sourdough cinnamon swirl bread that had been baked in a Dutch oven at the boutique, and Gretchen had bought a pair of earrings made of driftwood that fit her vibe perfectly.

He'd held her hand, and he'd kissed her every time they went back to the truck. He liked it when she sat on the seat, and he stepped into the space created by the open door.

Then, she was about his height, and she'd cup his face in her hand and kiss him, kiss him, kiss him. He could honestly kiss her all day, every day, and his male side told him to make sure she knew he was falling in love with her before the day ended.

He didn't know how to say words like that. He'd never said them to Tara, and he hadn't found out that she wasn't on the same page as him until he'd bought a diamond and dropped to one knee.

He wasn't going to do that again.

"Will," Gretchen said, her fingers going tight against his. "Look!" She pointed with her free hand, and Will followed it to see a woman descending from high up in the big top, the water starting to fall from the ceiling.

He'd been eating popcorn—one of his favorite foods —despite gorging on the taco-corn, the caramel corn, and the fruity pineapple corn at the boutique, but he forgot all about that now.

Designs appeared in lights against the falling water, and Will could only stare. The woman began doing tricks and tumbles using only the line she'd been lowered on, and Will decided then and there that he'd like to come see this show again.

By the time it was over, he knew he'd just experienced something unique, and by the beaming smile on Gretchen's face, she had too. They'd made this memory *together*, and Will leaned over to kiss her.

She kissed him back, but he kept it chaste, given that they were in public. The lights came up, and Will started to gather their soda cups and the now-empty bag of popcorn.

"I don't think I can eat another bite," he said. "I've eaten so much popcorn today."

Gretchen only shook her head, her smile cemented in place. "Now I know what to get you for your birthday. When is that, by the way?"

"May," he said. "You?"

"November."

He nodded, wishing her birthday sat closer than his. She'd said he didn't have to bring her so many gifts for

Valentine's Day, but Will wanted to fill her life with all of her favorite things. Absolutely all of them.

"You're not getting out of taking me to dinner," Gretchen said as they started down the steps that would take them out of the tent. "You promised me we'd try that fondue place."

"I know what I promised," he said, a single spark of irritation firing through him. He counted that as progress, because Will hated being reminded of what he'd already said or done, especially if it was in the very recent past.

They'd talked about where to go for dinner at the boutique, and she'd said she wanted to try Fondue Fusion, which had just arrived in Sweet Water Falls a few weeks ago.

Gretchen glanced at him as they left the tent, and Will gave her a smile. "Sorry," he murmured.

"I wasn't saying you'd forgotten."

"I know," he said with a sigh. "I'm not upset."

"Good." She released his hand and linked her arm through his instead. "It's about forty minutes back to Sweet Water Falls. Maybe you'll have digested a lot by then."

He smiled into the darkening sky, wishing he could somehow freeze time right now. Nothing else would move. No clock hands, no other people. Just him and Gretchen would get to continue with their day together, and it would never, ever end.

As it was, nothing froze, and about an hour later, he

pulled into the parking lot at Fondue Fusion. Before he could put the truck in park and hurry around to get her out, her phone rang.

"It's Jon," she said, looking up from her device to Will, her eyebrows up.

He flipped the truck into gear, his male protective streak rearing its jealous head. "Answer it," he said. "I'll be right around." He unbuckled and slid from the truck as she slid on the call and said, "Hey, Jon."

Will took his time, making his steps slow and measured, because he didn't want Gretchen to feel like she couldn't talk to her assistant. Jon meant a great deal to her, and she simply didn't see the man the way Will did.

He paused near the front of the truck and looked toward the entrance of the restaurant. It didn't seem too busy tonight, which was good. Though Will hadn't worked the farm today, nor had he run any miles at all, the same level of exhaustion ran through his system.

He turned when Gretchen opened her door. "Hey, I would've—"

"We have to go," she said, her voice loud and panicked. She dropped from the truck and ran toward him. Tears streamed down her face. "We have to go right now. Taffy is on fire."

"What?" Will received her into his arms and held her tight while she sobbed. That only lasted three seconds, and then she jerked back.

"Come on," she said. "We have to go." She ran back

toward the passenger door, and Will didn't even try to play gentleman. He hurried to get behind the wheel, and he'd pulled out of the parking lot and onto the street before he asked, "Did he call the fire department?"

The sound of sirens suddenly met his ears, and that was all the answer Will needed. Pure helplessness filled him as Gretchen continued to cry in the passenger seat, and no amount of pressure from his hand to hers could calm her.

All Will could do was drive, so he did that a little faster, hoping to get her where she wanted to be and praying that Taffy wouldn't be completely crispy by the time the fire engines arrived.

19

"The horizon is orange," Gretchen said, unable to stop herself.

"The trucks are ahead of us," Will said beside her. She couldn't see him, though the glow from the dashboard illuminated his features. All Gretchen could feel or see was darkness. Darkness everywhere—except where the horizon glowed orange.

She'd never get Jon's frantic voice out of her head, and she'd never forgive herself for taking a day off if she lost the candy shop completely.

Will pushed the truck faster, and the orange on the skyline decreased. When they finally arrived, the fire engines had the whole building illuminated with strong spotlights, and smoke rose from the back of it.

Will turned, seemingly on two wheels, and he'd barely

stopped in front of the shop before she jumped from the truck.

Jon stood on the front sidewalk with Jewel-Li, the woman who'd been working the front of the shop that afternoon.

Evening, Gretchen thought, surprised she had room for the thought in her mind.

"Jon," she said, and he turned. His eyes widened, and he released Jewel-Li and grabbed onto her.

"I called as soon as I hung up with nine-one-one," he said. "It was a sugar fire. I'm so sorry, Gretchen."

"It's fine," she said automatically. "Were there any customers in the shop?"

"Just one," Jewel-Li said, and Gretchen stepped away from Jon. "They left already. We've been out here maybe fifteen minutes. They got here really fast."

Will came up beside Gretchen, and she moved further from Jon to take his hand.

"The fire is out," Jon said. "But it's still smoking."

"Will someone come talk to me?" Gretchen asked. She'd never been involved in a fire.

"We should go around back," Will suggested, and Gretchen stepped with him, because she didn't have the gumption or strength to resist.

Thankfully, Will possessed the courage and ability to get her around to the back of the building, where the candy kitchen looked like someone had smeared dusty tar all over the clawed-out walls and roof.

She gasped, and her feet froze.

"Come on," Will said, tugging on her hand. "We have to talk to someone."

Gretchen let herself cry, because she'd only been at the helm of Sweet Water Taffy for eight months, and it had caught fire on the one day she hadn't come into work.

What would she tell Aunt Patty? How could she reclaim this and start over? It felt impossible and utterly overwhelming and like the very universe itself was pressing down on her with all of its galactic weight.

She let Will lead her toward a woman standing near the fire engine, barking commands at a couple of fire-fighters.

She let him ask her if the fire was out now. Yes, it seemed to be, but they were still checking for hot spots.

If they could go inside yet.

No, not yet.

What to do once the fire was out and the sun rose tomorrow.

The fire chief looked at Gretchen then, but she could only grip Will's hand and wait for the answer.

"I'd call a restoration company," she said. "Your land-lord, if you don't own the building. Find out what's still structurally sound, and what is lost. Then, you can decide from there." She turned as someone yelled, and Will backed Gretchen out of the way.

They stayed until the last of the smoke wisped into the sky, until the fire engines left, and until Gretchen felt sure she couldn't cry another tear. Will never left her side, and he took care of Jon and Jewel-Li too.

He put her in the passenger seat, and Gretchen stared out her window and into darkness as he drove back to her house. They hadn't gotten dinner, and her stomach felt as empty as her heart.

Will helped her down from the truck and he took her all the way inside the house and down the hall to her bedroom. Elvis streaked out, but Gretchen just shook her head.

"I'll go feed him," Will whispered in her ear, his lips landing on her neck for only a moment afterward. "You change and get in bed. I'll be right back." He removed his hands from her body, and Gretchen felt the earth sway at a million miles an hour.

Will left, his strides long and sure, and Gretchen wished she could rewind time just a few hours and tell Jon to close the shop early. Whatever he'd been making, he didn't need to make.

She moved like her joints had been replaced with wood, but she managed to get out of her clothes and into pajamas before Will returned. "What did you give Elvis?" she asked as he put one arm around her waist and drew her into his chest.

"Some chicken and those green peas in the fridge," he whispered. "Come on, baby. In the bed." He pulled down the comforter, and Gretchen started to cry as she climbed between the sheets.

"I have to call my aunt," she said.

"Tomorrow," he whispered, getting right into bed with her.

"My daddy."

"Tomorrow," he said again. "I'll call them both."

Gretchen turned to face him and curled into his chest, already crying again. He didn't say anything, and he didn't seem to mind as she soaked the front of his shirt with her tears.

————

THE NEXT DAY, GRETCHEN WOKE IN HER BED, ALONE. HER mind felt fuzzy and her mouth like she'd swallowed a bag of cotton. She reached up and touched her face, which felt crusty and tight, and she couldn't open her right eye all the way.

"Yeowl."

Gretchen kept rubbing her eye as she rolled over and found Elvis stalking into her room. The cat jumped up on her bed, his tail straight up.

"Are you hungry, buddy?" she asked. She couldn't remember feeding him last night—and her brain suddenly switched on.

She sucked in a breath and sat up, dislodging Elvis as she did. "The fire. Will."

She flung the blankets off her feet, realizing now why her eyes had been glued shut this morning. She'd fallen asleep crying. She'd probably cried all night long, and she raced into the hall and down toward the kitchen.

She had no idea what time it was, or where she'd put her cell phone. She needed to call Aunt Patty, Daddy, and then Jon. She needed to get the official fire report from the fire department, and she needed to call a really good restoration company.

No, she needed to call Kevin Barnett first, because he owned the building which housed Sweet Water Taffy, and he needed to know what had happened there. He'd likely have insurance, but she wondered if there'd be some fee or deductible he'd want her to pay.

She couldn't worry about that right now. As she entered the kitchen, Will came in through the front door, his phone at his ear. "...I'll let her know," he said, a half-smile on his face. "Yes, sir. I'm going to check on her right now."

He lifted his eyes in that moment, and their gazes met. He lowered the phone without saying goodbye.

Gretchen didn't know what to say to him, and he seemed frozen to the spot just inside her front door, which he hadn't closed.

She caught a streak of gray as Elvis saw his escape route, and she pointed and made some squeaking noise from somewhere inside her throat.

Will kicked the door closed, thwarting Elvis in his flight. The cat meowed in disagreement, and to her great surprise, Will stooped and picked the tabby cat up.

He cradled him in his arms, smiling down at the feline like they were the best of friends.

"I've entered another reality," Gretchen said.

Will smiled at her and approached. "We became friends last night. Slept together on the couch and everything."

Gretchen's eyebrows went up. "You didn't go home?"

"I couldn't." He arrived in front of her and with Elvis between them, he leaned forward and kissed her cheek. "How'd you sleep, sweetheart?"

"What time is it?"

"Almost seven-thirty," he said.

"Who were you talking to?'

"Your Daddy," he said, handing over her phone. "I called your aunt too, and answered all of Jon's texts."

Gretchen looked at her phone and back to him. "My shop really caught on fire." She wasn't asking, but she needed confirmation.

Will nodded, his lovely eyes filled with compassion and concern. "We'll figure it out, Gretchen."

She wanted to ask him how, so she opened her mouth and did.

"I don't know, Gretchen," he said, sighing. It wasn't his barking tone, or his sympathetic one. It was one that said he'd slept on the couch with her cat. "But we will, okay?" He set Elvis down and faced her. "I'm right here, and I'm not going to leave your side today. We'll figure everything out."

She nodded, because she wanted to believe him. Her mind misfired at her, and then she pulled back on her panic. "I need to call my landlord."

"Okay," Will said, trying to take the phone from her. "Tell me who it is, and I'll do it."

Gretchen didn't release the phone. "No, I'll do it." She took a deep breath, and then another one. "I can do it."

He'd called her aunt and her father, and she could do this. "What did Daddy say to you?"

"He said he'd call and cancel his appointments this week," Will said. "I told him I'd be there this afternoon to help with his oxygen tank."

Gretchen's eyes filled with tears again. She wanted to say thank you, but instead, she simply nodded and looked down at her phone. The letters on it blurred, but she blinked, and everything came into focus.

"I'll call Kevin right now." She headed for the front door, realizing why Will had gone outside to make the call. She needed more air than the house currently held, and she tapped to make the call as she stepped from living room to porch.

"Gretchen," he said, relief in his voice. "How are you? Are you okay?"

Instant tears filled her eyes, but she channeled her inner Will and said, "Yes, Kevin. I'm okay, and all of my employees made it out safely." She took a big breath, not even sure how she should start.

Thankfully, Kevin said, "I'm going through the

damage with the fire marshal at ten o'clock this morning, Gretchen," he said. "If you want to come down, we can talk more then. Get a better picture of what might happen."

"Sure," she said as brightly as she could. She had no idea how the sun rose each day, when something so terrible had happened in the night. "I'll be there at ten."

GRETCHEN PULLED INTO THE PARKING LOT WHERE HER candy shop still sat. The front of the building didn't look much different, besides the fact that she hadn't moved her candy apple truck in over two weeks.

The exhaustion she carried from dawn until dusk was the same. The worry about whether she could reopen continued day after day. The bad news just kept coming.

Or it had, in the beginning. The only employee she'd retained was Jon, and only because she'd begged him to please, please not quit, and then promised to keep paying him. She couldn't do that for any of her other employees, and all of them had quit.

They had to, and Gretchen understood why. They needed their jobs, and she couldn't pay them while the back of the unit on the end of the building got cleaned, dried, and then rebuilt.

Well, the rebuilding was still to come. Gretchen drove around the back of the building, which had been draped in plastic. The fire marshal had deemed the building stable enough to enter when she'd been there with Kevin and Will a couple of weeks ago. She'd been able to go inside with the marshal and collect the things she deemed valuable from her office, which included the computer, her recipe books, and all of her personal belongings.

Then, Kevin had called a fire restoration specialist, and they'd come in with their Dumpsters, shovels, and wheelbarrows. They cleaned out the south kitchen, where Jon had been making sugar art for the tops of the miniature cupcakes they'd needed for a birthday party. He'd gotten distracted when he'd dropped a tray of said cupcakes, and the sugar had burned.

He'd taken it from the flame in frustration, and when he'd dumped it in the trash can, the heat from it had ignited some brittle paper he'd put there earlier. Gretchen had asked him to stop there, because he'd then said, "You wouldn't believe how fast the flames kicked up," and she didn't want to imagine him in that kitchen, trying to put them out. Panicking. Breathing in the smoke.

The whole back corner of the building had been soaked with gallons and gallons of water, and that took a very, very long time to dry out. Wood, plaster, and anything that could mold got ripped out. That was basically everything down to the foundation. The wall separating the kitchen from the retail space in the shop had been torn back to the studs, and then the fans had blown and blown and blown.

Gretchen had barely gotten out of her car when the rumble of Will's truck came around the corner. She smiled at him, but she wasn't sure how she had the energy. She'd seen him every single day since the disaster, and if she'd known that was all it would take, she might've lit her candy kitchen on fire much earlier.

Not really, and she hated thinking that.

He pulled in next to her and got out of his vehicle. A paper bag rustled as he came around the hood, signaling that he'd been to town already. He lifted the pastry bag and said, "The cream cheese scone."

She took the bag from him and leaned into his kiss. "Thank you," she said.

They faced the building together. "They're not making much progress," he said, his voice tart to her ears.

"They have to dry everything out," she said.

"They've been drying it for over two weeks."

"I don't work for the restoration company," Gretchen said.

"Once it's dry, then what?" Will asked, taking a step toward the door. It was metal and hadn't been torn out. The kitchen where Gretchen created her truffles and caramels hadn't been burned, but it had been covered in water, so it too had been stripped, sprayed with mold preventative, and monitored for mildew growth.

She and Jon and Will had removed everything from the front of the shop as the professionals came in to deal with any smoke damage. They'd thrown away anything edible, because Gretchen anticipated the shop being closed for at least a month, and she wouldn't serve chocolates that were more than two days old, let alone thirty.

As she watched Will open the door and go inside the building, Gretchen knew the shop would be closed longer than a month. Frustration, annoyance, and a keen sense of being out of her league enveloped her, and she ignored Will as he asked something through the open back wall of the building.

Thankfully, the weather had been cooperative, and there had been no rain in the past couple of weeks. The restoration company had said rebuilding should begin this week, and Gretchen's disappointment cut through her sharply when she realized it was Friday morning and there had been no rebuilding begun this week.

Will came back outside. "Did you hear what I asked?"

She just shook her head, ready to go home and go back to bed. She was making a few treats out of her kitchen and fulfilling online orders only. It was enough to keep her and Jon busy during the day, and Gretchen had work to do today.

"I asked why they haven't even done the electrical yet," he said.

Gretchen rubbed her forehead. "I don't know, Will. I'm not a contractor or whatever." She turned toward her car.

"Have you asked them?"

"No," she said over her shoulder.

"Gretchen," he said, plenty of irritation in his tone.

The emotion fired through her too, and she spun back to him. "What, Will? You don't have to be here. I don't ask you to come here every morning, and I certainly don't need you to criticize me or what's being done."

He blinked, the frown between his eyes disappearing as he did. Gretchen pulled back on the lion roaring through her chest, but he couldn't be tamed completely. "You stress me out," she said. "Coming here and asking me questions I can't answer. Or insinuating I should've done something different." She took a deep breath and shook her head. "If you can't just put your arm around me and ask me how I'm doing, then don't come anymore."

Will simply stared at her, and Gretchen turned to get in her van.

"Wait, whoa," Will said, putting his hand on top of the minivan and crowding in behind her before she could open the door. "Don't go. Not like this."

She turned back to him and leaned into her van. She didn't have much choice or much space to do anything else. "I'm sorry," she said with a sigh. "I'm just tired, and you just came at me, and I don't know. I couldn't handle it today."

"I didn't mean to come at you."

"I know." She closed her eyes and tipped her head up toward him. "I don't want to argue with you, but I don't need more stress in my life."

"I'm sorry," he whispered. "I didn't mean to add more stress to your life."

She leaned into him and gripped the collar of his shirt in both of her fists. She opened her eyes and looked into his. His cowboy hat created a pocket of shade over the two of them, and she offered him a small smile. "I just want you to bring me pastries and stand with me. Listen to anything I have that's new, or anything I want to tell you, and then kiss me so I know everything will somehow, someday, turn out okay." Her heartbeat trembled in her chest, an indication that she was one breath away from a break-down.

She'd already cried so much in front of Will, and she didn't want to do so again. Not now.

Will swallowed, took a few moments, and asked, "Anything new or anything you want to tell me today?"

She shook her head and took his face in her hands. "I'm making caramels today," she whispered, tugging him closer to her. "I'll need dinner about seven. Doable?"

"Absolutely," he said, his voice as husky and as hitched as she liked it. "I'll be there, and I'll bring something for Elvis too." He touched his lips to hers, and Gretchen let her eyes drift closed again, the mess that was the back of her shop gone when she kissed Will.

He broke the kiss and took her into an embrace. "Someday, somehow," he said. "Everything will be okay. Okay?"

She couldn't verbalize anything right now, so she simply nodded while he held her.

20

Clarissa Rust told herself not to hope too hard. At the same time, she wondered why she couldn't hope to be pregnant. So she steadied her fingers, ripped open the package containing three pregnancy tests, and did what she needed to do.

She left the stick on the bathroom counter and headed down the hall toward the kitchen. In the cabins out on this part of Sweet Water Falls Farm, it only took four steps to get from the bathroom to the kitchen, and Spencer stepped into the entryway as if he'd been waiting for her.

Which, of course, he had.

"Well?" he asked, and Clarissa saw the bright ray of hope in his eyes. She carried it in her soul.

"It takes a few minutes," she said.

Her husband gathered her into his arms, a place she willingly went. "No matter what, it'll be okay," he said.

"I know," Clarissa said. She was six days late, though, and she couldn't help her feelings as they continued to climb through her. For a woman as regular as she was, she'd known the very first day she should've started her period and hadn't.

She hadn't said anything to Spencer until day four, and it had taken another couple of days to get to town to buy a test. Last time, she'd only bought one, as if she and Spencer wouldn't have to try for longer than one month to get pregnant.

This time, she'd smartly bought a multi-pack of pregnancy tests, but a writhing, desperate sense of discomfort inside her really didn't want to have to use the others.

"Even if you're not pregnant," Spence said. "That just means we get to keep trying." He leaned away and smoothed his hands down the back of her head, grinning at her.

She smiled back at him. "I don't think it'll be negative for a lack of trying."

"It's been a couple of months," he said. "Heck, we've only been married for four."

Three and a half, but Clarissa wasn't going to correct him. She nodded, because she knew when they'd said I-do. She also knew she was ready to be a mother. She knew he wanted to have a baby and be a father.

Something inside her flipped, and then flipped again, because Clarissa wanted Mama to be a grandmother before she passed away. Yes, she had Ford already, but she had more room in her heart for more grandbabies.

Selfishly, Clarissa wanted a little girl, so she could have a generational picture of the baby, her, and Mama.

"How long do we wait?" Spencer asked, and Clarissa turned to face the hallway with him.

"We can probably go look," she said, taking his hand. "I want you to check first."

He took a breath, squeezed her hand, and said, "All right." They went down the hall together, and Clarissa really wanted everything they did to be side-by-side, just as they were right now.

He crowded into the bathroom doorway in front of her. "Two lines is pregnant," she said.

"I remember," he said, committing himself by taking the first step inside. She stayed in the hallway and pressed her eyes closed.

She didn't dare pray, because God knew she wanted a baby. So much in her life was so perfect that she felt bad asking for more.

"There's two lines," Spencer said, and Clarissa's eyes shot open. Her husband turned around, the test in his hand and his eyes as wide as double moons. He whooped, threw his free hand into the air, and yelled, "There's two lines!"

He laughed as he grabbed onto her and swung her around. Her feet hit the door, and he quickly set her down. A smile had started in her soul, but she didn't dare let it show on her face yet. "Let me see," she said.

He handed her the pregnancy test, and Clarissa stared at it. One bright pink line sat on the right-hand side, just like last time. This time, a lighter, fainter pink line showed on the left. Barely there, but definitely there.

She grinned as tears filled her eyes. Her chin wobbled as she looked up and at Spencer. "There's two lines."

His joy streamed from him, and Clarissa finally let go of the happiness and hope she'd been clenching with such a tight fist. Tears flowed down her face as she tipped up to kiss her husband.

His touch was intimate, whole, and real, and Clarissa felt loved and cherished and so complete with him. She didn't have to ask him if he was happy—it came through in his eyes, his voice, his touch.

"I can't wait to tell Nate," he said.

"What?" Clarissa asked. "No, Spence, we can't tell anyone."

Confusion covered his expression. "Why not?"

"I'm what? Five weeks along? Maybe six." She shook her head. "No, you don't tell people until you're sure everything is okay."

"I don't know what that means."

"Like, the baby is okay, and I'm not going to lose it." She pierced him with a look that said, *don't argue with me on this.*

Spencer knew her looks by now, and resignation marched through his eyes. "How long does that take?"

"I don't know. Until I'm out of the first trimester?"

"Why does this sound like you're guessing?"

"Twelve weeks," she said with confidence.

Spencer frowned, clearly not a fan of that number. "So I have to wait six more weeks."

She nodded and made her voice as firm as possible when she said, "Yes."

"Fine." He pushed his hand through his hair, his smile returning. He took her into his arms again and kissed her. "Maybe we could celebrate by going back to bed."

"Mm." Clarissa didn't argue with him. She enjoyed feeling close to him, physically and emotionally. After they'd made love, she laid in his arms, her eyes closed and her heart full of gratitude.

Spencer's chest rose and fell evenly, as if he were asleep. She wasn't, but with her eyes closed, she pictured the future for the two of them.

Except now, besides the sunshine and the Shoppe and the sexy cowboy she got to kiss every day, there was a child. A beautiful child, who made Clarissa smile in a way she never had before.

"Spence?" she whispered.

"Hmm?"

"Maybe we could just tell Mama and Daddy," she said, not moving anything more than her lips. "That way, if Mama...goes soon, she'll know."

His arms around her tightened. "I'll do whatever you want, Rissa."

She nodded, wondering how she'd managed to get him to want to be right where he was. "I love you," she whispered.

"Love you too."

———

"HOW'S THE SHOP REBUILD COMING?" CLARISSA GLANCED over to Will, who sat at her kitchen counter on this weekday mid-morning. The farm Shoppe would open soon, but she was ready. Spencer had left hours ago to get a good chunk of his day worked before the sun super-heated everything.

Though it was only mid-March, Mother Nature had shown up for summer early in the Coastal Bend.

"I don't know," Will said, looking up from his phone.

Clarissa went back to measuring the coffee grounds into the filter. She and Will weren't as close as she was with Travis, but they had lived together and worked together on the farm for decades. "What do you mean you don't know?"

He'd talk more if she wasn't staring right at him, questioning him. She slid the now-ready filter into the coffeemaker and flipped it on.

"Gretchen asked me to stop coming around the shop," he said.

That brought Clarissa's attention back to him and surprise spreading through her. "She did?" She reached for the bagel she'd already toasted and slathered in cream cheese and took a bite.

"Yeah." He sighed and wiped his hand down his face. He hadn't shaved in a few days, and for Will, that meant a full beard. "She didn't like what I had to say, and she said I stressed her out."

"What did you say?"

Will pierced her with those bright eyes, but honestly, why had he shown up asking for coffee if he didn't want to talk? He did, and Clarissa knew it. She'd seen all the signs, and she'd been through this with him before. He just needed a little coaching.

"I tried not to say anything," he finally said, a sigh accompanying the words. "I just wondered why they didn't build the roof before they started on the inside. That made no sense to me. It rains in March and April."

Clarissa nodded and turned to get down a couple of mugs. She'd already had her morning coffee, and the baby didn't like it much. She had terrible heartburn now that she hadn't before, and she smiled internally at the reason why.

Having a baby was worth giving up coffee for a few months.

"She said I ask too many questions, and I pass judgment without knowing everything."

"Well." Clarissa turned back to him as the first drops

of his coffee hissed into the pot. "Sometimes we Coopers do that without meaning to." She knew Will, and she'd seen him with Gretchen. He hadn't brought her to a family dinner yet, but just the fact that he left the farm to see her spoke volumes.

"I know, and I hate that about myself." Will's eyes grew dark. "I hate that I can't control what I say. I'm trying. I swear I am, but honestly, Rissa, I don't think I'm ever going to be or do what Gretchen wants." He sprang to his feet. "I have to get back to work."

"Will," she said, hurrying after him. "Wait."

He did, pure anguish rolling from his broad shoulders. She stepped in front of him, anxious now. "I'm worried about you."

"I'm fine."

"Are you telling me everything?" Clarissa needed to know, and she'd risk her brother's wrath. "Did she break-up with you and you're just not saying?"

"No." He shook his head. "She just asked me not to come by the shop. We're still talking and stuff."

"You don't leave the farm much."

Anger blazed in his eyes, and he lifted his chin. "How do you know?"

"I'm guessing," she said. "But from that reaction..."

"I thought Travis might've told you."

"Travis and I don't talk about you and Gretchen."

"Really? Because he won't shut up about me and Gretchen at our house." Will spoke with so much venom in his voice that Clarissa fell back a step. "He's lecturing me constantly about what I should've said or not said—as if I don't know."

Clarissa didn't know what to do or say right here. She knew keenly how Will must've felt at his girlfriend's shop. "I'm so sorry." She stepped back into him and hugged him.

He gripped her tightly. So tight that Clarissa realized just how much pain he was in. Will was the strongest of them all. He'd eradicated his pre-diabetes within six months of learning about his elevated blood sugar. He'd lost fifteen pounds in the process, and then regained all of that and more in pure muscle as he lifted weights and ran around the farm.

He was smack dab in the middle of all of them, and he held their family together by sheer will. She had only seen him cry once, at least a decade ago, when the horse he'd raised from a colt, tutored in its care by their grandfather, had died.

Her worry doubled and then tripled as the man she considered made of rock, iron, and steel cracked and crumbled right there in her arms. She certainly wasn't strong enough to hold him together, but she sure did try.

Will finally stepped away, his eyes glassy. No tears came out, but his voice carried pure pain as he said, "I have to get back to work."

"Do you need to stay here with me and Spence for a few nights?" she asked, wiping at her own face. Only the slightest of tears came away with her fingers. "To get away from Trav?"

She was going to kill her youngest brother. He said plenty of inappropriate things too, thank you very much.

Will shook his head. "No, I moved in next door already."

Her eyebrows shot up. "You did? When?"

He cleared his throat. "Just today. Before dawn."

"By yourself?"

Fire moved through his expression, and she felt it filling her too. Right behind it came a wind so powerful, it could whip flames into tornadoes. Then a lashing, unrelenting rain, the kind that only came with hurricanes and tropical storms.

"Yes," he said. "By myself." He stepped past her, muttering something she didn't catch.

She turned, desperate to get him to stay. "Will."

He whipped back to her. "I want to do better, Rissa. I do. I don't know how. That's what I can't figure out. I know I've got this short fuse, and I've been trying to lengthen it. I know I speak harshly, and I've been trying to tame it."

"Just keep trying."

"I don't think I'm ever going to be as patient or as kind as she wants me to be." He shook his head again, what had turned soft and crumbly suddenly hardening in a single blink. "You'll not say anything to anyone about this."

"No, sir," she said.

"I have to get back to work."

"Yes."

Will opened the door and walked out, pulling it closed behind him. Clarissa moved over to the window that faced the cabin next door and watched her brother cross the greening grass between the two buildings.

She hadn't been able to pray for her and Spencer to have a baby, but she could absolutely petition the Lord to help Will.

"Please," she whispered into the glass. "He loves her, and he's such a good man. Please help him be exactly who she needs—and wants. Please."

21

W ill bent his ear closer to the construction foreman to hear the progress of the barn taking shape in front of him.

"...and then we'll get the roof shingled before that storm that's supposed to be comin' in, and then I'll have my guys out here to clean up, and then we'll get the stalls in."

"Just three," Will said, reiterating what he'd told Curtis several times now.

"Yep, three," he said, consulting his clipboard. "But the cement is cured now, and it looks great. We've got all the fixtures comin' in the week after next, and then it's paint."

"Perfect," Will said. He put a smile on his face and shook Curtis's hand. "Thanks for everything."

"Of course." Curtis went back toward the barn, where

he spoke with another man in a hardhat, and Will reached up to remove his. He did know a few things about construction, and he hadn't meant to sound critical when he asked Gretchen about why the crew at her shop did what they did.

Doesn't matter what you think you sounded like, he thought as he walked away from the barn. He'd fought hard to get this barn, as Lee and Daddy had wanted to spend the money on something else.

They needed this barn, and Will had been overseeing it's journey from foundation to completion. It wouldn't be done for another month or so, and Will could hardly wait. He was tired of squeezing their hay into the barn they had, and that barn was a mish-mash of equipment, tack, broken tools, and hay.

Will had to get that cleaned out, but he couldn't really do it until the new barn was finished.

"There you are," Travis called, and Will looked up from the dirt at his feet. He'd just tossed his hardhat into the back of his truck, and he just wanted to get on home to his new cabin. It wasn't new by any means, but he hadn't lived there for more than a couple of weeks. Maybe fifteen days.

"Hey," he said as casually as he could. He hadn't been getting along with Trav all that well, and he certainly didn't feel like talking to his brother right now.

"Goin' home?" Trav asked, coming closer.

"Yeah," Will said. And he wanted to go alone, so he didn't reach for his door handle. Trav wouldn't have much patience for talking out in the evening heat. Will certainly didn't. "What's up?"

"I'll tell Shay to come over there," he said, pulling out his phone.

Will sighed and opened his door and got behind the wheel. Trav joined him in the truck, his fingers still flying across the screen. That done, he tucked his phone under his thigh and focused on Will. "How's the cabin?"

"Just fine," Will said, not looking at his brother. "Yours?"

"I...you know what?" He sounded sour, and Will honestly didn't have the energy to deal with him tonight. "I don't like living there alone. You didn't have to move out so soon."

"You'll be married soon," Will said. He didn't owe Travis any explanation. True, he'd packed his things and moved out in secret, without talking to Travis about it at all. But again, Travis wasn't his father or his keeper, and Will didn't need his permission to move. He'd spoken to Daddy, and no one else needed the cabin.

"Not for two more months," Travis said, a growl in the words.

Will bumped down the dirt road. "I don't know what you want me to say."

"Why did you move out so soon?"

"Were you just assuming *I* would be the one moving out?" Will glanced over to Travis.

"I mean, I don't—no. I thought we'd talk about it." He frowned at Will, who quickly switched his gaze back out the windshield.

"Yeah, well, all you were doin' was yellin' at me about Gretchen. I didn't feel like talking about anything."

"I—" Travis started, plenty of punch in that single-letter word. He closed his mouth and breathed in through his nose. "How is Gretchen?"

"Fine, I'm assuming," Will said. "I don't want to talk about her."

"You're assuming? Did you two break-up?"

"No," Will said, when he could've easily said, *not yet.*

"When's the last time you saw her?"

"What day is it?" Will asked.

"Will," Travis said, heaviness in his voice. "She's your girlfriend. You have to make her a priority,"

"Thanks, Mom," Will said, unable to keep the sarcasm out of his voice. "I already said I don't want to talk about her." He drove past Clarissa and Spencer's cabin and parked in front of his.

He threw Trav a dirty look and got out of the truck. His door slamming sounded like an angry exclamation point, and so did Trav's. "Will," he said, jogging after him.

"Travis, go on home," Will said.

"You should go see her," he said, coming up the steps right behind Will.

"I don't need to be lectured tonight." He barreled into the house. He'd lock himself in his bedroom if he had to. Pressure built in his chest, and he suspected he needed to let it all out before it made him explode. So no retreating to his bedroom.

He opened the fridge and pulled out a bottle of water. He tossed one to Travis, along with one of his hottest glares.

"You might as well say it," he said. He'd known Trav for his whole life. He knew when Travis had something on his chest, and he knew when he needed to let him scream his frustrations into the sky. He wouldn't leave until he spoke his mind anyway. Might as well get it over with.

Will took a long drink of his water and recapped the bottle. "Are you mad at me?"

"You know what?" Travis asked. "Yeah, I am. You moved out without saying a single thing to me. How do you think I felt when I realized you weren't coming home at night, and then that you had a whole new home and I was all alone?"

"Is this about you or me?"

"It's about me," he said. "Right now. We'll get to you."

"Can't wait," Will said, immediately wishing he hadn't. He met Trav's eyes, and thankfully, he and Trav could communicate with just their eyes.

"You didn't have to move out," Travis said. "I would've told you that if you'd talked to me."

"I know that place is for you and Shay," Will said. "I

saw you two there, a couple of months ago. I knew then that she'd come live on the farm with you, and I'd need to find somewhere else to live."

"But not for two more months," Travis said. "And I didn't know that. Shay and I just barely talked about where we'd live."

Will finished his water and waited while Trav drank too. "I didn't mean to lecture you about Gretchen," he said.

Will nodded, because he did love his brother. "I shouldn't have moved out without talking to you."

A knock sounded on the door, and Travis's gaze flew in that direction. "That's Shay."

"Let her in," Will said. "I'll find something for dinner."

Travis went to open the door, and Will rustled up some frozen chicken cordon bleus from the freezer. He had a bagged salad, and that would have to do for tonight.

He set the oven and then finally turned toward the front door. Shay was just starting to move away from Travis, and relief filled Will. He didn't want to watch his brother kiss his fiancée, not when Will hadn't even texted with Gretchen that day.

He probably needed to go see her. It was Thursday, so she was real busy with her daddy tonight, but he could ask her to dinner tomorrow. Even just taking her one of her favorite meals would count, and Will didn't mind his time in his truck if he got to see Gretchen at the end of the drive.

"Hey, Will," Shay said, smiling at him as she walked through the living room.

"Howdy," he said. "I have chicken cordon bleu. It'll be about forty-five minutes."

"That's fine," Travis said, following Shay and slinging his arm around her as she sat at the bar. "Right, baby?"

"Sure," she said. "You don't have to feed us at all, Will." Shay had always been kind to him, and Will did his best to smile at her. She saw the effort, and her smile slipped. After a quick glance at Travis, she asked, "How's the barn coming?"

"Great," Will said.

"Oh, you know what?" she asked. "I got those new running packs. I should've brought you one."

"I'll come by this weekend," he said, turning when the oven beeped to alert him that it had come to temperature. He slid the frozen chicken into the oven and started for the couch.

"You're still running, right?" she asked.

Will yawned, thinking of his four-thirty alarm. "Yes, ma'am." He collapsed on the couch, his eyes falling closed.

Travis said something, but Will didn't have any more brain cells to converse. They could stay or go, talk or not. He didn't care. He just wanted to sleep until dinner.

When he slept, he didn't have to think about Gretchen. He didn't have to beat himself up for being who he was—and that he'd never be the man she wanted him to be.

All he did was dream of a cabin in the woods, with trees that had leaves that turned yellow in the fall. There were two deck chairs there, and Will had the distinct feeling in the dream that he'd built them for him and his wife.

They sat on the edge of a river that flowed out of a natural spring and into a pond down the hill a little way. Trav and Shay lived by the pond, but Will and his wife had the spring.

The woman came toward him, carrying a couple of glasses of sweet tea, and Will looked up at her, his heart filled with love and belonging.

Then the woman disappeared, and he never could get a good look at her face. He sipped the sweet tea, alone in the deck chairs, with the yellow leaves and the bubbling spring.

Always alone.

———

THE FOLLOWING WEEK, WILL PULLED INTO THE PARKING LOT at Sweet Water Taffy. He hadn't been here in weeks, though he had found his courage and seen Gretchen last weekend. Mama had asked about her on Sunday, telling Will to invite her to their Sabbath Day dinner.

He hadn't done it yet. He didn't get to see her all that

often, and when he did, he didn't want to share her with his family.

The shop looked good from the front, and Will parked and went toward the glass door. It opened, though the shop wouldn't re-open to the public until tomorrow. Will's heart pounded as he went inside, much like it had the first time he'd come here.

Now, he wasn't nervous about buying too many treats and what they'd do to his blood sugar, but he was still anxious to see Gretchen.

She lifted her head from where she studied something at the small, two-person table right beside the front window. "Hey," she said, her voice clear and bright.

Will relaxed the way he always did around her. "Hey."

She stood and embraced him, and that one hug might've been the thing to push him over the edge and fall all the way in love with her. That thought, and those feelings, sent his pulse to racing again, and he stepped away.

"Take me on a tour?" He looked over to the familiar candy cases. "You've got chocolates in there."

"Yes," Gretchen said. "Jon's been in the candy kitchen all day."

Will watched her as she spoke, and he'd never thought she liked Jon for more than a friend and employee. Will didn't have a problem with Jon. It was Jon who didn't like Will.

"He's in the back?" he asked, glancing toward the swinging door that led back into the two candy kitchens.

"Yes," Gretchen said, reaching to close her book and pick it up. She didn't reach for his hand, and he waited for her to lead the way toward the back of the retail space and around the register.

They went through the swinging door, which squeaked and annoyed Will. For some reason, he wanted to be here as much as he didn't. He told himself that Sweet Water Taffy was extremely important to Gretchen, and he could swallow his discomfort for the next few hours.

For her, he absolutely could.

Her candy kitchen hadn't been touched by the flames, but they'd ripped a lot of it out as the smoke had gotten into the walls and had to be cleaned out.

"It's all the same appliances," she said. "And the tables. Only the walls are new."

Will swept his eyes around the kitchen, seeing it as it had been before. "It's great," he said, slipping his hand into Gretchen's.

"The office," she said, taking him past the short hallway where he'd kissed her weeks and weeks ago when he'd brought her lunch.

He'd been in her office too, but it was much brighter now. "Wow," he said. "This is great."

"I had them put in the bright white," she said. "And I bought that gray desk."

She'd also added a row of three filing cabinets, the middle one holding a potted plant. There were no windows, but she'd put a big picture of what looked like windows being opened to a beach scene behind her.

Her computer sat on the desk, the screen dark. Gretchen loved to plan in her notebooks and journals, and Will had been doing some online research about the best ones so he could get her an elite planner for her birthday.

"I like it," he said.

"I love how it turned out." She smiled at him, and Will leaned down to kiss her. She kissed him back, and Will relaxed even more.

"Are you excited about the grand re-opening tomorrow?" he asked.

"Nervous," she admitted.

"I think the moment of 'someday, somehow' has arrived, Gretchen," he said. "You did it. It's almost all okay again."

She nodded, her anxiety evident. "And the small kitchen." She went across the hall to the candy kitchen where the fire had started. Jon worked in there, and he looked up as Will and Gretchen entered the room.

"Hey," he said, going back to wiping the counter. "Almost cleaned up."

"Just giving Will a tour," she said, throwing Jon a smile. Will watched the exchange, but he couldn't tell anything different between her and Jon.

"Have a good night," he said. "I'll be here at eight."

"Okay," Gretchen said, and she looked at Will. "Take me to dinner?"

Hope burned through his chest, and he wondered if all of his doubts had just been his own demons trying to chase him to the edge of a cliff, where he'd throw himself off.

"Sure," he said, his voice somewhat choked. "Anywhere you want."

22

Gretchen didn't want to go out. Her very bones ached, and she was so tired of thinking. Everyone around her had so many questions, and everyone looked to her for the answers.

She led Will out to the back parking lot, but his truck wasn't there. "Oh, you came in the front."

"I can walk around," he said. He ran his hand up her arm and along her neck. "Gretchen, you—we don't have to go out. Do you want to just go home?"

Tears pricked her eyes, because Will did know her so well. She nodded, and Will did too. "I'll follow you there," he said. "I can go get something in town and bring it out."

"Okay," she said, closing her eyes. The past six weeks had been a living nightmare, and sometimes Will had eased her stress, and sometimes he'd added to it. She felt stretched thin, and she wasn't sure how much more she could take.

She told herself it would all be over tomorrow, because Taffy was going to re-open in the morning. But she knew what her bank account looked like, and she knew what the business books looked like, and she'd be paying for this fire for a long, long time still.

The nightmare wasn't over yet.

"How about that wood-fired corn pizza?" she suggested.

A shadow crossed his face, but he said, "Okay. I'll see you at your house in a bit." He didn't kiss her before he turned and went back into the shop through the back door.

Gretchen didn't have the mental energy to analyze his behavior. She had enough other things to worry about, and he was a grown man.

She went home, calling her daddy along the way so she wouldn't have to think about him once Will brought dinner. She fed Elvis and texted Max that his cat missed him. *How are you?* she asked her brother, because he'd been telling her about an upcoming talent show for his oldest daughter, who really wanted her mother to come see her tap dance.

She sat and texted with Max for quite a while, not realizing how much time had passed until Max said he had to go so he could get his youngest to bed.

"Bed?" Gretchen asked herself, looking up from her

phone. She glanced at it again, realizing she and Will had split ways over an hour ago. Almost ninety minutes, in fact.

She tapped to call him, but his phone only rang once before going to voicemail. It was probably dead, and Gretchen got to her feet, which ached as she did.

Her stomach growled at her, and she cracked the front door, the whine of the hinges still loud enough to alert Elvis that a door had been opened.

She quickly stepped outside, a hint of worry gnawing at her. Just then, bright LED headlights cut through the darkness, and she recognized the rumble of his truck's engine as he turned the corner at the end of her street.

He arrived in her driveway a few seconds later, and he got out, slamming doors left and right. Oh, boy.

He came toward her with two pizza boxes in his hands and the power of darkness in his eyes.

"I tried calling you," she said. "Your phone must be dead."

"Yeah, because I waited at Pizza Five-Twelve for the last two hours." He stomped up the stairs, and Gretchen suddenly didn't want him there.

He went into her house, leaving the door open, and she caught a streak of gray tabby cat as she turned.

Her own anger sprang to life, and she followed Will into the house. "You let out Elvis."

"Sorry," he said, but he didn't sound sorry. He tossed the pizza on the counter and wouldn't look at her.

Gretchen usually didn't mind her grumpy cowboy. He'd respected her wishes these past few weeks, and he'd asked her about Taffy all the time. He'd taken her away from the chaos on the weekends, and he hadn't left her side in some of the worst moments of the past six weeks.

"Just go home," she said, joining him at the counter.

He looked at her then. "What?"

"I can't handle your grumpy side tonight," she said, trying not to be cruel. "Thank you for the pizza. But really. Just go. You've probably been up since four, and we should've just had something here." She opened the top box to find the wood-fired corn pizza she liked. The dobs of ricotta all over it made her mouth water.

"You want me to go?"

"Yes," she said, glaring at him.

"Fine." He ripped the box out from underneath the corn pizza. "I don't know how to be who you want," he said. "I really don't." He walked away, leaving Gretchen reeling for a moment.

When she finally caught up to what he'd said, she dashed after him. Will had long legs, and he'd reached the bottom of her front steps by the time she gained the porch. "Will."

"What?" he yelled into the night. "Don't come by the shop, Will. Don't give me your opinion, Will. Go get me some dinner, Will. Be happy about wasting almost two hours in a stupid pizzeria when you could've been with me, Will." He opened the back door and all but threw the pizza in the back seat.

He glared at her where she'd frozen at the top of the stairs. "I don't know what you want from me, Gretchen. I'll admit I have a temper, but I swear to you, I've been trying to tame it."

"I know," she said, but she hadn't spoken nearly loud enough for him to hear.

"I am who I am," he said. "I'm not perfect. I know that, but I have been trying *so* hard. I don't think I'll ever be who you want."

Gretchen didn't know what was happening, so she just stood there and looked at him.

"I'm going to go," he said. "Good luck with your re-opening tomorrow."

Her mouth dropped open. "You're not going to come?"

"I have to pick up some stuff in town," he said, opening his door and getting behind the wheel. He paused there, and their eyes met through the windshield.

He got back out and said, "I'm sorry I haven't been able to live up to your standards. Honestly, I am." He paused right at the front corner of his truck, the head-lights now flooding the entire front of the house. "I think if your shop hadn't burned, I might've been able to somehow convince you to stay with me. But I can see now that I won't be able to, because I'm simply not who you want."

"Don't say that," she said, her chest catching on to what he was saying.

"I'm loud, and I have opinions, and yes, I get mad when I waste my whole Friday night waiting for a pizza instead of kissing the woman I love." He stopped and shook his head. "This doesn't matter. I have to go. Good luck tomorrow."

With that, Gretchen stared as Will got behind the wheel of his truck, took a second to buckle his seatbelt, and then backed right on out of her driveway.

Right on out of her life.

———

THE NEXT MORNING, GRETCHEN'S FACE FELT AS CRUSTY AND as swollen has it had the morning after the fire at Sweet Water Taffy. She hadn't been able to find the courage to text or call Will last night, and foolishly, she searched the crowd who'd gathered in the front parking lot for him instead.

He wasn't there, at least not that she could see. He wore such a blindingly white cowboy hat, she didn't think she could miss him. Truck after truck pulled in, and then people started parking down the road.

Gretchen clutched her notecards, her stomach trying to claw its way into her brain.

"Gretchen," Jon said, and she blinked away from the sea of faces. He looked like he'd been trying to get her attention for more than a moment, and she gave him a quick smile.

"Yes," she said. "I'm ready."

"I wasn't going to ask that." He nodded to someone to her left, and she looked that way, an insane amount of hope shooting to the back of her throat. Of course Will wouldn't stay away from this, one of the most important events of her life.

She found a tall Cooper man standing over that way, but it wasn't Will. By the look on Travis Cooper's face, his brother wasn't coming.

Gretchen's emotions shook and shattered, and then Jon stepped in front of the mic and said, "Welcome everyone. We won't waste your time this morning. I give you the tireless and fearless owner of Sweet Water Taffy, Gretchen Bellows!" He looked at her with a perfectly charming smile on his face, the one he used for all the customers.

She could see the urgency in his eyes too, telling her to *dwell on Will later. Re-open the shop now.*

So she glued a smile on her lips and stepped over to him. "Thank you, Jon," she said, taking a moment to arrange her notecards on the podium in front of her.

Her next thought was, *Why is there a podium here? It's a candy shop.*

Rattled, she looked up from her notes, utterly lost.

Then she met a pair of eyes she'd know anywhere. They followed her into her dreams, and she knew exactly what they looked like when he smiled, when he was fixing to kiss her, and when he wanted to rage about waiting too long for pizza.

Will had come.

She wanted to run to him, but the crowd shifted, and she lost sight of those pretty ocean-colored eyes she wanted to dive into and swim around in for the rest of her life.

The woman I love.

She wanted to question him further about what he'd said last night, but her bravery had failed her once again. She wasn't perfect either, and she hated that she made him feel like he had to be in order to be with her.

"Gretchen," Jon hissed out of the corner of his smile.

She looked down at her notecards and took a great, big breath. "Wow," she said as she looked up. "Thank you so much for coming out to support our grand re-opening. I sure hope we have enough caramels inside..."

23

Travis Cooper adjusted the jacket over his shoulders, knowing it didn't quite lay right. He left the dressing room anyway, the three men waiting for him out in front of all the mirrors looking his way the moment he did.

Lee's eyes scanned down to Trav's boots, as if it mattered what the jacket looked like with these jeans. He'd worn these to urge Berthas into the milking chutes this morning, along with the boots. He'd literally run back to his cabin, put on a bunch more deodorant and a different shirt, and hopped in Lee's truck ten seconds after that.

Will kept his eyes on the jacket, but Trav couldn't tell if his brother liked it or not. Will glared at everything these days. Positively everything, as Trav had caught him eyeing

Mama with daggers when she'd asked about Gretchen's grand reopening.

That event was a week old, and Will still hadn't gone to get his girlfriend back in his life. If Trav had been living with him, he was sure Will would be just as sighy and just as slammy as Trav had been after he'd broken up with Shayla.

The salesman who'd helped Travis find this jacket nodded appreciatively and approached first. "We can let it out in the shoulder," he said, brushing his hand along the offending part of the jacket. "But this looks great with the hat."

Travis had found his wedding cowboy hat first. He wanted his tux to match it, and that was the purpose of today's visit. Shay had told him if he didn't get to town to order his tux today, she'd call off the wedding. She'd agreed to be married on his family farm, but she would not allow him to show up in jeans and a plaid shirt.

He'd demanded to know what was wrong with his clothes, and then she'd started kissing him, so he'd forgotten everything after that. She sure knew how to get what she wanted.

"Guys?" Travis asked, throwing his arms straight out to his sides. "What do you think?"

"Looks great," Will said disinterestedly. Honestly, Travis wasn't sure why he'd brought him along. He hadn't cared where they'd gone to lunch either. It was like the usually-opinionated-and-didn't-hold-back Will had disappeared.

With a jolt, Travis realized he had. "Will," he said. "Really. What do you think?"

Will looked up from his phone again, his eyes dark with irritation. Travis didn't care; he'd weathered darker looks than this. "I think it matches the hat really well," he said.

"Me too," Lee said, and that was that. Trav knew he wouldn't get much more from his brothers.

"You guys said you wanted to come," he said, frustrated with them.

"You said you'd buy my lunch," Will said, an attempt at a smile touching his face.

"Like you can't afford your own lunch," Trav shot back at him.

"I had to drive to town to get Ford from his birthday party," Lee said, and he sank back into the luxurious red recliners outside the men's dressing rooms.

Travis heaved a great big sigh and looked at the attendant. "I think this is the only one I need to try on. I do want the shoulders wider, and I need more room in my underarm."

"Yes." The man whipped out his tape measure like it was a sword and started taking down numbers.

Travis stared at his brothers, one standing and one sitting. Neither of them seemed to care about his laser glare. It probably wasn't as strong as theirs.

"Can you make the pants into shorts?" he asked, not removing his eyes from his brothers. Neither of them moved or even looked at him. Lee looked like he'd passed out in two seconds flat, which he probably had.

"Shorts, sir?" the salesman repeated, looking up with surprise.

"Yeah," Travis said, raising his voice. "I saw these really hip *shorts* on a guy online. They went all the way down to his knee, and he wore the usual attire up top. I'm thinking *I want to wear shorts at my wedding.*"

At least the yelling got Will to look up. He blinked and asked, "What?"

"Not a good idea," Lee said, opening his eyes.

"Shay will murder you in front of everyone," Will added. He shook his head, no smile in sight. "He's kidding. He doesn't want shorts for his wedding."

"What's with you guys?" Travis asked. He shook his head at the salesman. No, he didn't want to upset Shay at the wedding. He'd totally wear shorts to get married. Maybe he wasn't as hip as the couple he'd seen online, but he'd still do it.

Shay *would* fillet him if he did; Will was right about that.

"Nothing," Lee said.

"Let me go check on the alteration schedule," the salesman said, glancing at Will and Lee in distaste before he nodded at Travis. "You can give me that."

Travis shrugged out of the jacket and handed it to the

man, who couldn't seem to get away from them fast enough. That was probably a good thing, as Travis was about to lose his mind.

"You know what?" Lee asked. "I take that back. I know what's wrong with me, and that's that I don't want to go to this stupid wedding—no offense, Trav—alone." He looked from Travis to Will. "I need a date."

Will put away his phone and exchanged a look with Travis that comprised a whole conversation. "Yeah? Who are you going to ask?"

"I don't know," Lee mumbled, but his face grew redder every half-second.

Travis's first inclination was to tease him, but he bit that back when he saw Will shake his head just once. "You can bring someone," he said instead. "I won't tell Shay you said the wedding was stupid."

Lee flashed a smile. "You know what I mean. I don't really think it's stupid. I'm the stupid one who's thinking about it every second, and it's not for two more months."

Six weeks, but Travis wasn't going to correct him.

"Someone on the app?" Will asked, his voice much cooler than Trav's would've been.

"No," Lee barked, getting to his feet and looking around like the three of them were planning to rob this tuxedo shop. "I'm not using the app anymore."

Will frowned. "Who'd you meet then?"

Travis waited silently, because it was an excellent

question. Lee left the farm less than Will, who hadn't been off of it in a week.

Lee cleared his throat. "I think you should talk to Gretchen."

"Yes," Travis said, jumping in to agree. "I think that's an excellent idea."

"How did this get on me so fast?" Will asked. "You're just deflecting, because you don't want to tell us who you're sweet on."

"I'm not sweet on her," Lee said with plenty of disgust, as if liking a woman was the worst thing a man could do. "I've only met her once, that's all."

"Bet you can't stop thinking about her," Travis said, shooting a look at Will. He started to open his mouth, but Travis cut him off with, "Just like Will can't sleep, because he lays awake in bed, thinking about Gretchen."

Will turned his blue-green daggers toward Travis.

"Or how he hasn't gone running one day this week," Travis said, deciding if he was going to die today, it better happen at the hands of one of his brothers as he called them out. "Because even running with everything he has doesn't drive Gretchen from his mind."

"Stop it," Will growled.

"He's right," Lee said. "I haven't seen you running."

"I'm just taking a break," Will said. "I've already got the alarm set for Monday morning."

"Show me," Travis demanded, and Will gripped his phone tighter.

"Listen," he said, his face turning pale a moment later. "I mean—this is none of your business."

"Yeah, like when you sold me out in front of everyone about my behavior when me and Shay were split."

"This is different," Will said. "You had a misunderstanding. Gretchen doesn't—she can't—she...I'm not good enough for her."

"You saw her at the re-opening," Travis said. "I know you did, and how much she brightened when she saw you."

Will leaned forward, anger streaming from him. "I'm not talking about this here," he hissed, his voice so menacing that Travis shrank back.

Will straightened and looked left and right. He seemed to gather himself back together and smooth the emotion from his face. "Let's help Lee. I'm beyond help."

"You are not," Lee said. "I saw her last Saturday too, Will." His voice came out much gentler. "She looked at you the way—" He went mute and cut a look at Travis.

"Go on," Travis said, because he really wanted to know what Lee would say too.

"Yeah," Will said slowly. "Go on."

"She looked at you—however briefly, because you scampered away—the way Shay looks at Trav. The way Mama looks at Daddy. She loves you too, Will."

"I'm not in love with her," Will said, but the words came out flat and without life.

"Liar," Lee and Travis said together, and a grin spread

across Travis's face. This was how the Cooper brothers talked. They didn't let each other get away with anything.

"It doesn't matter," Will said, most of the fight leaving him. "I'm not going to talk to her, so unless she shows up at the farm begging me to be with her, it's over." He cleared his throat and looked at Lee. "Who's got you sighing and flustered?"

Lee narrowed his eyes and looked between Travis and Will. Travis pressed his palms together and batted his eyelashes. "I won't tease you."

"I met this woman at Ford's math night," he said. "Rosalie Reynolds?" He mumbled the name, and Travis looked at Will.

"Did you get that?"

"I did not," Will said.

"Rosalie Reynolds," Lee barked. "She's this super-smart, super-attractive, way-out-of-my-league game developer. There's no way I can ask her. We don't run in the same circles at all."

Travis's mind spit all kinds of ideas at him, but it was Will who said, "This is easy, Lee. She was at Ford's math night? Why?"

"She did a demo on this math facts video game."

"Did you buy the game for Ford?" Will asked.

"No," Lee said. "It was—" His brain obviously caught up to his mouth, because he once again cut off, his eyebrows flying toward the ceiling.

"Buy the game for Ford," Will said. "Then, you'll have

a reason to contact her. Next thing you know, you have the woman's number."

"Then you'll ask her to the wedding," Travis said, grinning at Lee.

"This isn't that easy," Lee said, but the wheels were obviously spinning in his mind.

"All right," Travis said, plucking Will's phone from his hand as he had it out again. "Now, let's talk about how you're going to make up with Gretchen…"

"Travis," Will growled. "I was texting with one of our cowboys about his vacation days."

"Come on, bro," Travis said. "This is way more important than that."

"I agree with Trav," Lee said. "You shouldn't walk away from her just because a few things got hard while she rebuilt her shop."

"That's not why I walked away," Will said.

"You're who she wants," Lee said, and when he spoke in his older-brother, caring tone, Travis usually sat up and listened.

Will did too, and he looked past Travis as they arrived at the check-out counter to order his tuxedo. "You think so?"

"I know so," Lee said. "You're just like Trav—you get too far inside your head. You've invented all these reasons you can't be together, none of which Gretchen has actually said."

Travis nodded in an overdramatic way, and Will

sighed. "Fine," he said. "So how do I get her back?"

Travis took his credit card back from the salesman. "I have a few ideas," he said. "Actually, these come from Shay, but she's going to be so proud of me for finding a way to suggest them today." He beamed at his brothers, but for some reason, they didn't smile back.

24

Lee couldn't sleep, and he spent a good thirty minutes tossing from left to right before he got up. He paused in the doorway of his son's bedroom, the silver moonlight falling across the floor but not touching the boy.

Ford meant the world to him, and Lee questioned whether he should try to bring another woman into either of their lives. He had Martha, his mother, and she didn't seem to worry about dating or the men she introduced into Ford's life.

He leaned into the doorway, the chill of the air conditioning kissing his bare chest. Lee had never felt so torn in his life. He'd always known he'd inherit Sweet Water Falls Farm and the accompany dairy operation, Cooper & Co. Always, and he'd always wanted it.

He loved working outside, loved cows and horses and dogs and goats and chickens, and he couldn't remember a day he didn't love putting on his cowboy boots and hat, finishing his coffee, and heading out into the dawn of a new day.

When he'd married Martha, he'd not had a single second thought. When she'd filed for divorce only a couple of years later, he'd been expecting it. He even paid her back for the fee to do so. Lee never doubted what he felt or what the next step should be.

Until now.

Ford was almost nine years old. He'd be moving into the fourth grade this year, and he understood things Lee didn't want to explain to him. At the same time, Lee could admit he was lonely—only to himself—and he wanted to try to tame the temper-tantrum-beast inside him and find someone he could kiss in the evenings. Someone who would bring him hot tea when he didn't feel well, and who'd curl into him when he tossed and whispered that she was right there and everything was okay.

Sighing, he turned away from Ford's bedroom and padded down the hall in only his boxer shorts. He wanted to be someone's soft place to fall too. He wanted to hold his wife while she cried and reassure her that he was right there, and he'd make sure whatever had upset her, he'd fix.

Right now, in his dark kitchen, he opened the fridge

and flooded his retinas with light. Squinting, he pulled out an energy drink and popped the tab. If he was lucky, he'd get down a few swallows, find his cowboy courage, and get Ford's backpack from the boy's bedroom.

Lee drank a lot of coffee during the day, but his energy drinks had twice as much caffeine, and he felt it infusing him with strength to get this job done. Travis's wedding sat on the calendar, almost like a death date to Lee. A noose around his neck he felt tightening centimeter by centimeter.

He took another swallow of the grape-flavored drink and slammed the can on the countertop. A bit splashed out and hit his hand, but he just wiped it on his shorts as he strode back toward the back of the cabin. Ford slept like the dead, and it wasn't hard for Lee to step into the bedroom, cross it to the corner desk, and lift the backpack from the floor.

His son hadn't closed it, and Lee wasn't surprised when the front of the pack flopped open and several papers fell out. He stooped, scooped them all back in, and kept going.

Out in the kitchen again, Lee switched on the light and dumped the backpack upside down. Everything inside came clattering or fluttering out, his heart beating the same way against his ribs and down into his stomach.

It had been weeks since the order form for Fire-breathing Facts had come home. Ford had mentioned it once, and Lee couldn't even remember what he'd said about it. Maybe Martha had bought the program for their son; he honestly didn't know.

She did most of Ford's homework with him. She signed the permission forms. She dealt with ninety-percent of the school stuff. As he sifted through old, graded homework papers, a note about a field trip that was three weeks past, and the handwriting sheets he found so insufferable, he didn't find the note about the software.

Desperation built inside him until finally, he had to admit it wasn't there. He shoved everything back inside Ford's pack and very nearly tossed it out the window in his frustration. He pulled back on his own inner fire-breathing dragon, his chest heaving, and forced himself to *think*.

"You have the Internet," he said right out loud. Because he lived in a three-bedroom cabin and didn't have much space, the computer sat on the edge of the living room carpet, almost in the dining area of the kitchen. Lee wanted it where he could see what Ford did too, and he picked up his energy drink and went toward the machine.

It brightened, and his fingers flew across the keyboard as he searched for the software Rosalie Reynolds had been selling at math night almost seven weeks ago now. With the combination of her name and what Lee remembered about the program, the website for Curious Kids appeared before his eyes.

Fire-breathing Facts sat right at the top, and he clicked to learn more about it. The price nearly knocked him back to bed, and he was sure the flyer he hadn't been able to find had contained a discount.

"So what?" he muttered to himself, actually leaning forward to see the screen better. He'd just gotten glasses last week, and he still wasn't used to wearing them. "You think you can't afford it?"

He could, and he put the software in his cart. Hesitation gripped him, and he paused, the mouse clicker hovering right over the purchase button. "Who else are you going to ask?"

He bought the software, and an announcement came up that said he'd have a confirmation email already and his product in hand very soon. He navigated to his email, and sure enough, the receipt for the math facts software sat there.

It had a customer service number, the website, and email address. Lee's pulse pounced through his body, and his throat felt so, so dry.

"She probably has people who answer her customer service emails and phone calls," he said. He didn't have access to her personal line...yet.

That pesky *yet* touched his mind and wouldn't let go. He went back to the Curious Kids website and poked around a little bit, finally clicking past all of the other products—only one other computer game—to the About page.

He sucked in a breath at the full-color, smiles-for-miles photo of Rosalie. The dark curls, the pink lips, the mesmerizing eyes. In the picture, she was clearly laughing, and Lee couldn't take his eyes from the joy radiating from her.

When he finally did, he started to read the beginnings of her company.

Rosalie Reynolds has been developing educational games for almost two decades. She started when she was ten years old and her younger sister, who is autistic, needed a way to learn how to add and subtract. She finally launched Curious Kids in the Coastal Bend of Texas after developing and designing educational games for Pearson Parents and Educational Leadership for five years.

She is the sole employee and wears every label from CEO to shipping consultant. If you have a problem with any product from Curious Kids, when you call, you'll get Rosalie personally.

Lee leaned away from the screen, his eyes unable to see the small text. His mind whirred, spitting back facts he'd read.

She has an autistic sister. So she'd be patient, right? Lee needed someone who could be patient with him, patient with Ford, and patient with farm life.

When he calls, he'll get her on the other end of the line. If he called. Not when. *If.* Lee felt like he'd need an entire case of his grape energy drinks to dial Rosalie's number, company or personal.

His brain misfired then, screaming something about how *she's only thirty years old.*

"That can't be right," he muttered, leaning forward and squinting to be able to read the top of the paragraph again.

Rosalie Reynolds has been developing educational games for almost two decades. She started when she was ten years old...

That didn't mean she was only thirty. Or "almost thirty," which would be far worse. Surely, she hadn't gone all the way back to age ten, and then added the two decades. It meant from the time she'd started working for the other companies.

"Has to," Lee whispered. He was forty-two and not getting any younger. Down the hall, the alarm on his phone started to sing, and Lee groaned as he picked up his energy drink and went to turn it off.

He'd done what he could for now. He'd ordered the software. He could continue to grapple with himself for another day.

———

"Dad!" Ford came barreling into the administration building. "Look what came!" He waved a box left and right as he entered the office where Lee sat with Will. He still hadn't spoken to Gretchen, and Lee didn't know how to bring it up the way Travis did. The shopping trip only a few days ago had been excruciating for Lee too, but in a different way.

"What's that?" Will asked, but Lee knew what it was. He let his heart bang and beat as Will whipped out his pocketknife and cut through the tape on the box.

"It was on the porch," Ford said. "It didn't even have a shipping label." He looked from his uncle to Lee. "It just had my name on it."

Will met Lee's eyes, and Lee simply folded his arms across his chest so his heart wouldn't beat right through skin and bone. Will pulled out the box with the giant, red, fire-breathing dragon, and Ford yelled.

"You bought it?" He spun and grinned at Lee, and he couldn't keep his face straight when his son looked so happy. "Thanks, Dad!" He came around the desk and launched himself at Lee, the two of them laughing.

"Can I go put it on the computer right now?" Ford asked. "When did you get it?" He searched Lee's face, and Lee had never been much of a liar.

"I ordered it on Saturday night," he said. Sunday morning. Whatever. It was still dark when he'd put in the order.

"It came in one day?" Will asked, flipping over the shipping box. He looked up and met Lee's eyes. His curiosity knew no bounds, and Lee shook his head just once. A silent plea for his brother to please wait a minute.

Since Will wasn't Travis, and the man had more sense

than even Lee himself, he snapped his mouth shut and went back to examining the shipping box.

Ford returned to Will and took the box with the disc inside. "I'm going to go put it on right now."

"Okay," Lee said. "But you can't play for long. You have to go feed Queenie and help Grandpa with the steaks."

Ford groaned and his shoulders slumped, but he'd do what he was supposed to do. He'd been working around the farm all day today, as it was a professional day for teachers and the students didn't have to go to school. Lee would take him to school in the morning, and Martha would pick him up from there.

Then his son would be gone until the weekend.

Ford took his new prize and left the office. Lee watched him go, then waited for the outer door to slam closed. He flinched when it did, closing his eyes.

"You ordered it on Saturday night?" Will prompted. "And it was hand-delivered to your door by Monday afternoon."

Lee wasn't about to tell him it had been ordered about five a.m. on Sunday morning. He opened his eyes and met his brother's. "Yes," he said. "Apparently."

"Who do you think delivered it?" He turned over the box again and held it up as if Lee hadn't seen it. "Without a label?"

Lee swallowed, because he knew who. *She is the sole employee and wears every label from CEO to shipping consultant. You'll get Rosalie personally.*

"I don't know," he said, and Will's eyebrows shot toward his hairline.

"Lee—"

"Have you gone to talk to Gretchen?" Lee asked, glaring at his brother.

Will glared on back, his eyes throwing ninja stars and stabs of darkness into Lee's face. "She's busy on Mondays," he said.

"Yeah, I'll bet," Lee said, standing up. "I'm going to go monitor my son on the computer. You keep lying to yourself."

"I'm not lying to anyone," Will yelled as Lee left the office. But he was. He knew he was, and Lee knew he was. Lee also knew he was lying to himself as well. When he arrived at the cabin, he pulled out his phone and searched his email for the receipt he'd gotten from Curious Kids.

The phone number sat right there. He could just call and say thank you for hand-delivering the game, right? That would be appropriate, wouldn't it?

Before he could, Ford came running out of the front door, the box in his hand. He skipped several stairs on the way down, causing Lee to have a mini-heart attack when he felt sure his son would trip and break both legs.

He hastened to get out of the truck, and he said, "Ford."

The boy hadn't even looked toward the driveway, but he did now. "The game doesn't work," he said, holding it up. "It just sits there and spins and doesn't do anything."

"You sure?" Lee asked, and Ford gave him a withering look, worthy of any Cooper. He reached his son and took the game. "Let me just try, okay?"

They went back into the house together, and sure enough, when Lee put in the disk, it spun. And spun, and spun. It never loaded, and it never prompted them to install the game. He wasn't sure if his stomach was sick from excitement or all the caramels he'd been eating that afternoon. He'd gone to Gretchen's re-opening, and he may have bought too many sweets.

"I'll call them," he said, pushing the button to make the tray spit out the disk. He had to call now, and his insides shook as he looked around for his phone. "Shoot, my phone's in the truck. C'mon."

"Are you going to call?"

"Yes," Lee said, irritation shooting through him. "I paid a lot of money for this game." He followed Ford back to the truck. "I'll get you over to Grandma and Grandpa's. Then I'll call."

"Dad."

"I said I was going to call," he barked at Ford, who fell silent. Regret lanced through Lee. "Sorry, bud," he murmured.

"Sorry it doesn't work," Ford said.

"It's not your fault." Lee looked over at his son, but he stared out the side window. "Hey, Ford."

He turned and looked at him. "It's not your fault. I'll call, and they'll send another one. That's all."

He nodded, and Lee wished he could bring back the excitement and joy from only fifteen minutes ago. They pulled up to the white farmhouse, and Lee nodded toward it. "Go on now. Be helpful to your grandparents this afternoon."

Ford opened his door and got out. Lee rolled down his window and waited for Ford to round the truck. "Ford," he called, and his son turned back to him. "I love you, bud. I didn't mean to get upset."

"I know," Ford said, smiling. "Love you too, Dad. Thanks for the game." With that, he bounced up the front steps and into the farmhouse. Lee wished he could bounce back from the difficult and trying things in his life as easily as an eight-year-old.

With a sigh, he picked up his phone and dialed the number for Curious Kids. The line rang twice, and he almost threw his phone right through the windshield.

"Curious Kids," a woman said, perfectly pleasant and professional. Perfectly Rosalie. "This is Rosalie Reynolds. What can I help you with?"

Lee sat there, frozen, the sound of her voice so melodic and so beautiful.

"Hello?" she asked.

"Yes," he blurted out. "Sorry. This is Lee Cooper, and I ordered that dragon computer game?"

"Yes, Lee," she said as if he hadn't fallen into a trance. His face burned, and he reminded himself he was on the phone with her. She couldn't see him. "Did you get it? I dropped it off today."

"Why didn't you mail it?" he asked.

"It's cheaper to bring for someone local," she said. "There are all these taxes for computer software and the postal...anyway." She cleared her throat. "Is there a problem?"

"No," he said. "I mean, yes." He pressed his eyes closed and told himself to *calm down. Think. Talk like a normal person.* "First, thank you for bringing it. I could've come to get it if I'd known that was what you'd do. Second, we put it in the computer, but it doesn't load. It doesn't install."

"Okay," she said without questioning him further. "I can do a swap. Is there a time you'll be home?" Something banged on her end of the line. "I have tomorrow or Wednesday..."

"I can come do the swap," he said. "You don't need to drive out here again." His mind screamed at him to ask her out. They could do the swap over dinner or even coffee. *Lunch!* his brain yelled. *Ask her to lunch!*

"Okay," she said easily. "I have a tiny office off Church Street. Can you take down the address?"

"Is it in the email I got when I bought the game?"

"Oh, sure," she said with a light laugh. "It's there too."

"I'll come tomorrow," he said.

"I'll be here all day," Rosalie said, and the call ended.

Lee let his phone drop to his lap, everything inside him going quiet and dormant again. He hadn't asked her out, and if he couldn't do it over the phone, there was no way he could get the right words to come out in the right order when faced with her.

No, it would be better to go to Travis's wedding alone. He just needed an escape plan for anyone wanting to fix him up with their niece or daughter or even their mother...

25

Gretchen finished with the edible gold dust and stepped back to admire the company logo she'd just applied to the chocolates. She'd hand-painted the H and the J, but the ampersand between them glittered in gold.

They made her smile, but they didn't bring her joy. Not the way monogrammed and personalized caramels once had.

She wiped her hair back out of her face, the tears she'd been fighting for days always so close to the surface. She started boxing up the caramels, as the lead secretary for the marketing firm Henry & Jenkins would be here in about thirty minutes.

After that job finished, Gretchen needed to get caramelizing the apples that had been delivered that morning. The re-opening of the shop had been a spectacular event, and Taffy had sold out of almost everything before closing time.

She'd stayed at the shop until almost eleven that night, mostly to restock the cases, but also afraid to go home. She just knew Will would come to the shop, and she didn't want to miss him.

They were closed on Sunday, and on the way home every day last week, Gretchen had actually convinced herself that Will would be waiting on her front steps. He wouldn't want to make a big scene at the candy shop.

He hadn't been there either, and she'd gone out to Daddy's to help with the oxygen tank, with his meds, and their traditional Thursday night sandwich date had continued without a hitch.

Nothing in Gretchen's life felt put together right. Without Will, she didn't care about Taffy the same way. She couldn't be herself. Last night, she couldn't bear the thought of going home and not finding him, and she'd slept at her daddy's. Elvis had been none-too-pleased with her when she'd shown up that morning to feed him, and Gretchen couldn't blame him.

She was none-too-pleased with herself.

She finished with the boxes and took them out front for Carmen, one of the new cashiers, to give to Bridgette Barker when she came in.

Gretchen untied and retied her apron. "I'm going to be working on the caramel apples next," she said, moving down the case to see what they had left. "Looks like the Oreo and the apple pie ones are the most popular."

"And the one with all the tiny M&M's," Carmen said. "With the milk chocolate."

Gretchen nodded and returned to the cash register to pick up a notebook. She didn't mean to take a full inventory, and she caught herself in time to stop doing so. She simply wrote down the apples they had, and the ones they didn't. She'd make a plan from there.

She went through the swinging door, studying her notes. Gretchen knew instantly that something was different in the candy kitchen, and she jerked her attention up. Was there another fire?

"Howdy, ma'am." Will reached up and tipped his hat at her.

Gretchen's whole body lit up, and she lost the ability to hold her notebook. It tumbled to the floor, but she just stood there, staring at the delicious cowboy in her kitchen. She hadn't smelled smoke; she'd smelled his cologne, and she'd known instantly that something was different.

In that moment, she knew she was different too. She wasn't the same woman she'd been when she'd smashed caramel into Will Cooper's shirt at the drugstore. He wasn't even close to the same man.

"Listen," he said, clearing his throat. He flicked his gaze toward the doorway that led into the other candy kitchen. His eyes came back to hers. "I'm just going to do what I do best, okay? And that's say all kinds of inappropriate things. The difference is, I've thought about all of these, and I want to say them."

Gretchen absently tucked her hands in her apron, her heartbeat speeding through her veins. *The woman I love.*

Was he going to take that back? Had he meant to say it?

"I am who I am, Gretchen," he said. "I know I'm not perfect, and I know I can be this growly, barky beast. I'm trying to do better about that, and I'm going to keep trying. I want to keep trying, because I want you in my life."

He took a breath, and she realized how nervous he was. "I want you in my life, because I love you."

Tears filled her eyes, but she still couldn't get her voice to work.

"One thing I've learned over the past couple of months. Three months. Whatever. Is that I need to be more patient, and that starts with myself. I want to be this perfect man for you. I want to protect you from hard things, and bad things, and sad things. All I wanted when I came to the shop was to be here for you. I didn't mean to ask the wrong questions or seem like I was being too critical."

Another deep breath. "I just wanted to maybe shoulder some of the *huge* burden you were carrying. I did a real bad job at that, but I'm going to try again. I mean, if you'll let me." He cleared his throat. "I'm going to be patient with myself as I change, and I'm going to be patient with us, and I'm going to be patient with Elvis."

Gretchen broke, her eyes finally closing and releasing the tears she'd kept inside by pure will.

"I am, Gretchen," he said softly. "If you'll just give me another chance, I'll show you that I can be kind enough, and quiet enough, and patient enough for you. I can. I *know* I can."

She shook her head, the image of him blurry through her tears. She blinked and wiped at her face, squared her shoulders, and took a step toward him. His countenance had fallen, and she wasn't sure why.

"You better not, Will Cooper," she said, her voice as flinty as she could make it.

He lifted his eyes back to hers. "Excuse me?"

She advanced toward him, and a vein of fear crossed his expression. That gave Gretchen power, and she seized onto it and used it to fuel her next words. "You better not," she said. "I don't want a different version of you." Her nerves shook, but she plowed forward. "I love your temper, and I love your mouth, and I love that you just say what you want. It took me a while, but I realized you were trying to support me in the way you knew how, and I'm really sorry I made you feel like that wasn't good enough."

"Don't apologize to me," he said, that grumpy cowboy she loved shining right through. He clenched his jaw and shook his head. "Please, don't."

"Then don't you apologize to me," she shot back. She

reached him, and with only a couple of feet between them, Gretchen could see the amazing flecks of color in his eyes. "I don't want a watered-down version of the man I fell in love with. I just want the real Will Cooper, and it's okay that you're loud, and opinionated, and that you sometimes lose your cool when you have to wait for a pizza for two hours."

Those pesky tears filled her eyes again. "I'm sorry about the pizza. I'm sorry I asked you to go. That wasn't me asking you to change."

Will reached out with one hand, sort of lobbing it toward hers. She grabbed onto him, wishing they'd clung to each other when things had gotten really hard. A sob worked its way toward the surface, but she wasn't done talking yet. "I hate this place," she whispered.

He looked right into her eyes. "No, you don't. You love Sweet Water Taffy."

She shook her head. "Not without you. I hate coming here if I can't talk to you about it. I hate leaving here, knowing I won't hear your voice later. I hate it. I hate that I let this stupid candy shop come between us, and I hate that instead of letting you help me the Will-Cooper way, I pushed you away."

"You didn't," he said.

"I did," she insisted. "And blast you, Will Cooper, you let me."

Anguish crossed his face, and then he wrapped her up in those arms she missed so much and held her right against his chest while she cried. "Someday," he whispered. "Somehow, I'm going to make this okay."

Gretchen pulled back her tears once again and looked at him. "You just did. Today."

Hope shone through the clouds in his eyes. "Yeah?"

"Yeah."

He pressed his lips to her forehead, which wasn't where she wanted them at all. "Can we go back to that bit...I thought I heard you say...maybe it was something like... *I don't want a watered-down version of the man I fell in love with*." He raised his eyebrows, and Gretchen smiled for the first time since she'd gotten the call from Jon that Sweet Water Taffy was on fire.

A real smile. One filled with hope, and joy, and William Cooper.

"What about it?" she challenged.

"Do you mean that?"

"Did you?" she asked. "When you said you'd fallen in love with me?"

"I did," he said. "Mean it, I mean. I do." A smile spread across his face, reaching clear up into his eyes. "I love you, Gretchen. I won't be happy with anyone but you."

"And I won't be happy with anyone but you," she said. "*You*, Will Cooper, just as you are now. Not whoever it is you were saying you were going to become."

He searched her face, but she didn't know what he was trying to find. "I'm worried you won't like him for long. That he's not good enough for you."

"Will," Gretchen said. "I liked you from the very moment I laid eyes on you. There you were, in the drugstore, and you seemed so...I don't know. Upset. I thought you were upset. I thought maybe I could brighten your day with a caramel apple. Then I smashed the whole tray into your chest, because, well, because you smelled so good, and your eyes were so mesmerizing."

"Stop it," he said, his smile faltering.

"Don't you dare change for me," Gretchen said firmly. "You change if you want, but you do it because it's what *you* want. Not because you think I want someone besides the grumpy cowboy I met in that drugstore."

"How could you possibly want him?" Will asked, and she detected true surprise in his voice.

"Because he's perfect for me," Gretchen said. "And he loves me, flaws and all. So I'll love him, flaws and all."

Will chuckled and shook his head. "You're my favorite person."

"Oh, I am not," she said, pressing further into him.

"No?"

"No, that's your mama, who I still haven't met, by the way." She lifted her eyebrows, clearly asking him when he was going to take her to the farm to meet everyone.

"Mm, we can fix that." He kneaded her even closer to him, and Gretchen stumbled as she tried to get her shoes between his boots. Their whole relationship had been filled with stumbles, and she embraced this one as they smiled at one another. "It's Rissa's night to cook. It's a good day to come."

He slid his lips along her neck, and Gretchen roared to life. "One more thing," she said, her voice hardly her own as airy as it had become with the reintroduction of his lips into her life.

"Yeah? What's that?"

"Stop kissing me everywhere but in the right spot." She tipped up and matched her mouth to his, the flames between them fueled by passion, love, and acceptance. Oh, how Gretchen missed kissing Will, and she hoped she'd never have to go another day of her life kissless.

26

W ill couldn't have planned a better kiss. This time, Gretchen had him pressed against the wall in the candy kitchen, but he didn't mind a bit. He'd missed her far too much to focus on anything but her. Anything to let her know he wouldn't disappear again. He wouldn't walk away when she was stressed or when things got hard, even if she asked him to.

He broke the kiss and whispered, "I love you," before forming his mouth to hers again.

She kissed him back in ways that said, *I love you too, Will,* but when she pulled away and said, "I love you too, Will," it sure was nice to hear. Beyond nice.

He smiled at her and touched his lips to her cheek. "I can't kiss you here?" He moved his mouth to her ear, and she shivered in his arms. "Oh, this feels like a bad spot."

"Stop it," she said with a giggle.

Will sobered and looked at her. "You help your daddy on Tuesdays. Do you think he'd like to come to dinner at the farm too? He'd be welcome."

Her eyes widened, then filled with those tears again. Will's heart couldn't take more crying, because he knew every tear was his fault. "Don't cry, baby," he said sweetly, wiping her eyes for her. "Please, I hate it when you cry."

Gretchen smiled, and she was the loveliest creature in the whole world. "Don't be so amazing then."

"I can go get your daddy. I took the afternoon off on the farm."

That sobered her up. "You did? And you didn't ask me to skip work and go with you?"

"That didn't turn out so hot last time," he said. "Or maybe it was too hot." He shook his head and told himself to stop being cute. "Lee wanted me to switch out this game he bought, so I did that, and I've been thinkin' about calling you or showing up at your house with your favorites, but then I just couldn't drive by this place again without talking to you."

"Again?" Gretchen teased. "How many times have you been by?"

"Just the one, to take the game back," Will said. "And it was torture. Honestly, Gretchen, my life has been pretty terrible without you."

She smiled at him and took his face in her hands. When she did that, and coupled it with a smile, he felt seen and cherished at the same time. "I love you, Will Cooper."

He grinned back at her. "Are you going to call me Will Cooper from now on? Both names every time?" She'd done it a lot before kissing him.

She burst out laughing and shook her head. "No."

"Shoot," he said. "I kinda like it. Sounds real sexy." He kissed her again, giggles and all, because it sure felt nice to be loved, and to love another person, and to not have to be perfect to do either.

———

"HELLO," WILL CALLED INTO THE FARMHOUSE. "WE'RE here." He kept a real steady hand on Reginald Bellows, who leaned on his cane on the right side and towed along his oxygen tank with his left hand.

"Right over that little bump," Will said. "You got it." Reggie went in the house first, muttering about how of course he knew how to enter a house.

Will smiled behind him and followed him into the farmhouse. Daddy came into the formal living room and foyer, his face all lit up. "Howdy," he boomed. "Welcome to the farm."

"I'm not deaf," Reginald said, and that made Will laugh. If Gretchen were here, she'd probably die from embarrassment and then chastise her father. Will had left her to do her caramel apples, and she'd promised to boogie out to the farm as soon as she could.

"Daddy," Will said through his chuckles. "This is Reginald Bellows. He's Gretchen's daddy. Reggie, this is my father, Wayne Cooper."

"It's so nice to have you here," Daddy said, still smiling. He had taken the volume of his voice down a notch, which was just more evidence that all the Coopers could change at any given point in their lives. He took Reggie's arm as Will released him. "Come sit with me and Chrissy on the back porch. There's a beaver in the pond building his hideout."

Reggie said something in his low, old-man voice that didn't register in Will's ears. He watched the two older men shuffle through the kitchen and past the long dining room table where the Coopers gathered for dinner every evening.

"Lord, help us tonight," Will murmured.

Daddy and Reggie went outside, and Mama turned her head toward them. She tried to get up and couldn't, which sent Will's heart to the back of his throat. Daddy couldn't manage them both, and Will jogged through the kitchen and outside.

"Mama," he said, arriving a bit breathless, though he'd definitely run much longer distances. "Let me help you." Together, he got her to her feet, where she faced Reggie, plenty of her Texas charm flowing from her.

"How wonderful you came," she said, almost sounding

like a queen. "Will has been telling us about you for weeks."

"My mama," Will said. "Chrissy. Mama, this is Reggie."

He sure seemed to like her, because it was impossible not to love Mama the moment you met her. Will had seen it time and time again, especially before she got sick. Somehow, her losing her hair and not being able to get up only endeared her to others faster, and Reggie took her hand and kissed it before they all sat down.

With their heavy sighs lifting up into the air, they faced the little pond off the back of the deck. No one said anything, and Will couldn't wait to get old so he wouldn't be expected to talk.

"Oh, there he is," Mama said, pointing. "See the ripples, Reggie? Will?"

"I see 'em, Mama," Will said, watching the water ripple toward the shore. In that moment, he realized the pond he was looking at was the very one he'd dreamed about several nights ago. A month? Who knew when.

But he'd seen this pond. There were no trees, like in the dream, and he walked to the edge of the deck and leaned over the railing. No deck chairs for him and Gretchen to sit in and watch the beaver build his den.

"Will," Mama said, and he turned back to her. She gestured for him to come sit down. "It's your day off, son. Come tell us how Gretchen is doing."

He swallowed and shot a look toward Reggie. He wore the same disgruntled look on his face that he had when

Will had shown up at the little house in the country. Will had asked him if he felt well enough to get in the truck and ride for twenty minutes and then put up with a very loud family dinner.

Reggie hadn't hesitated at all. He'd said, "I need my shoes," and together, he and Will had located them and put them on.

"She's doing pretty good," Will said. "I mean, I don't know. I was there for maybe twenty minutes, and most of that was me yelling about her taking me as I am, her crying, a lot of apologizing, and then quite a bit of kissing."

He grinned at his mother as he sat beside her. She and Daddy sat on a swing bench that Daddy kept moving with his toe. Reggie sat beside Daddy in a zero-gravity chair, and Will had one on Mama's right.

He leaned it back, still smiling up into the sky. Well, he would if the back of the house didn't have a huge roof that hung over the deck. That way, Mama could still sit outside if it was raining.

"Oh," Reggie said, blurting out the word. Will sank back to the ground, looking past his parents to find Queenie nosing Reggie's hand. Or she had been. He'd pulled it back and was wiping it on his pants.

"Queenie," Will said, jumping to his feet. "Leave 'im alone. Come sit by Mama."

"She can stay," Reggie said, reaching out to pat the golden retriever now. "She probably just smells Howl. I once had a dog named Eastwood. He went everywhere with me."

"Even into the Army?" Will asked, returning to his chair.

"I got 'im from the Army," Reggie said as if Will should've known that already. "Retired war dog. Came home with me when I retired too."

"That's wonderful," Mama said, and she was willing to let Queenie sit by Reggie and get scrubbed. It sure seemed like Reggie needed the dog, and Will smiled at them too.

"Is that why Max named his cat Elvis?" Will asked, leaning his chair back again. He got it into the best napping position and locked it there.

"Elvis?" Reggie chuckled. "No, Joan named that silly cat Elvis because she loved Elvis."

"Oh." Will didn't know what else to say. Max and his wife were separated, as far as he knew, and Gretchen was taking care of Max's cat, because he had his hands full with three kids and no wife.

"Max didn't want to keep him after Joan left," Reggie said, just stating facts. "Gretchen took the cat, and she doesn't even like cats."

"Gretchen helps everyone," Will said absently. He wanted to be the one to help her, and he wondered how he could do better at that. Bringing her father here surely would help, he hoped.

"He could come live here," Daddy said, surprising Will. He actually turned his head and cracked his eyes to look at his father. "We always need mousers in the barns."

"He's an indoor cat, Dad," Will said. "You should see what Gretchen feeds him. It's like cut up salmon and mashed potatoes and peas."

Both Mama and Daddy looked at Will, about equal expressions of surprise there. "You're kidding," Mama said.

"Mama," Will said back. "What did you feed Queenie this morning?"

"That's different," Mama said, squaring her shoulders and looking back out to the beaver den. "She needs her joint supplement."

"Yeah," Will said dryly. "She *needs* it stuffed inside a peanut butter and banana sandwich."

"Used to feed Eastwood raw steak," Reggie barked out. "That dog *loved* steak."

Will started laughing, and when his dad joined in, he felt freer and happier than he had in a long, long, long time.

Now, he just needed Gretchen to show up so he could introduce her around to everyone in the family. He'd already sent them a stern text about being on their best behavior that night, to which Travis had replied with a laughing emoji. Lee had promised he would if Will wouldn't say anything about taking the game to town for him, and Ford wouldn't be there tonight so there'd be no oily dogs and no muddy boys.

Mama was always nice, and Daddy was getting better. Clarissa and Spencer weren't a problem, and Clarissa had given him permission to bring both Gretchen and Reggie to dinner. She was cooking, so Will only thought it fair to let her know there'd be two more mouths to feed.

His mind drifted, and he imagined the Sunday family dinners with everyone there. Mama and Daddy, Clarissa and Spence. Trav and Shay, and him and Gretchen. Lee had a brunette at his side, and even Cherry had come home to celebrate...something.

Will didn't know what. He just knew he was happy in the vision, and he had Gretchen at his side, and all he needed was her, and all she needed was him.

27

Gretchen smelled the evidence of something brown, something baked, and something bite-worthy as soon as she got out of her van. She saw the handsome, grumpy cowboy coming toward her, and she promptly forgot everything else.

"Sorry," she said as Will enveloped her in a hug. "I had to go home and change. I couldn't come meet your mama and daddy wearing chocolate-caramel clothes." She giggled as Will swung her around, her feet coming off the ground.

"It's fine," he drawled as he put her down. "Rissa says the meatballs are just comin' out, and she can hold the sauce as long as we need."

"But we don't want to," a man yelled from somewhere inside the house. Gretchen looked past Will in surprise, expecting to see Travis on the porch, his arms folded. He wasn't there. "So kiss her quick and let's eat."

The sliding sound of a window closing echoed through the farm stillness, and Will grumbled, "I'm going to kill him in his sleep, don't worry."

"That actually does worry me," Gretchen said, though she knew he was kidding. "But you better do what he said."

"Kiss you?"

"Yeah," she said, walking her hands up the front of his shirt. He hadn't been home to change since she'd seen him at the shop a few hours ago. "But don't do it quick."

"You want a mutiny on your hands," he murmured right before he touched his lips to hers. No, Gretchen wanted to taste the strength in his mouth, and she wanted to feel the strands of his hair through her fingers, and she wanted to be enveloped in the warmth of his arms for a good, long while.

She kissed him back for several long moments, and then a dinner bell filled the air. Will pulled away, chuckling and saying, "You did want to meet them."

"Who's doing that?"

"That's Rissa's subtle way of saying dinner is ready, and I've been kissin' you for long enough." He took her hand and led her the rest of the way to the steps. "They're nice people," he said, as if he needed to explain before they went in. He paused just outside the closed front door.

It could use a wreath, but Gretchen would excuse it's nakedness for now.

He looked at her, helplessness in every inch of his face. "They're just Coopers."

"I like Coopers," Gretchen said, squeezing his hand. "You don't need to apologize for them."

"All right." He sighed as he opened the door, and Gretchen entered the farmhouse first. The foyer seemed like it belonged to people with money, and shock blipped through her. She'd never thought of Will as rich, but she probably should've.

"Howdy," a man said, and Gretchen's eyes flew toward the arched doorway that clearly led into the kitchen. A hallway branched off the foyer in the opposite direction too, but it sure felt like it didn't get used very often.

"That's Lee," Will said, taking a step forward and bringing Gretchen with him. She moved, her legs feeling a bit wooden. "He's the oldest brother. He's got a son, but Ford's with his mom tonight."

"I've met Lee," Gretchen said, smiling as she relaxed. Honestly, getting her voice to work was a major accomplishment. "Nice to see you again, Lee."

"I've been sick on caramel for days," he said with a grin, and he leaned in and kissed both of her cheeks when she arrived in front of him. There was no spark in his touch, not like there was with Will, and she beamed at him as Lee turned and went into the kitchen. "The crazy is in here."

"Get out of here!" a woman yelled, and Gretchen suspected that was Clarissa, Will's sister. "Travis, I swear, I'm going to chop off your hand in the night."

"See?" Will said. "Killing him would be far more humane."

Gretchen smiled and kept it on her face. She and Will stepped through the arch, and the house opened up on this side. The kitchen had been designed by someone who knew how to put the appliances, the sink, and the counter space in exactly the right place for a chef.

Rissa was currently waving a towel at Travis, who danced out of the kitchen area. "Get over here," another woman said, and she wore a look of displeasure as she reached for Travis.

"That's Shayla Nelson," Will said. "Have you met her?"

"Yes," Gretchen said. "She and Travis were at the New Year's Beach Bash." Shayla looked her way, and Gretchen could've sworn she looked relieved to find another non-Cooper. That was what streamed through Gretchen at the moment, and she lifted her free hand in a shoulder-high wave.

"Plus, I catered the tent reveal, don't you remember?"

"Oh, right," Will said. "Duh. I think that's when I started thinkin' about you day and night." He grinned at her and leaned forward like he might kiss her.

"Don't you dare come in here again," Rissa said. "Lee, get Mama and Daddy. Will, go get Reggie. Travis, sit down." Rissa gave him a final glare before she switched her gaze to Gretchen. Her bright green eyes took her in after a single breath, and then she softened.

"My," she said, pressing one hand to her chest as the men mobilized.

"Rissa," Will said. "Don't." He'd released Gretchen's hand, but he hadn't moved yet. "This is Gretchen Bellows. Gretchen, my sister, Clarissa. The younger one." He stayed for one more minute, until Gretchen nodded at him that he could go. Once he had, Gretchen stepped right into Clarissa.

"It's so wonderful to meet you," she said.

Rissa hugged her back. "You're so beautiful," she said. "So perfect for Will. Have you two seen yourselves together?" She stepped back and searched Gretchen's eyes. "Just...wow. He loves you so much."

"The feeling is mutual," Gretchen said, finding it odd that Rissa was...crying over this. She glanced toward the back wall of windows, where Will had gone, but he hadn't quite made it outside yet.

Rissa released her, sniffling, and said, "Go sit. Will usually takes a seat by Daddy, but I think he'll put your daddy there tonight. So way down on the right side there." She nodded in the general direction, but Gretchen detoured toward Shayla.

"Good to see you again, Shayla," she said, extending her hand.

"Oh, girl, get in here for a hug." Shayla took Gretchen

into a hug too, adding, "We'll have to stick together, me and you. This family can eat you alive."

"They can?" Gretchen asked.

Shayla nodded as she pulled back. "Just wait. If not tonight, then another time. They're ravenous."

"I know I am," Travis said from where he sat. He twisted and smiled at Gretchen. "And we don't eat people...usually."

"It's meatball sub night," Rissa yelled as Will entered with Gretchen's father. Watching the two of them froze the clock for her for the second time that day. Will had turned toward her father and leaned down slightly to hear him better. Daddy moved with his oxygen tank trundling along behind him, but his cane nowhere in sight. Instead, he'd looped his hand through Will's arm, and the very sight of them together made Gretchen emotional.

Her dad could be a lot to handle, and here was Will—the grumpiest of them all, supposedly—smiling at him gently and moving with him as if he were a precious kitten.

People moved around her. Chairs scraped the tile floor. Rissa kept yelling something about the freshly baked bread and the sauce she'd been working on for hours. But Gretchen didn't look away from Will and Daddy until Will had him seated on the corner of the table. Then he looked up to search for her.

She walked toward him, and he slid his hand into hers. "Mama," he said as Lee came inside with their mother. Will lifted Gretchen's hand and kissed it, his lips still somewhat curved into a smile. "This is Gretchen Bellows."

"Oh, my dear." His mama took a moment to steady herself, and Lee hesitated to release her. He did, and she grabbed onto Gretchen, who silently vowed she would not drop this woman. "It's so lovely to meet you."

Gretchen positively melted into her touch, the memories of her own mama flowing thickly through her whole soul. She didn't mean to, and she was going to ruin her makeup, but tears came into her eyes. She missed her mother so much, and Will's mama smelled so much like her. She sounded like her. She could *be* herself.

"I'm sorry," she said, her voice pinched as she stepped back. She swiped hurriedly at her eyes while Will and his mother watched her. She put a smile on her face, foolishness filling her. "My mother—" she cut off as her face scrunched.

"It's okay," his mother said, taking both of her hands into her papery ones. "Will told me your mama died a few years ago." She wore such a kind smile, and she reminded Gretchen so much of Daddy.

She was sick, but she was fighting hard.

Gretchen just nodded and took deep breath after deep breath. Will lifted his chin toward the door leading out onto the deck, but she shook her head. Besides, a dog came in that way, and Gretchen crouched in her maxi skirt to pat him.

"Hello, there," she said to the animal, who smiled at her like he'd been waiting for her to walk into the room. "What's your name?"

"That's Queen Elizabeth," Will said. "Mama's therapy dog. We call 'er Queenie."

"Are we eating or what?" someone bellowed, and Gretchen straightened.

"I have to introduce Gretchen to Daddy," Will yelled on back. "You won't starve."

"I might," Lee said as he slid into the chair right in front of Gretchen. She edge around him and Will's mama to his daddy.

"This is my daddy, Wayne," Will said. "Mama is Chrissy. I don't think I said that. Daddy, this is Gretchen."

He took her into a hug too, and Gretchen didn't understand what Shayla meant about getting eaten alive. "I see how well you go together," he said. "No wonder Will was so devastated after you two broke up."

"Daddy," Will said with plenty of warning in his voice. "I wasn't devastated."

"He was," Travis said.

"I agree," another man said, and Will whipped his gaze to him.

"Spencer," he said, shocked. "I expected you to be on my side."

"Will, you yelled at me every day last week," Spencer said, grinning at him. "Trust me, you were devastated."

"Can we eat?" Lee asked. "The meatballs are going to be stone cold in about five seconds."

"They're fine," Rissa said, slapping his hand away from the huge vat of meatballs she'd put on the table. Will led Gretchen past her father, and they sat next to him, facing Lee, Travis, and Shayla.

Clarissa cleared her throat. "Spencer and I have an announcement." She slapped Travis with an oven mitt as he moaned.

"Shape up," Shayla said crossly. "Your sister is trying to talk, and all you're doing is delaying dinner even more." She glared at him as the room fell into silence.

Gretchen stared at her, her mouth open slightly. Shayla moved her gaze off her fiancé's, finally realizing that she'd caused the quiet in the farmhouse. Redness crept into her cheeks. "Go on, Rissa."

"Thank you, Shay," Rissa said. "Spencer and I are going to have a baby!"

If Gretchen thought the Coopers had been loud while the introductions got made, what with people yelling to each other, slapping oven mitts around, and scraping chairs, she'd been wrong.

Will whistled through his teeth, and that alone made Gretchen cringe away and clap her hands over her ears. Lee pounded his fists on the table, and Travis whooped like a police siren as he stood up and engulfed his younger sister in the biggest hug of the night.

Gretchen looked at Wayne and Chrissy, who both

clapped with all they had. Chrissy wasn't making much noise, but tears streamed down her face. Wayne got to his feet and raised both hands above his head. The noise subsided, but it took a few moments to happen.

"When is the baby coming?" he asked.

"November," Rissa said, beaming at everyone. Travis sat back down, and Rissa turned to her husband. "We're thrilled, and we can't wait to share him or her with all of you." Just as quickly as she'd transformed earlier, she picked up a pair of tongs and pointed them at Will. "You can't get married in November. Or October for that matter." She started to lower the tongs. "You know what, let's just say no fall weddings. All right?"

Will's mouth gaped, and then he scoffed. "I'm not going to get married in the fall."

Gretchen reached for the napkin beside her plate. "We're not?" she asked, and once again, the entire room went silent. She quite liked the power of that, and she calmly spread her napkin in her lap and looked right at Will. "So do you want a summer wedding or a winter wedding?"

"It's kind of quick for summer nuptials," Lee said, and Gretchen nodded seriously though she'd heard the teasing undertone in Lee's voice. She shot him a smile and found him grinning too.

"It's April already," Travis said.

"I know what month it is," Will sniped at him. He looked back to Gretchen. "I...don't know what to say." He picked up his napkin and snapped it open. "Can we eat already? Jeez, I've been starving for an hour."

The whole room burst into laughter, Gretchen included. Will didn't seem to think anything was all that funny, but she put her hand on his knee anyway. He smiled then, and she leaned her head toward his.

"I would marry you tomorrow," he whispered among all the chaos of his family around them.

"Better get me a ring and get down on one knee then," she said just as Wayne quieted everyone again so they could say grace.

28

W ill walked into the jewelry store, feeling like the whole world could see him. The two walls of windows did that, and the natural light spilling inside made every gem shine and glitter.

"Ah, Will," Darrell said. "Here for the ring?"

"Yes, sir," Will said. He swiped off his cowboy hat, his nerves running rampant through him. "Louisa called and said it was sized and ready."

"Yes, I think I saw it in the back." Darrell gave him a smile and went that way. "I'll be right back."

Will nodded and watched him go. A little further into the shop, a woman stood behind the case while a couple looked at the rings inside. Other than that, only salesmen littered the floor. He started to sweat despite the cool temperature inside the shop, and he had no idea why.

Probably because the calendar hadn't even flipped to May yet, and here he stood, buying a diamond ring to propose with. His relationship with Tara had not advanced this quickly, and Will shook the woman out of his head.

After watching Rissa and Spence, then Travis and Shayla, fall in love, Will knew that when a person met their one true love, it didn't take long to want to spend forever together. He and Gretchen were simply meant to be, and he didn't want to wait to be with her.

He also didn't want to wait until December to marry her. If Clarissa really wasn't going to let anyone get married in the fall months, then Will figured he might as well ask Gretchen now and they could get married in August.

He hoped three full months was long enough for her, and panic paraded through him while his brain screamed at him that he should've asked her how long she needed to plan her wedding. For all he knew, she'd send off for a custom dress from the shops in Paris or Milan, and that could take months.

"Here you go," Darrell said, reappearing in front of Will as if by magic. He held out a smooth black bag with white tissue poking out of the top.

"Thank you," Will said, his voice grinding through his throat. He nodded at the man, put on his cowboy hat, and headed for the exit. He needed to get out of this place and stop spiraling.

Gretchen wasn't going to order her wedding dress from Europe. She wasn't that kind of woman at all. She probably would want to make sure she didn't have any events on her candy calendar, and she'd want to make sure her brothers could be there.

Will hadn't met them yet, as they lived some distance from Sweet Water Falls and both he and Gretchen were quite busy with their work. His heart sat heavy in his chest, like someone had filled it with water and it had bloated to twice its normal size.

He had no idea where he and Gretchen would live once they got married. Would she want to live on the farm? In her house in the country? Could he stand having Elvis around all the time?

"Stop it," he told himself as he drove. "It's all going to work out fine." He sometimes hated the way his mind circled and spun, and he'd gotten a lot better at slowing it enough to see reason.

He glanced over to the bag riding on the passenger seat. He didn't know where to hide it or put it. He didn't want to hold onto it. He'd bought it for Gretchen, and he wanted to give it to her.

A quick glance at the clock told him that he could be at her house before she left Sweet Water Taffy, and he started making the right turns to get him there. He'd left late enough in the day to not put out anyone on the farm, and he quickly dialed Travis, knowing his brother would be on the last round of milking.

"What's up?" Travis asked, clearly using the speaker on his phone.

"I got the ring," Will said, kneading the wheel. "I don't know what to do next."

Travis chuckled, but Will didn't appreciate that. "Sure you do," he said.

"Don't I need flowers or something?" Maybe he could stop real quick. Another glance at the clock told him not to. It was Friday, and Gretchen never stayed late on Fridays. She went in so early on Saturdays and again early in the week that by Friday, she did the bare minimum and went home.

It was almost four, and Will actually pressed on the accelerator.

"No," Travis said. "I mean, it's nice if you have flowers or something, but no. You have a *diamond ring*, Will. That's all she needs."

"What if she hates it?"

"Okay, I'm hanging up," Travis said. "Where are you, bro? You've never struck me as unsure of yourself or about what to do."

Will took a deep breath and nodded to himself. "You're right. Okay, yeah. I'm going over to Gretchen's now."

"Good luck," Travis said. "Not that you need it. I think she's been waiting for you to ask her for a while now."

Will nodded again and said, "Thanks, Trav." He let his brother hang up, and he made the rest of the drive to Gretchen's as fast as he could.

His heart sank when he came around the corner and her van already sat in the driveway. "Doesn't matter," he told himself, though he definitely could've stopped for flowers. And pizza. He suddenly couldn't show up without food, and yet, he turned into her driveway and parked behind her.

He picked up the bag and took the ring box out of it. "It's just me and you," he said, hoping the pair of them together would be enough. He flipped open the box and gazed at the ring he'd chosen. It said Gretchen to him the moment he'd seen it, and he smiled softly at the bright gold band which flourished up to hold the diamond.

It was actually shaped like a diamond, and two more tiny gems sat along each of the four sides. They were pink diamonds, and for some reason, Will thought of Gretchen when he looked at the ring.

Somehow, his booted feet took him up to her porch. He swept his cowboy hat off his head one more time and knocked. Elvis meowed behind the closed door, and Gretchen's female voice shushed him.

A couple of moments later, she cracked the door.

"Just me," he said, holding his hat against his chest with one hand, the ring box concealed behind it.

A smile bloomed on her face. "Hey." She opened the door even further. "I wasn't expecting you until later." She licked the corner of her mouth. "I was just having a snack."

He grinned at her. "One of Jon's haystacks?"

She giggled and backed up so he could come in. "How did you know?"

"I can smell the chocolate on your breath," he said, entering the house and closing the door so Elvis couldn't make one of his feline escapes. Gretchen retreated into the kitchen and plucked another haystack from the box on the counter.

Faced with her, Will wasn't nervous at all. He lowered his cowboy hat and dropped it on her loveseat as he passed. He couldn't look away from her. "Gretchen," he said, and she looked at him, half a haystack in her hand, the other half in her mouth.

He held up the ring box, and she froze.

He grinned at her. "That day at the drug store last year changed my life. I want to be yours, and I want you to be mine. I love you." He opened the box with strong, sure fingers and turned it toward her. "Will you marry me?"

Her eyes widened as she looked at the ring. She shook her head, which made Will's chest cave in.

"No way," she said. "You're not down on one knee."

"Are you kidding right now?"

She hastily set down her uneaten haystack and dusted her hands. "I'm wearing the ugliest shirt I own."

"So what?" Will couldn't believe this. Travis had said none of this would matter.

Then that teasing glint came into Gretchen's eyes. She flung herself into his arms, and he dang near dropped the diamond that had carved a hole in his bank account. "I'm kidding, Will Cooper. I love you, and of course I want to marry you."

She kissed him while relief ran through him, and it took Will a couple of seconds to catch up to the situation. "Not funny," he murmured in the moment he pulled away. Then he kissed her again—a real kiss this time, with both of them aware of what was happening.

When he finally had the decency to pull away, Gretchen grinned at him with glassy eyes. "This is how we are, Will. Things are little hectic. Cats run away. Caramel gets burned. You seem to have it all over you and the most inopportune times." She held out her left hand. "We're awkward, and I love that about us."

"Mm." He slid the ring on her finger, and they both gazed at it for several long seconds. He looked up at her again and found love streaming from her. "What are you thinking?" he asked. "Like August? Or are we waiting until December?"

She put her arms around his shoulders and clasped her hands at the back of his neck. "Oh, we can't wait until December."

"I wouldn't think so," he said, already sliding his mouth along her jawline.

"I don't need very long," she said. "I'll look into a venue, and then get a dress. It won't be hard."

"So...maybe next month?" Will asked, pulling back and grinning at her.

Gretchen giggled and said, "Listen," in her stern-Will-

Cooper voice. "We're not getting married in the same month as Trav and Shay. They deserve their own spotlight."

"Yes, ma'am," Will said.

"But maybe June or July..." She tilted her head to the side. "I'll check the calendar and talk to my brothers."

Just as he'd known she would. "I'll talk to Mama," he said. "Do you want a venue? We can get married here. At the farm. At your dad's place. His backyard is beautiful."

Gretchen's face lit up on the last one, and Will knew they'd be getting married in Short Tail. "Could we get married at Daddy's?"

"Of course," Will said, leaning down to kiss her again. "Whatever you want."

"I love you, Will Cooper," Gretchen whispered.

"Love you too," Will said just before kissing his fiancée.

———

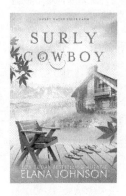

KEEP READING FOR A SNEAK PEEK AT the next book in the Sweet Water Falls Farm series, **SURLY COWBOY**, which features the last Cooper brother, Lee! *You can preorder it now.*

SNEAK PEEK! SURLY COWBOY CHAPTER ONE:

Lee Cooper pulled his shirt over his head and tossed it in the general direction of his bed. It landed short and fell to the floor, but he didn't bother going to retrieve it. As frenzied as his mind was, the one thought he landed on was, *No wonder Ford is a slob. It's genetic.*

He ripped open the closet doors, everything inside blurring for some reason. Probably because he hadn't taken a proper breath in the past minute. Maybe two. Fine, ten.

Lee closed his eyes and slowed down. He dropped his hands to his sides and took a long breath in through his nose. He watched a morning affirmation channel online every day, and the woman who led the group did breathing exercises like this.

In through the nose, he heard in her voice. *Hold it.*

Longer. Really take a moment and slow down your mind. Your heart. Release those muscles. Okay, out with me.

Five, four, three, two one, zero.

Lee opened his eyes when he got to zero, and the shirts took on individual form in the closet. "Okay," he said. "You're fine. Ford is fine. His teacher just wants to talk to both you and Martha on a weekday evening. It's not a big deal."

He'd gotten off the phone with his ex-wife ten minutes ago, and he'd hurried to finish an email that had to go out today. Then he'd dashed home, and he wasn't any worse off by taking twenty seconds to center himself again.

With a bright red shirt covering his upper half and a peanut butter sandwich in one hand, Lee dashed back out the front door of his cabin and down the steps to his truck. The old girl was starting to show her age, with rust wearing through around the wheels and the engine chugging to life like it would rather not.

Lee knew how she felt, and he patted the dashboard. "I'll let you retire soon, okay? But Ford needs us tonight."

He had no intentions of buying another truck, though he had plenty of money to do so. Lee rather liked this one, and he saw no reason to spend money on something when he already had one that worked.

The drive to Sweet Water Falls passed in a blur, and Lee had no idea where his mind had wandered. He blinked, and the dark-haired image of Rosalie Reynolds flashed in his mind. Ah, so he'd gone down *that* path again.

He hadn't been brave enough to drop by the woman's office, even when she was expecting him to. He'd sent Will instead. *Begged* was a better word. The proper word. Familiar loathing and disgust built within Lee, and it was all directed at himself.

His heart pounded right now, though Rosalie wasn't anywhere near him physically. He wasn't sure why she affected him so thoroughly, only that she did. They'd only met the one time. He'd only spoken to her twice, once in person and once on the phone. He'd looked at her picture plenty of times on her website, and he was taking that knowledge with him to the grave.

He didn't need to add "stalker" to the list of names he'd been called over the years. Grumpy, sure, he could own that. Short-tempered, yes. What Cooper man wasn't? He could hardly be blamed for that one. It was genetically inbred in him to get angry or frustrated at the drop of a bale of hay or the first sign of oil leaking from a tractor.

Meticulous, he actually counted as a compliment. Anal-retentive was a bit of a stretch, but Lee didn't even mind that one. He worked with a lot of papers that held a lot of numbers, and someone had to be detail-oriented and obsessive about checking them to make sure things got done correctly.

Money in, money out—Lee took care of that.

Paychecks due, new orders received—Lee took care of that.

New clients and their contracts, established accounts and their renewals—Lee took care of that.

Lee ran Cooper & Co almost single-handedly these days, and most of the time, he let an inch of pride into his heart at how proud Daddy was of him. At how much Daddy trusted him to take over the generational operation that had been supplying milk to the people in Southern Texas, Louisiana, and Arkansas for over a century.

He pulled into a spot at the elementary school, spying Martha's car a few spaces over. She and Ford weren't in it, which meant Lee was late. His ex-wife would give him the stink-eye for that, but he'd come as soon as he'd been notified of tonight's meeting.

As he jogged toward the entrance of the building, he tucked in his shirt and he dang near pulled off the door as he opened it.

"Dad," Ford said, jumping to his feet from a cement bench across from the entrance.

Lee's whole face lit up, and he couldn't be mad at his son no matter what. He opened his arms to him, glad when Ford flew into his embrace. He always wanted Ford to be able to come to him for help, for the good, the bad, the anything.

"Hey, buddy," he said. "What am I doin' here tonight, huh?"

"Your son got in a fight," Martha said, and Lee looked

over Ford's head to meet her eye. She didn't look too terribly upset, and Lee kept hold of Ford in one arm as he leaned forward to touch his lips to Martha's cheek.

He settled awkwardly back on his feet, even putting another few inches between them. "I got here as fast as I could."

"We've got five minutes still," she said, nodding down the hall. The three of them started that way at a much slower pace than Lee had used coming inside. He'd loved Martha once-upon-a-time, and sometimes when he looked at her, he only saw the good things they'd experienced together.

It didn't take long for him to remember the things that had driven them apart, and he certainly wasn't interested in getting back together with her. Lee simply took a long time to forgive—himself and others—and he wasn't sure he'd ever be able to get over infidelity.

Something about it just cut him right to the core, and even now, he worked against the feelings of betrayal and mistrust of all women.

Ford's teacher—a Miss Bair who was easily a decade younger than Lee—stepped into the hall. She smiled at Ford and then Lee and Martha. Lee didn't want to be in her shoes, and he gave her a smile back so she'd know they were going to agree with her.

Lee was, anyway.

"Evenin'," he said when no one else spoke. "I hope you weren't waiting long for me. I live pretty far out."

"Not at all," Miss Bair said. "Come on in."

Martha went first, then Ford, and Lee held the door for the teacher and entered last. She'd set up some chairs around her desk, and he sat in the last one.

"Did Ford tell you what happened today?"

"I heard most of it," Martha said. "Lee hasn't gotten much information. I didn't find the note or hear the message you left until about forty minutes ago."

"Ford?" Miss Bair prompted.

The boy squirmed in his seat, and Lee put his arm around his son. "Hey," he said real quietly. "Remember the roof? And the stars?"

Ford looked up at him, his innocent eyes so wide and so beautiful. He nodded, and Lee smiled at him. "Go on then." He ignored Martha's questioning gaze and glanced at Miss Bair.

She smiled at him, but Lee felt no spark of attraction to her. She had dark hair too—his preferred type—and nothing. Absolutely nothing like what he felt when he looked at Rosalie.

He had to call her again. Stop by her office. Something.

Travis's wedding was in ten days. Could he ask Rosalie to go with him? Maybe he could offer to pay her, or pay for her dress, or something.

Nope, he told himself. *You're not paying a woman to go out with you.* Either she'd say yes or she wouldn't.

But not if you don't ask.

"...so I told Simon to leave her alone," Ford said.

"Wait," Lee said, coming back to the conversation at hand. He really couldn't let his mind wander in situations like this. "Simon Alvarez?"

"Yes."

Lee glared at Ford and then Miss Bair. "I thought Simon and Ford weren't going to be allowed to be together."

"It was lunch recess, Dad."

"I don't care," Lee barked. "You're not supposed to be near him."

"He was teasing Lily," Ford said, his eyes welling with tears. "He had her up against the kindergarten fence, and I helped her."

Lee opened his mouth, but nothing came out. He looked at Martha, and she stroked Ford's hair off his forehead. "But you hit someone, baby. That's not how you solve problems."

"Your mother's right," Lee said, swallowing afterward.

"But it got Simon to leave Lily alone," Ford said, looking from him to Martha and back. "And then I was able to help Lily to the office. She was having a panic attack."

"Whoa," Lee said. "What?" He looked at Miss Bair, who wore a look of sympathy on her face. "Is she okay?"

"She's asthmatic," Miss Bair said, giving Ford a maternal smile too. She wasn't mad at him, Lee realized, though she certainly couldn't condone him hitting another student. "Once the nurse got her inhaler, she calmed right down."

Lee nodded, suddenly so tense. "So now what?"

Miss Bair leaned forward and put her fingertips on Ford's knee. "What did we decide, Ford?"

"That I won't hit people," he muttered. "Whether it's to help someone or not."

"That's right," she said. "Instead?"

"Instead, I try to get Lily away from Simon, or I start yelling for help from the sixth grade aides or the recess monitors." He hung his head, as if this option was the worst thing imaginable.

"Simon won't have lunch recess for three school days," Miss Bair said, pulling her hand back. "Unfortunately, I have to do the same to Ford."

"No suspension?" Martha asked.

Miss Bair shook her head. "I can't do that," she said, and while she couldn't say more, Lee heard it all. She actually agreed with Ford, and she'd do what she could to protect him. She looked from Martha to Lee. "Any questions?"

"No, ma'am," Ford and Lee said together, and they looked at one another and laughed.

"I think that covers it," Martha said, and the three of them stood. Lee took his son's hand in his as they left the classroom, but he waited until he was all the way outside before he crouched down in front of his eight-year-old.

"I don't think you should hit people, bud," he said.

"But I'm so, *so* proud of you for standing up for Lily." He grinned at Ford and nodded once. "Okay?"

Ford nodded and reached out to touch Lee's cowboy hat. "I don't want to tattle to the recess monitors."

"Just stay away from Simon."

"But what if he's hurting someone?"

"Ford," Martha said, kneeling down in front of him too. "You'll get suspended next time, I promise. You can't hit other children."

He nodded again, his chin so low.

"Hey," Lee said. "Chin up, son. Look at me."

Ford did, and he seemed so lost and looking for Lee to guide him. "Do you want the other kids to think of you as a bully?"

"No."

"You can't hit other kids, not even if you're standing up for someone." He smiled and tapped Ford's nose. "Plus, if you get suspended, I'll work you like a dog on the farm. Is that what you want?"

Ford grinned too. "Can Queenie come with me?"

Lee laughed, realizing that his "punishment" for his son getting suspended wasn't a punishment at all. He exchanged a glance with Martha.

"Come on, Ford," she said. "Give your daddy a hug. We have to get going."

Ford wrapped his skinny arms around Lee, and he held his son just as tightly. He whispered, "I love you, son.

You be good for your momma, and you obey your teacher."

"Yes, sir," Ford said.

Lee stood and watched Ford link his hand in Martha's. She met Lee's eyes, and so much was said between them. Then they went to their car, and Lee went to his truck.

He drove back to the farm alone. He made dinner for himself, and he ate it alone. He hated being alone, and he wanted to do everything in his power to change his single status.

He got out his phone and let his thumb hover over the icon for the dating app he'd once used. He couldn't tap on it; he just couldn't.

He only wanted to go out with one woman, and she was Rosalie Reynolds.

Therefore, the following afternoon, Lee went through a similar routine as the previous night.

He changed his shirt. He washed his hands. He loaded himself into his truck. He drove to town.

Everything blurred around him, because when Lee focused on something, it was all he could see. All he could think about. All he could taste. And right now, that was a certain curly-haired brunette with gorgeous eyes. She'd rendered him mute once, and he was determined not to let that happen today.

He swallowed as he flipped on his blinker, scanning for the Curious Kids office. A small sign sat on the roof announcing the location of his destination, and he dang near stomped on the accelerator to get away.

"No," he coached himself. "You've come all this way. You're just going to go in there and tell her how stunningly beautiful she is, and then you're going to ask her to your brother's wedding."

The pit in Lee's stomach roared at him, but when there was a break in traffic, he made the turn into the parking lot.

No one sat in front of Curious Kids, and Lee took the spot directly outside the door. He killed the engine. He got out of the truck.

It was almost like his mind was moving through a checklist. *Do this. Do this. Do that.*

Go inside, check.

Find Rosalie, check.

She stood from the smaller of two desks, off to his left. With a smile on her face, she said, "Lee Cooper," in that melodic voice he couldn't get out of his ears.

Ask her to the wedding.

Wait.

Tell her how gorgeous she is.

No.

Say you can't stop thinking about her.

Creepy.

Do something.

Lee couldn't do anything. He felt like he'd entered the presence of an angel, and he stood there, frozen and mute.

SNEAK PEEK! SURLY COWBOY CHAPTER TWO:

Rosalie Reynolds had never been happier for her self-imposed dress code when she came to the office. She currently wore a pencil skirt that fell just below her knees, and she felt every inch of herself as Lee Cooper's gaze moved from her low heels and up along her skirt to the bright candy apple red blouse she'd chosen this morning.

She wasn't sure why she'd gone with red. Maybe she thought it accentuated her lips, which always seemed a bit too pale pink to her. Or maybe she'd been told a time or two—or twenty—that red complimented her darker skin tone and hair. She wasn't sure.

What she knew was that her phone blared at her again, the sound of an airhorn she hated but had also set. It was her sister, Natasha, and Rosalie's heart bobbed in her throat. She'd been texting her sister about perhaps joining a dating app now that James had made the move to California and he was good and truly gone from her life.

The face of her sweet daughter flashed through her mind. James would never be good and truly gone, but Rosalie also wasn't dealing with him on a daily basis anymore. Part of her languished in indescribable sadness, and the other part kept urging her to move forward with her own life.

Maybe with Lee Cooper, she thought, her face burning as the cowboy's eyes finally latched onto hers. His were just as foresty as she remembered, and she itched to see some of that deep, red-gold-brown hair.

"Can I help you?" she asked as professionally as possible. After all, he'd shown up—unannounced—at her office. The last time she'd seen a Cooper, it had been his brother, William. He'd been the one to bring the faulty game back and make the trade. "Is everything okay with your new disk?"

Rosalie cocked her head as her phone yelled at her again. She honestly didn't have time for Handsome's staring. Her heart told her not to send him away, but she wasn't sure what else to say. Natasha's notification went off again, and Rosalie swiped her phone from the edge of her desk. She tapped out a quick, *With a customer. I'll text you right back*, and looked back to the gorgeous, if not a little... strange cowboy.

Strange wasn't the right word. It almost looked like he'd fallen into a trance.

"Lee," she said, really snapping out his name.

He blinked a couple of times and looked around the office, as if he'd driven here while asleep and just now realized where he was.

"Are you okay?" Rosalie took a step toward him, but when those delicious eyes came back to her, she paused. "I was just about to leave, so is there something I can do for you?"

He cleared his throat, and praise the heavens, she was going to get to hear that low, growly voice of his again. "Yeah, I was just thinking about something."

"Okay," she said.

He folded his arms, something shuttering over his face. "Ford doesn't really like the game I bought."

Rosalie blinked now, his statement a complete surprise to her. "Oh," she said, her brain whirring quickly. She wanted satisfied customers, but her return policy didn't include "didn't like it."

"Well," she said smoothly, her policies flying into place. "You're outside of the thirty-day, no-questions-asked refund period. So...I'm sorry."

"You're sorry?"

Rosalie squared her shoulders against this surly cowboy. "Yes," she said. "I can't just refund everyone's money because they don't like something."

"He hardly plays the game."

"I'm sorry about that," she said, breaking her eye contact with him and returning to stand behind her desk. She looked down at the papers there, but her concentration had broken completely. Handsome had a way of making her feel like the only woman in the world, and Rosalie hadn't felt like that in a long, long time.

She dared to look at him again, the frown between his eyes making him even sexier. She wondered what it would be like to kiss him when he wore such an unhappy look, and she could imagine a fight ensuing between the two of them for the control of *that* kiss.

She shook her head and muttered, "Keep it together, Rose," as the image of Lee pressing her against the very wall behind her and kissing her senseless continued to play through her mind.

"What?" Lee asked.

"Nothing." She looked up at him again, her phone blaring out at her again.

"What is that awful noise?" he asked. "It's happened like five times."

Rosalie could handle her company being insulted. Fine. Not everyone liked her games. She understood that from a consumer standpoint. She could even handle a critique of her personally, though she worked hard to keep her imperfections concealed behind the closed doors of her house.

But no one, not even Handsome, would criticize Natasha.

She took one step toward him, feeling every cell in her body light up with fire. The angry kind. "That is my notification for my sister," she said, hearing the danger in her own voice. "She has some special needs, and I need to be able to hear my phone whenever she texts." She had a similar notification sound attached to her daughter's babysitter, as well as her neighbor, both of whom helped Rosalie with Autumn now that James was gone.

"So if you don't need anything, *Mister* Cooper, I really have more important things to do than stand here and be insulted by you." She'd taken several more steps toward him, and he hadn't backed up an inch.

The man was muscle from head to toe, and she'd seen him soften before. She really wanted him to back down now too, because then she'd feel powerful and strong. At the same time, her eyes dropped to his mouth, and wow. That was what power and strength looked like.

She yanked her eyes back to his, and even through the lenses on his glasses, they fired at her. "Or stared at," she added.

"I wasn't staring," he said.

"You've been here for at least five minutes," Rosalie said, lifting her chin. "And have said twenty words."

"You know what?" Lee asked, but he didn't finish his challenge. He simply growled—yes, growled—and spun around. He stalked the three steps to the door and went out onto the sidewalk. As the glass door swung closed behind him, Rosalie's heartbeat shook through her veins.

He yelled something as he got in his truck and slammed the door. Rosalie stayed very still, wondering why she wanted him to come back inside. He reminded her of a feral cat—skittish, unsure, but oh-so-wounded. She wanted to help all the strays in her neighborhood, and she couldn't help wondering if Lee had strayed into this part of Sweet Water Falls specifically so she could see him.

She sure had been thinking about him a lot. She'd almost called him after he'd gotten the second disk to make sure it worked. At the very least, she'd wanted to make sure he'd gotten it from his brother. Deep down, Rosalie knew both of those were covers simply to interact with Handsome again.

Lee didn't pull out, and Rosalie turned away from the door. Her legs shook as she returned to her desk. She still had some work to do, but it would be there waiting for her tomorrow. It always was.

She bent to get her purse from the bottom drawer, and she dialed Natasha while her eyes darted back to the front windows. Handsome's old, rusted truck still sat outside, and Rosalie wasn't sure she wanted to leave all of a sudden.

"Rosie," Natasha said in her thick tongue. "You're working?"

"Yes," Rosalie said. "Always working." She wiped her hand through her hair, but her fingers always caught in her curls. She wasn't one of those women with the perfectly straight hair that shone like sunlight off snow-fall. She'd been trying to grow out her curls, but they never made it much further than her shoulders.

"Mom says I can come visit this weekend," Natasha said, and that made Rosalie smile. "She said I have to ask you first."

"This weekend is great," Rosalie said, already feeling tired. But just like she couldn't say no to Autumn, she wouldn't deny her autistic sister her first trip to the beach. At least this year. "Maybe you could come stay with me this summer."

Rosalie had an extra bedroom, and Autumn loved Nat. James was gone, and why not? Rosalie didn't have anything else going on in her life. Her parents might enjoy the break, and Nat would get to go to the beach everyday. Truth be told, Rosalie could use a beach day every week too.

"Don't tell her things you can't do." Mom's voice came through the line, the Jersey accent still thick though she'd lived in Texas for almost three decades.

"I'm not, Mom," Rosalie said, smiling as she pictured her mother. They had the same curls, and Rosalie loved her parents with everything she had. "I miss you guys. Will you stay the weekend too?"

"If we can come," Mom said.

"She said I can come," Nat said, her argumentative tone strong.

"I know what she said," Mom shot back. "But she really needs to think about it. So think about it, dear."

"Okay," Rosalie said. "I'll check my calendar when I get home." A quick glance toward the windows showed her that Handsome still hadn't left. What was he waiting for? "But I don't think there's a conflict."

As she watched, Handsome opened the door on his truck and got out again. Rosalie's heartbeat went wild, and she said, "I have to go, Mom. Nat, there's a customer coming in."

"Text me back about that picture," Nat said.

"She has to go," Mom said, and the call ended just as Handsome yanked open the glass door again.

Rosalie took a moment to stuff her phone into her messy purse, and she tugged on the zipper. It wouldn't quite slide, because she might have stopped by the store and bought Autumn a couple of packages of new underwear. Princess style, so the girl would remember to stop playing and go to the bathroom when she needed to.

Her face heated as the zipper caught on the plastic, the sound unmistakable. She abandoned the idea of closing her purse and faced Handsome.

His chest lifted and fell in the way it would had he just run a couple of miles. "Rosalie," he said, and it sounded like a bark. "I don't care about the game. That was just a stupid thing I said, because I couldn't figure out how to say what I really wanted to say."

Rosalie's pulse fell to the soles of her feet, but she still managed to ask, "What did you want to say?"

Lee took another breath and blew it out. "My brother is gettin' married next weekend. The fifteenth?"

Rosalie did know the date, so she nodded.

"I was wonderin'... See, the thing is, Rosalie, I've been thinking about you since that blasted math night months ago. Then I started thinking maybe you and I could go to the wedding together."

Whatever she'd been expecting him to say, it wasn't that. She opened her mouth to reply but ended up simply fishing her mouth closed and open. Closed and open.

I've been thinking about you since that blasted math night months ago.

Warmth slid through her, and the brightness of the sun started to fill her when she thought about being on this cowboy's arm at his brother's wedding. Her mind misfired about when Nat was coming, and what date the wedding was on, and if she could really go out with a man right now.

A smile touched Lee's mouth, and he cocked one eyebrow. "Who's staring now?"

The fire inside Rosalie flared, and she folded her arms the way he had several minutes ago. "Really, Lee?"

The smile fell from that mouth. "No, ma'am," he said, lifting his hat and smoothed back his hair. "You stare all you want."

She would, thank you very much, and she let her gaze drip down his bright coral shirt, past his belt buckle, and along his jeans to his cowboy boots. His hat was the same dark brown one he'd worn to math night a couple of months ago, and it made the saliva in Rosalie's mouth turn to sand.

Her eyes came back to his, and he raised his eyebrows, a silent *Well? What do you think? Will you go to my brother's wedding with me?*

She opened her mouth to answer, feeling more alive than she had in twenty months and so many things streaming through her mind that she couldn't sort through them fast enough to find the words she wanted to use.

———

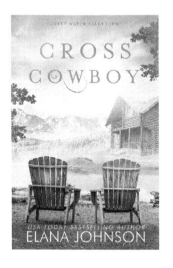

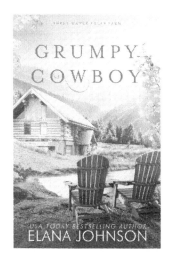

Grumpy Cowboy, Book 2: He can find the negative in any situation. Like that time he got upset with the woman who brought him a free chocolate-and-caramel-covered apple because it had melted in his truck... Can William and Gretchen start over and make a healthy relationship after it's started to wilt?

filled with joy?

Surly Cowboy, Book 3: He's got a reputation to uphold and he's not all that amused the way regular people are. Like that time he stood there straight-faced and silent while every-one else in the audience cheered and clapped for that educational demo... Can Lee and Rosalie let bygones be bygones and make a family

BOOKS IN THE HOPE ETERNAL RANCH ROMANCE SERIES

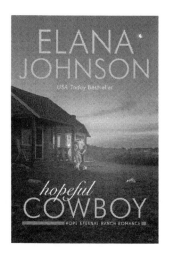

Hopeful Cowboy, Book 1: Can Ginger and Nate find their happily-ever-after, keep up their duties on the ranch, and build a family? Or will the risk be too great for them both?

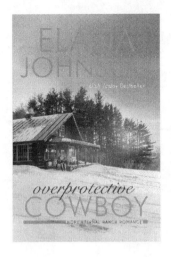

Overprotective Cowboy, Book 2: Can Ted and Emma face their pasts so they can truly be ready to step into the future together? Or will everything between them fall apart once the truth comes out?

Rugged Cowboy, Book 3: He's a cowboy mechanic with two kids and an ex-wife on the run. She connects better to horses than humans. Can Dallas and Jess find their way to each other at Hope Eternal Ranch?

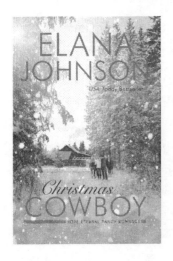

Christmas Cowboy, Book 4: He needs to start a new story for his life. She's dealing with a lot of family issues. This Christmas, can Slate and Jill find solace in each other at Hope Eternal Ranch?

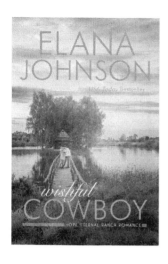

Wishful Cowboy, Book 5: He needs somewhere to belong. She has a heart as wide as the Texas sky. Can Luke and Hannah find their one true love in each other?

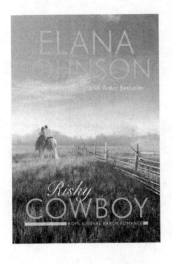

Risky Cowboy, Book 6: She's tired of making cheese and ice cream on her family's dairy farm, but when the cowboy hired to replace her turns out to be an ex-boyfriend, Clarissa suddenly isn't so sure about leaving town... Will Spencer risk it all to convince Clarissa to stay and give him a second chance?

BOOKS IN THE HAWTHORNE HARBOR ROMANCE SERIES

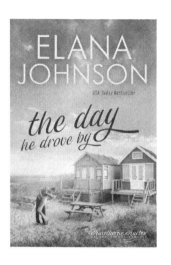

The Day He Drove By (Hawthorne Harbor Second Chance Romance, Book 1): A widowed florist, her ten-year-old daughter, and the paramedic who delivered the girl a decade earlier...

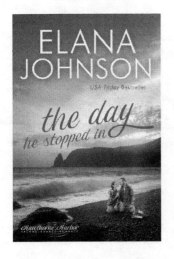

The Day He Stopped In (Hawthorne Harbor Second Chance Romance, Book 2): Janey Germaine is tired of entertaining tourists in Olympic National Park all day and trying to keep her twelve-year-old son occupied at night. When longtime friend and the Chief of Police, Adam Herrin, offers to take the boy on a ride-along one fall evening, Janey starts to see him in a different light. Do they have the courage to take their relationship out of the friend zone?

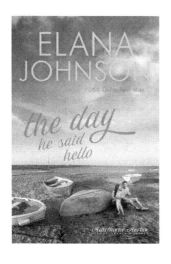

The Day He Said Hello (Hawthorne Harbor Second Chance Romance, Book 3): Bennett Patterson is content with his boring firefighting job and his big great dane...until he comes face-to-face with his high school girlfriend, Jennie Zimmerman, who swore she'd never return to Hawthorne Harbor. Can they rekindle their old flame? Or will their opposite personalities keep them apart?

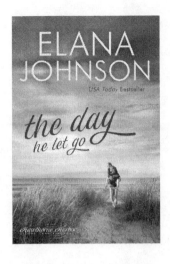

The Day He Let Go (Hawthorne Harbor Second Chance Romance, Book 4): Trent Baker is ready for another relationship, and he's hopeful he can find someone who wants him and to be a mother to his son. Lauren Michaels runs her own general contract company, and she's never thought she has a maternal bone in her body. But when she gets a second chance with the handsome K9 cop who blew her off when she first came to town, she can't say no... Can Trent and Lauren make their differences into strengths and build a family?

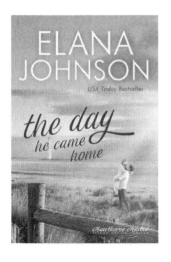

The Day He Came Home (Hawthorne Harbor Second Chance Romance, Book 5): A wounded Marine returns to Hawthorne Harbor years after the woman he was married to for exactly one week before she got an annulment...and then a baby nine months later. Can Hunter and Alice make a family out of past heartache?

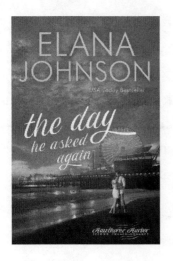

The Day He Asked Again (Hawthorne Harbor Second Chance Romance, Book 6): A Coast Guard captain would rather spend his time on the sea...unless he's with the woman he's been crushing on for months. Can Brooklynn and Dave make their second chance stick?

ABOUT ELANA

Elana Johnson is the USA Today bestselling author of dozens of clean and wholesome contemporary romance novels. She lives in Utah, where she mothers two fur babies, taxis her daughter to theater several times a week, and eats a lot of Ferrero Rocher while writing. Find her on her website at elanajohnson.com.

Made in the USA
Middletown, DE
04 November 2024

63879267R00213